GOING

NOWHERE

Nick
Pretnar

Holy Grail
Publications

Holy Grail Publications LLC
1411 Bass Avenue #200
Columbia, Missouri, USA 65201

http://www.holygrailpublications.com/

Going Nowhere

First Edition Trade Paperback

Cover art by Jon Norman.

Special thanks to Sarah Byrne, Scott Ross, Steve Woods, Joe Donaldson,
Nancy Anderson and Meredith Berkowitz for their consultation.
Without them, this wouldn't be as good as it is.

Set in Liberation Serif.

To contact the publisher:
call, 217-972-1901 or e-mail, nick@holygrailpublications.com

To contact the author please write:
randolphwolfram@gmail.com

ISBN 978-0-9829688-0-2 (trade paperback)

Library of Congress Control Number: 2010935634

Printed by:
The Country Press Inc.
1 Commercial Dr.
Lakeville, MA 02347

To Julia,

You're going to be really, really, really, really ...

good.

To those who seek

Contents

1

Going Somewhere ...

Genesis

In the beginning when Time was once upon us and the best and worst were yet to come, there were a Man and a Woman who by sheer happenstance became Father and Mother thanks to a great Yadi-Yada that occurred long long ago in a galaxy far far away. Way back in that yonder, a Star was forming from an assortment of matters that may or may not have included tadpoles given to a Virgin by wise men, who for centuries have followed this here light ...

Never forget!

And we won't.

For should old acquaintance be forgot and never brought to mind over matter, Mother wouldn't need a knife or a dose of morphine, just the unhindered flow of adrenaline and a big *thrust* ... so that her baby boyden slips-n-slides right on out into same yonder light ...

"Randolph," She said. "Randolph Wolfram." Gotta nice ring to it, eh? Of course, Who would've known back then that you would be sitting here today beneath yonder light reading about our little hero. You see, there was a time when Randy could've grown up to be an ordinary man. But that was long long ago, much before he began to grow ...

The whippersnapper was a quick learner, reciting the alphabet at eighteen months. Father recorded the spectacle on an analog cassette as baby Randy sat in Mother's lap chanting A-B-C-D-E-F-G-H-I-J-K-L-M-N-O-P-Q-R-S-T-U-V-W-X-Y and Z ...

Not long thereafter young Randolph found himself amongst all the little runts running rampant around the big trees of the playground, figuring he should be running too, because isn't that what everyone is to do? It did seem so, but Randolph never really enjoyed running around and around and around, instead preferring to just watch the around and around and around, just like the big trees anchored into the soil, reaching to heaven, growing ever so higher and higher, until one day ...

A flash of lightning!

A crack of thunder!

Randolph began to wonder ...

What grows up must come down ...

So he walked away from that cumbersome metaphor and into the dark forest where he figured to think about this and that and everything else and maybe even what he could do with it all. What could he do?

Hmmm ...

This and that and everything else ... but especially *this*.

Because you see, Randolph had a big idea about destiny. He thought if he did it all he would be great, and so he thought about doing it and dreamed about living it just strolling along thinking ...

Indeed he was thinking so much and dreaming so much that he didn't know he was being followed by a giant monster until the hideous thing swallowed him.

And there sits our little Jonah. There is our Pinocchio trapped in the belly of a whale with everything to think and nothing to see ...

And so we begin our narrative, sometime not too long ago, but certainly not now and definitely not here, as our hero, Master Randolph Wolfram, tells us about Everything.

~~ RW ~~

It all started with a compliment that I took way too far: "You're a good writer," he said. Hideki Yamamoto was a Japanese sociology professor at Schaumme University in Columbia, Missouri. Fall semester 2006, I was a sophomore

3

enrolled in his 'globalization' course. He convinced me to write a research proposal, apply for an undergraduate grant, and toil night and day over every transition, clause, and ink blot in the damn two-page report.

For my tedious efforts I was awarded three-thousand dollars. If not for his methodical motivation, positive reinforcement, and strategic initiative, I never would've gotten the money, never would've gone to Cairo, Illinois, and never would've gotten myself into what I got myself into. I otherwise would have spent my summer smoking too much pot, drinking too much beer, and tripping too much acid. This gave me something to do and focus on, and I got money for it so all the better. Besides, alls I had to do was give a five-minute presentation to the board of research facilitators or whoever-the-hell at the end of the summer. That was the easy part, the boring part. The hard part, the fun part was doing the damn fieldwork especially when I didn't even know what-the-hell I was looking for ...

A causal explanation for racial residential segregation ...

At least that's what my proposal said. Really though, I wasn't looking for anything other than a damn good story, and I even had a hard time finding that, searching under all of these rocks and talking to all of the little roly-poly worms, trying to put together bits and pieces of everyone's stories into a big puzzle. Of course, none of the damn pieces fit, so I had a buncha little pieces to a buncha different puzzles but not all of the pieces to one puzzle. On top of that, I was trying so fucking hard to find some sortta meaning, some sortta rational explanation that would explain everything so thoroughly and logically nothing would matter ...

... click-click-a-tick-a-rick ... click-click-a-tick-a-rick ... click-click-a-tick-a-rick ...

... which I would've found had my intuition not been completely nollied by the skeptical questioning of all the damn Devil's advocates. I was trying to find the answers outside rather than listening to them screaming at me inside, all the

4

while ignoring my faith in the story — that it will always have a conflict, climax, and resolution. And I'm not just talking about something written in a book; I'm talking about any series of events that can be connected, however remotely, to form a story — maybe something you would tell your friends over beers or even something you might write down one day.

I was so caught up trying to draw conclusions from my discoveries that I failed to see the conclusion itself. You see, the problem was I was in an academic mindset — a scientist looking for hypothetical causalities and trying to support my findings with data that doesn't really mean anything, like this:

> As of the census of 2000, there were 3,632 people, 1,561 households, and 900 families residing in Cairo, Illinois. The population density was 515.1 people per square mile (198.9/km^2). There were 1,885 housing units at an average density of 103.2 per km^2 (267.3 per sq mi). The racial makeup of the city was 35.93% white, 61.70% black or African American, 0.08% Native American, 0.72% Asian, 0.03% Pacific Islander, 0.36% from other races, and 1.18% from two or more races; 0.74% of the population were Hispanic or Latino of any race. The median income for a household in the city was $21,607, and the median income for a family was $28,242. The per capita income for the city was $16,220. Of the population as a whole, 33.5% lives below the poverty line, as compared with 27.1% of families. Out of the total population, 47.0% of those under the age of 18 and 20.9% of those 65 and older were living below the poverty line.

Thank you Wikipedia for presenting the demographic statistics in trite declarative sentences as if saying, 'Here are the facts. That's just how it is.'

Alright.

But isn't it ridiculous that these 'facts' count the number of people with a specific skin color? Sixty-two percent of people in Cairo, Illinois, have 'black' skin. Okay, what the fuck do I care?

But let's be honest here: whether or not you care, once you've read that this community consists of primarily impoverished dark-skinned individuals, you have formed an idea of the place's appearance based on the stereotypes already present in your mind. Perhaps your material idea of Cairo is something like this:

... the storefronts are boarded up, buildings abandoned, young males in baggy jeans and doo-rags huddle in empty parking lots barking at the females who wear shirts that reveal their cleavage furrows and they're all passing a blunt around a basketball court surrounded by a high chain-link fence while the jolly elders sit on porch stoops sipping big bottles of malt liquor from brown paper bags and sucking on Newports and Marlboro Menthols as the 1980s sedans float by on chrome rims with deep thumping basses reverberating from the subwoofer in the trunk as a gang banger pops a cap in somebody's ass because everybody's always stoned and high and cracked out and everything like that ...

So is that what you thought when you read that Cairo, Illinois, consists of a high population of impoverished people who happen to have black skin? You damn stereotypical racist! Now do you see what 'facts' do?! They reinforce these thoughts in our heads. They are the images we see on television or stories we read in the newspaper, and that's just the surface. You gotta dive in to discover the turds at the bottom of the pool. Seriously, public swimming pools are full of band-aids and shit, but you can't see any of it unless you dive down to look.

That's what I did when I went to Cairo: I swam in the deep end and found a buncha stinky shit. Of course, before I could dive down I had to break the surface, and you know what I saw?

... the storefronts were boarded up, buildings abandoned, baggy jeans and doo-rags and cleavage furrows and blunts and basketball and malt liquor and menthols and stoners and crack heads and spinning hubcaps ...

I saw all of it as I drove into town for the very first time, and I fucking freaked the fuck out because they were all standing around looking at me ...

I remember riding with my mom through a rough part of Saint Louis as a kid. "Don't look at anyone," she would say. "Lock your doors."

And all of these black people standing on street corners gazing at us as if wondering what this white soccer mom and our minivan were doing in their part of town, much as a white person in a subdivision would wonder if black people were spotted in an '85 float-boat. But you see there's one big difference: in the white part of town, people are suspicious of those that don't look like them because they're pry gonna rob somebody, whereas the black people look at us whiteys and shrug their shoulders because what would we want from them anyway?

Nothing. My mom was just afraid some black guy was going to shoot us because we were white, but you don't ever hear about anything like that ever happening. It's mostly about gang shit and drug deals, so if you're not dealing drugs or messing with gangsters you're probably not going to get shot unless you blatantly insult someone and then you probably deserve it anyway, because you see, it doesn't matter what color your skin is, what you dress like, how you talk or dance or what music you listen to or anything like that. It only matters that you respect everyone for who they are, who they have been, and who they choose to be because they are alive on this planet just like you and me, and no matter how smart we think we are or how much we think we know, we really don't know shit.

So this is for everyone who doesn't know shit. By the time you're done reading, I hope you understand Everything a little bit better.

~~ RW ~~

You're pry still wondering who-the-hell I am, so here's a little background ...

I got started in journalism when I was just twelve years old writing junior high sports stories for the local newspaper — an outfit with a circulation of about five thousand in Montdale County, Illinois. You see, I sucked at sports, so I kept stats instead. In fifth grade (Spring 1998 to be exact) I was tallying a basketball tournament which my fellow classmates won when Kathy Samardzja, the publisher of *The Montdale County Examiner,* approached me to help her spell everyone's names for the caption of a team photo. I did, and then she asked me if I would be interested writing for them in the fall. I told her I'd think about it because I had to talk with my parents. They of course thought it was a great opportunity, so I called her and said, "Sure," and thus began my tenure with *The Examiner.*

From sixth grade through eighth grade, I went to all the junior high basketball games and wrote the stories. My dad would edit the stories and tell me how to talk about the game's ebb and flow instead of just rambling scores and stats. He and Kathy were always critiquing me and challenging me to expand my vocabulary and describe the game play in concise detail, so that when I got to high school I was skilled enough that Kathy gave me more responsibility and my own desk. When I got my driver's license, I started traveling to other high schools in the county, meeting and interviewing new people while writing for a broader audience. I did that for my sophomore and junior years — sports writing during the school year and writing about old quilt-knitting homemakers during the summer.

I got pretty comfortable at *The Examiner,* propping my feet on the desk while talking on the phone, just pimpin out at sixteen and seventeen years old — a big shot sports writer with an office on the courthouse square in beautiful downtown Hamilton.

One day, Kathy's husband Edgar, an orchid-obsessed recluse, approached me really passive and matter-of-fact. "We have some news for you," he said. "You will no longer have a job with *The Montdale County Examiner* come Monday."

"What?!"

"You won't be working for us anymore." He was standing over there fiddling with a screwdriver in the light switch.

"Uhh — why?"

"Because we're merging with *The Hamilton Journal* to make a new newspaper — *The Journalaminer*." ... him over there screwing me ...

I rose because the tears were starting to come and my heart was tearing apart: here's this asshole profiting off a merger that not only destroys my soul but the entire social fabric of the community.

You see, Hamilton had been one of the only small towns in America to sustain two local newspapers into the twenty-first century. Subscribership was split amongst Hamilton's five thousand citizens and the other twenty-five thousand that lived elsewhere in the county. At *The Examiner,* we specialized in *real* stories whereas *The Journal* published what Mary Sue baked for the First Baptist Church potluck. Obviously the world was ending ...

And then, "You're going to be the sports editor."

Plopping back, "What?!"

"You and Jim Pritchard will be running the sports department."

Jaw dropping.

"There will be an entire sports section in the newspaper devoted to all four county high schools, and there is even a possibility to print the front page of this section in four-color."

Gaping.

"You will be writing your sports column and covering all of the best games, and since our circulation will be doubling, many more people will be reading your stories."

... !!! ...

"We're going to be the biggest newspaper in the county," and finally he looked up through those coke-bottle glasses.

"A monopoly on news," I gasped.

"Ha!" he barked. "Something like that. The first edition is Monday. We move into the new office on Thursday, and we will of course, desire your help moving if you wouldn't mind putting in some time and getting paid for it."

"Yeah yeah! Of course."

"Well, okay." And that was it. He left.

I just sat there and gaped at the world as all of the changes morphed into idyllic possibilities within my mind. I could see it all! And this was just another necessary steppingstone on my path destined to be a bigger big shot than I already was.

But before all of that, we had one more edition of *The Montdale County Examiner* to publish, so I wrote a long feature story about some of my friends and their band. The story and a color photograph appeared on the front page, just below Edgar's historical narrative on the adventures and exploits of Professor Otto Von Funk, "the traveling troubadour," who in 1910 grabbed his fiddle and a knapsack and walked across America.

The next day, we packed up all of the essentials — the computers, the desks, etc. — and hauled it all two blocks down the street to *The Journal's* spacious office building. After everyone was set up and the computers all networked, we were ready to publish a brand new edition of a brand new newspaper. My first assignment was to grab a camera and hop in a plane with Bob Smelcher, WWII pilot, to snap some aerial shots of Hamilton for a full-spread photo/feature story to occupy the front page of the B-section. On the eve of my senior year of high school, I was soaring ...

For the rest of that year, I probably spent more time at that damn office than I did at my house, and not because I was swamped with work or anything like that — I just liked it there. You see, the people I worked with weren't relatives or classmates but real people with families and houses and lots of debt. I was just a kid, so I felt different and I liked it because it was an escape from all the responsibilities of being a kid.

You see, I was one of those 'perfect' kids whose parents were pseudo 'society' people (my dad was an attorney), so I was always participating in copious extracurricular activities: I played golf to release sexual tension, was the all-state captain of the Scholastic Bowl team, sung in the choir, played in the band, was President of Key Club, and on top of all of those 'extra' things, I was enrolled in the most advanced of the most advanced classes that Hamilton High School offered — Advanced Placement Chemistry, Calculus, Spanish IV, and Advanced Placement English Literature. But you know what (and I don't wanna sound like a prick here), it wasn't hard. I did it all, and I don't how I did it but I did.

If anything, it all taught me how to manage time. I would teach myself derivatives and logarithms while passing between classes or sitting at the lunch table. Of course you can speed through calculus problems and as long as you understand the thematic concepts of finity and infinity you'll be fine. Literature, however, is a-whole-nother story cuz you have to read the book all the way through, front to back, and if you're trying to hurry or worrying about what else you have to do, you're going to miss something because a book, much like looking at a painting or listening to music, is an aesthetic experience that requires full and unabridged sensory devotion. Literature was my hardest subject. I had too much else going on in order to appreciate it. I struggled through essays and papers, toiling into the wee hours of the morning, trying to figure out why why why, but I could never calculate it so I cheated with SparkNotes.

I cared too much. But by the time second semester came around and Schaumme U had accepted me, I said fuck it! I would do what I wanted and liked — basketball games, news stories, idiotic adventures to creepy abandoned shacks, and road trips to obscure fast-food restaurants in far-off towns.

That's what we did for fun on Friday and Saturday night. Everyone else went out and got drunk at Will's farm or stoned down by the Red Bridge. What were we missing there? Not a

11

thing. All those idiots were just debaucherous hicks and we were all better than them. That is until one Friday night in early May (it was May 6, 2005, I remember the date exactly), all of us idiots were driving around smoking cigars ('stogies' we called them) when we happened to encounter a group of rowdy rubes en route to some lake-lot party north of town. They beckoned us, and we nervously stumbled around with our excuses before submitting.

Thank God we didn't cop out like pussies! I'd probably still be a pimple-faced know-it-all had I not gone out there and seen all of them sitting in the back of pickup trucks, huddled around a bonfire encircled by tiki torches, chuggin plastic cups of red kool-aid stuff while the muddy water lapped at the sandy beach ...

Paradise!

I drank a couple cups of the kool-aid and mixed and mingled until somebody yelled out, "Randy! Randy! Wud er ya doin 'ere?! Nice ta see ya! Really is." And you know it was nice to be there and just have fun and forget about all of the worries and stuff-to-be-done cuz you know life ain't that serious, and all that bullshit that's got you tied up and clogged up, well it ain't that important cuz the only thing of any paramount significance is love — an I-love-you, a lovely maiden, or just a lovely time. And for the first time in my life, on that night — May 6, 2005 — I felt love, not for one particular person, but the general love that accompanies honesty, acceptance, and freedom!

Out there guzzling jungle juice and screaming and grunting, nobody gives a fuck except to fuck all that shit that stresses you out and freaks you out and makes you think or hurt or whatever. Fuck it all! It doesn't really matter. But it was a strange, new and unfamiliar sensation ...

... just hanging out around the fire and looking up to see them standing in the darkness looking down on us and the lake lapping behind, then the flicker of light from the silhouettes above, Vinnie whispering, "Nate wants ta show you somethin," and my heart pounding following him through the darkness to their faces illuminated by the flickering fire below — Nate Fox, Jared Parmley, and Atty Dahling — Nate hands it to me, "Smoke it," and so I do and I cough, "It tastes like scrambled eggs," and Vinnie laughs as it passes around the circle and then all the way back to me for another and Nate says, "Wow! I just got The Wolfman ta smoke pot!" and all of them chuckling warmly like 'welcome!' ...

Oh what a relief to stand there with those gentlemen as just another one out of many! Yes, I succumbed to peer pressure, not because I was easily manipulated, not because they threatened me or anything like that, but rather because I was afraid of not being loved, of not feeling significant.

After that party, I hunkered down and finished my schoolwork for the next few weeks until finally came the last day of school. I remember it specifically — a Tuesday. We all cried on each other's shoulders and said goodbye to our underclassmen friends as if we would never see anyone ever again. Nobody went to class or did anything except take pictures and talk about all of the upcoming graduation parties. The day concluded rather anticlimactically. I mean sure, there were burnouts in the parking lot and a lot of cursing but it was nothing more than an extremely glorified version of what happened everyday after school anyway.

Like always, I just went up to the office to get some work done, then home for supper. I had settled down at my computer to stare at internet porn for the rest of the evening when my cell phone rang: it was Lauren Gant, one of the first girls I ever had a crush on way back in Misses Graham's first-grade class. I hadn't spoken with her much in the past few years, so I was surprised to receive the phone call. Nevertheless, she informed me of a party out at Tony Barnrooster's lake lot and that if I wanted to come, I should drive out to the North Marina in an hour.

After cajoling my parents, I drove all the way out there to find a singular fishing boat idling at one of the docks. Justin

Tobin and Andy Rosenstein chugged Natty Light at the helm. Fraternal greetings ensued before I hopped into the boat. We waited for someone else to arrive (I don't exactly remember who) before Tobes fired up the engine and powered us into the murky darkness of the calm lake waters ...

... the orange streetlights of the parking lot fading behind us, the stars twinkling in hordes up above, faint orbs flickering through the blooming trees on the far shore, and all of us blossoming flowers opening to embrace the world and freedom! ... our hair blowing in the wind, cruising beneath a bridge and around a bend, back into a cove to idle to a dock at the base of a steep incline atop which was a fire flickering back in the woods ...

We were all alone. Fifty of us together, sitting around a fire, drinking beer and passing a bowl ... all alone ... together celebrating the Apocalypse, tasting our freedom ...

If only we would've known what the world was about to throw at us ...

If only we would've known how much turmoil and pain, trial and tribulation we would each undergo trying to make it on our own ...

If only we would've known that freedom isn't all fun and games ...

If only we would've known ...

Maybe we wouldn't have been celebrating. Maybe we would've been cowering in the corner, crying on momma's shoulder, begging her not to make us go.

~~ *RW* ~~

Back on that playground the little sapling was blooming as they all merrily merrily went round and round shouting, "Faster! Faster! We need another master!" summoning all the boys to come push until it spun faster than anyone could run. Those stranded atop the whirling wheel either laughed or cried but everyone got dizzy and nauseous in front of the gawking gallery ...

Somebody runs up and gives a mighty heave and somebody jumps off and they all shout, "Wussy!" If they didn't like you they would chase you into the trees where you would have to hide with the dirty bumpkin kids who sat in holes, chewed on sticks and wailed in tongues ....

Down in the meadow, far from the mystical drama above, were the soldiers of the kickball field and soccer pasture fighting with and against the same friends and foes day after day after day ...

Then you get a little bit older, and now you're in fourth grade when everyone's growing bigger and badder and wiser. You're still just kids, though tiny little hairs are sprouting and new body parts growing and strange new odors fermenting. It's all becoming more sensational. Some are more awkward and others more expressive and flamboyant ...

The great social production of elementary school is coming to an end. Roles are changing: the popular, cool kids struggle to maintain their social status or elevate themselves to new levels of immature maturity. The dynamics are fluid: everyone is growing faster but in different ways at different paces. Alliances come and go; new armies and new friendships are quickly cemented and just as quickly crumble away. Junior high is nearing, and so are 'teenagers' ...

Oh that word! Adults shudder and children shiver upon its utterance ...

Fifth-grade year, the armies are dissolved and the petty infighting ends. We spend our last days on the playground discussing the future and everything it has to offer. What will junior high bring? ...

"My brother says there's four differ'nt lunch lines n one of em has fries ev'ryday!"

"I heard you kin git ice cream ev'ryday!"

"Awesome!"

"Can' wait ta have my own locker!"

"Yeah dude! We should try ta git lockers next ta each

other."

"Yeah!"

"I don' think ya git ta pick em though."

The Big Gulp! ...

Everybody bows and kicks the dirt, feeling that empty hole open inside, like something you've always taken for granted is missing ...

A profound sense of loss, a brooding hopelessness ....

But it's not like any of us actually understand any of this when we're eleven years old. Hell no! Junior high is coming. We're all growing up and that means more freedoms, like french fries and lockers. And then you get to junior high and what do you worry about?

How you smell and how you look and who likes you and who doesn't. For me it was most people — that is, that didn't like me.

I was getting louder and more 'right' all the time. Hair was growing down there and I didn't know what to do about it, so I just let it all grow including the dirty-Sanchez mustache, and since my voice was cracking like Mickey Mouse everyone always had a reason to laugh at me, especially my 'friends.' Then every single God-damned night, the erections, and how good it felt just to rub it, discovering that orgasmic ecstasy humping the bed and then waking up the next morning wondering what-the-hell that white stuff is all over the sheets, but oh well, only to jerk it again the next night and feel that weird tingling sensation on the tip like piss, until finally one night you say to yourself, "Fuck it! It feels too good, I'll just pee on myself," and that's when the cum splooges all over your chest and you lie there in the darkness, heart pounding, wondering what you have just done! You can't get caught with this sticky stuff all over you!

So you wipe it up with kleenex and hide the wad under your bed until the next morning when you personally take it out to the trash barrel so your mother doesn't find it cuz what would she think if she saw this huge wad of crusty kleenex in

16

the trash can in your room?

The worry and fear go on like that until you get a girlfriend who finally makes you feel god (good) about yourself and you stop caring so you start splooging everywhere — all over your chest and bed sheets and boxer shorts and the wall of the shower. Then one day you splooge all over the girl and you really don't care because you are the strutting cock, the bad boy in the leather jacket whom every parent of every teenage girl should be afraid of ...

But who are you afraid of? And what are you afraid of? And who is ever gonna stop you from fucking the world?

Exodus

Along came a spider, but he seemed innocent enough — just a shy and quiet boy of fair skin who happened to sit next to Randy in homeroom on the first day of sixth grade. They had never met nor seen one and/or other, yet they regarded each other as another lost in his own loneliness. Of course on that first day of junior high, everyone was shy and awkward. In fact Randy didn't learn the boy's name (and vice versa) until Misses Ratwurm paired the nervous students with a partner for their 'acquaintanceship' project. Lo-n-behold, Randolph met Elmo!

On the outside Elmo was bright as light, his albino skin as pale as the fluorescent tubes lining the ceiling. Still there was something dark and mysterious about Elmo that piqued Randy's curiosity, so he befriended him, and Elmo befriended Randy ...

What was it that struck Randy about this spider? And what struck Elmo about our hero?

Perhaps just the lonely need for a friend ...

Perhaps a shared longing ...

Perhaps ...

~~ *RW* ~~

So there are quite a few dimensions to this thing. It certainly isn't a simple linear story with a beginning, middle, and end; a conflict, climax, and resolution, oh no! Because this thing has multiple climaxes and revolutions and in the end I hope it all resolves itself. Anyway we'll get there, I promise.

So just bear with me here because we still got a long way to go ...

Back in summer 2006 I was nineteen years of age and the world outside of Montdale County couldn't have been more frightening and enticing to me. Following my freshman year of college, I returned to my hometown, the 'City Upon a Hill' sprouting from the countryside, to find some solace in a familiar place and familiar people. Having tasted freedom and the world without the comforts of home, life had suddenly become an adventure or even a quest, though I had no idea what I was looking for. I had begun to wrestle with grandiose ideas involving divinity and prophecy thanks in part to my relationship with Elmo Sargent, a.k.a. Sarge. Eight years after initially meeting Sarge in Misses Ratwurm's class, we discovered a mutual interest in concepts of 'knowledge' and 'philosophy,' very vaguely speaking of course. We just had these random discussions about various political and religious theories and conspiracies and god and willpower and prophets and supermen. You get the idea.

Anyway, one night in mid-May after Sarge and I and everyone else we went to high school with had returned home from college or trade school or whatever-the-hell, we set up this big meeting at Sarge's house to plan for the end of the world. Obviously shit was going to hit the fan real soon and we needed to be prepared, so we mapped out battle formations and planned an order of hierarchy for when I would have to take over Hamilton and convert it into a city-state. We would have to build a huge wall around the town or make alliances with other neighboring communities, except Niemanville because they would be who we would invade since they were our arch rivals in football — it all made perfect sense! We just had to wait for the world to end ...

When we got all that crap figured out, we all went out back to get stoned and further debate about what to do next. Giby, the quick and skinny white boy (we were all very white), volunteered one of his dad's unoccupied rental houses for a smoke out. Everyone thought it was a great idea and proceeded one by one over to wherever-the-hell. Sarge and I were the last ones remaining because we had to discuss a few top secret matters of the utmost importance.

Well, I start talking about all of the plans and potentials and crap, and he nods and says yes and no and maybe-so, just sitting there in a lawn chair, white as a ghost. When the lecture is over, we each hop in our respective vehicles and proceed toward Giby's house, me following Sarge figuring he pretty much knows where to go ...

Directly to the cemetery.

I pull up beside him, "Dude, d'you not know where this house is?"

Nodding 'no,' so I tell him to "follow me" and confidently lead us to Giby's house on Franklin Street ...

The dark house was laden with junk and rotting furniture; voices echoed beneath the floorboards. We walked around to the basement stairs and then down the dark steps into a cool candlelit cave where everyone was sitting on crates and boxes that surrounded a mirror supported by a couple crates, positioned in the center of the chamber. On the mirror-table were strewn plastic soda bottles, sacks of weed, cigarette packs, glass pipes, and birthday candles. Shadows danced on the surrounding walls; a filmy haze of smoke floated about the room; soft voices erupted in roaring laughter as the topics of conversation ebbed from the thought-provoking possibilities of conspiracy theories and flowed into the ordinary events of everyday life ...

"Me n Jared went fishin yesterday," Giby began. "N we fuckin jus' smoked a shitloada pot n I had an eight-ball n some whiskey n —— "

"Where'd you guys go fishin?"

"Jared's grandma's lake lot. Jared caught this huge catfish," putting the cigarette between his lips so he could gesture how huge, "n the hook went through its eye so Jared popped it out."

Bouts of chuckling laughter, Giby smoking cooly, smiling wryly, then turning inside out ... "Then he jus' poked out its other eye n threw it back." ... stupututup ...

"Nice," Whitey said, crossing his arms to screen himself from the invisible force tickling us all.

Giby sparked the bowl and inhaled the specter, leaving us together alone in silence, passing and puffing until someone knocked it clean ... mercy ... forgiven from sin, ascending to life everlasting, Giby rose ... the priest bowing before the altar ... his reflection in the mirror.

"Check this out," beckoning us to join him in reverence ... the disciples of nobody-who-so-ever staring up at us from the flickering candle light at the bottom of the well ... then from the darkness behind, that phantom shoved each into his own abysmal void, blinking in unquestioning perplexity of nothing | what | so | ever ... to be again seated before the consecrated altar resuming our chitchat about something-or-other ...

Sometime during the whole farce Sarge had disappeared, so I went searching and found him at the top of the stairway gazing out over the backyard into the fiery wash of a singular halogen streetlight burning against the silhouettes of the pitch-roofed houses. Behind the little triangles the shutter clicked one flash of lightning then more flashes ... and the cold fingers tickling my spine ...

"So Randy," Sarge said. "Wha' d'you think about the Devil?"

It wasn't the first time ...

"What about him?" ... cackles from the peanut gallery ...

"D'you think he exists?"

The mask contorting hmmm ... "The Devil is a concept, like half'f the whole thing, ya know?"

I didn't ...

"So d'you think he's real?" ... flashbulbs, cackles, and the burning city ...

"I don' know dude, I mean I've heard a lot about him. But I can't really say, per se, I've ever met him."

"What if I would tell you," turning to face the true _____, "I saw the Devil?" ...

And then somebody flushed the toilet and it all disappeared except for the hurgley-gurgley morphing into syllables and words ...

Is Sarge the Devil? Is he the Antichrist? Maybe, and then the Devil is just an idea planted in Sarge's brain by the Matrix Master, and now he is possessed, trying to get me to convert to the dark side and sell my soul in exchange for his ... what? I mean seriously, everyone else is downstairs talking about catfish and here we are up here watching the lightning talking about the fucking Devil?!

I turned to him standing there all melancholy and serious, "So — uhhh — you saw the fuckin Devil?" ... a flicker a flash ... "Dude?"

... itsy bitsy spider up your spinal spout ...

"Back there," he said, "when we were standing on the porch at my house n ev'ryone else was ——

"Yeah dude! You looked like you had jus' seen a ghost er somethin!"

"Jus' lis'en okay."

"I'm lis'ning."

"Alright," scolding school teacher, "just lis'en."

"Okay I'm lis ——

"Lis'en!"

"Dude I'm ——

"Randy!"

... the storm clapping distant thunder, the applause and laughter from the audience below, the fire up and down and all around, and the flash bulbs from the flickering invisible orb ...

The moment! Oh how beautiful and awesome! This was hell! And it was absolutely magnificent and ominous and overwhelming and inviting but frightening. The Devil whispered in our ears, offering us Lordsmanships, Crowns, Gardens, and Superpowers! One singular taste of the salt of the Earth and your mouth waters for more ...

"I saw it," he said.

"Saw what?"

"Back on my porch," abruptly dramatic, "it was there, standing by your car."

"What was it dude?" ... a monster, a red-faced man with a trident, Hitler, or Bello ...

"Next ta your car door, jus' standin there leanin against your car."

"Was it the Devil?"

"I don' know. I couldn' tell."

"Well what-the-hell was it? Wha' did it fuckin look like?"

"Nothing," shrugging dumb. "It was *nothing!*"

"How could it've been *nothing?*"

"It was just an outline, like a shadow of a man leanin agains' the car."

"Like a silhouette?"

"Yeah," gaping at me ...

"How tall was this shadow?"

Up and down, head to toe, "About your height."

I chuckled and pulled a cigarette from my pocket. "So," I said, holding back the monster. "This shadow was *my* height, standin next ta *my* car."

"Pretty much."

"Hmmmmm." I couldn't help myself, "Well I guess that makes me the Devil!"

... ||| ... ||| ... |||

A couple weeks later we were walking in the woods when it started to rain. Sarge said, "If we put our minds together, we can stop the rain." I thought about stopping the rain — got fucking pissed off at the rain thinking, 'You fuckin stop rainin you — *you* — YOU MUTHAFUCKER!' ... But it didn't stop so I got more fucking pissed at it for not heeding my commands. I was burning up inside and then those voices started questioning and doubting, making me think I couldn't do it, so I got fucking pissed off at them until I was totally peeved at everything and I couldn't fucking take it anymore, so I let go and raised my arms to heaven, embracing every falling drop, breathing slowly and deeply in and out and in and out and in and out ...

I closed my eyes and saw the cloud and felt myself flying up to it then through it out into the atmosphere, the stars up above and the cloud down below, the raindrops on my hands and arms a-drippity-drippity-droppity-droppity-droopity-dwindling-dur to no more, and opening up to see the stars through the parting clouds as a cool contented breeze blew everything away ...

We kept walking with the Bibles we had purchased from Dollar General and the stick-scepters Sarge had made because he fancied himself a hobbit or something; I was just a royal ass. Anyway, we each had a different Bible (his idea not mine): he had a white one, and I had a black one, but somewhere along the line (probably right before we were about to read the Book of Revelations by flashlight in the depths of the dark woods) I said, "You're the black Bible," and handed him my testament.

He looked at it repugnantly, "No no. 'Member? We talked about this."

"No dude, seriously. You're black. I'm white."

"Rand ——

"Elmo." ... crickets and a coyote howl ... "Seriously, I jus' know. You're black n I'm white. That's just how it's gotta be."

"Okay," tangling himself into reason, "so what makes you think I should 'ave the black one?"

... Ding Ding Da-dong Da-ding Da-dong! ... "Well, that's very simple actually" ... Ding-a-Ling-a-Ring-a-Ling-a-Ting-Ting-Ting! ... "I'm white. N since we have two Bibles n one is black n one is white" ... Ding-a-Ling! ... "ipso-fatso" ... Ring-a-Ling-a-Ting-Ting! ... "you're black."

Forcing the black one on him, I grab the white one from his dangling arm as he stands there gaping speechlessly. "So dude," I say, gazing out beyond, "What er we doin 'ere again?"

Flying saucers in his eyes, "This way." I follow him deeper into the darkness, climbing over thorn bushes, ducking through whippers and snappers. He stops at a steep ledge and opens the Bible to the Book of Revelations, flipping through the pages with his flashlight-hand. I creep behind him with my light, shining it over his shoulder and on to the page ...

"Aha!" turning to me, "the four horsemen."

"Oooo ...

He read Revelation 6:1 thru 6:17 real slow like he were reading "Mary Had a Little Lamb" to first-graders ...

... little lamb little lamb, his fleece was white as snow ...

"And he said to the mountains and the rocks, 'Fall on us and hide us from the face of Him who sits on the throne and from the wrath of the Lamb! For the great day of His wrath has come, and who is able to stand.'"

"So ——

"Wha' d'you think it means?"

"Well," I thought. "Christians would have us all believe that Jesus is on his way n we should all repent n hide or something, but what about those who don' hide?"

"They face his wrath."

"Well, are we —— I mean —— who —— where is he?" ... woopity-woopity-glooooo ....

"Wha' d'you mean?"

"Think about it dude, if you're hiding, you're scared, right?"

"Sure, kind of, I see ——

"Just hold on, lemme finish."

"Okay."

"Well, if you're fucking scared you're obviously not the savior, the Lamb, whatever, or one o' those proclamating angels or somethin, or even one o' the fucking horsemen: these are the players on the chessboard, the actors on the stage; ev'ryone else is just a spectator that has ta hide because the spectacle is so fantastic n bright n awesome that it's practic'ly blinding!"

"I see what yer saying," chuckling to himself. "That's very interesting. I never really thought of it that way."

"Well, it's fucking prophecy, it's not gonna be straightforward two plus two equals four. I mean seriously! We're talkin about angels n devils n gods n saviors n shit! None o' these things are fucking *real!* They're mythological! But that doesn' mean that we *can't* derive meaning, either symbolic'ly, existentially, or whatever from them. I mean, all this shit was written down by somebody sometime so at least he thought it was important; therefore it's worth a fucking look."

"But it doesn' always have ta add up."

"Exactly."

... two plus two equals five or six six six and sevens too ...

The heavens were thumpundering somewhere not too far off but not here because we were hiding from the war and Satan's wrath when, who knows, he may have greeted us with open arms.

"You ready?" he asked.

"Yeah."

Bolting!! ... past the trees and through the underbrush, up the side of the hill clamoring towards the moonlight ... the hum-drum and far-far-boom-a-looms cracking and fizzling in the electric hellfire ... *dadaDA!! dadaDA!! dadaDA!!* ... the revelating whistles and squeaky applause of the forest creatures ... breaking through the tree line into the light spectacle of Her Holiness Luna, the twinkling flashbulbs of the fireflies, and the electrical surge brewing in the Devil's workshop deep within a supercell across the deserted plains ...

Here was the End! All hail _____!

With our books and scepters we proceeded across the meadow toward the brewing storm then paused to Idol our God. Sarge started to giggle maniacally, so I patted him on the shoulder because he was just a mad scientist who had planned this entire scene.

You see, he had set up the whole thing, from the Bibles to the reading from Revelations in the dark woods to the storm even. The guy is a marvelous director. His sheer presence erases the bounds of time. Alongside him I have beheld unadulterated beauty and felt the incessant ebb and flow of the universe. That night may indeed have been the climax of our summer's long quest.

Maybe ...

Coming back down into town, Sarge said, "That was exactly how I pictured it."

"What was, dude?"

"The storm." ... plappidy-slappidy ... "Randy, I had a dream las' night."

"About the storm?"

"I had a dream that we were both standin there, holding our Bibles n that same storm was in front of us n the moon was behind us, jus' like it was! Jus' like it happened!"

'Wow!' I thought. "Wow!" I said. Because I believed it! After Everything happens anything is possible ...

We walked along the gravel road without speaking. The big drops came in spurty waves, ceasing all together then coming again. It was very dark except for our flashlights and the occasional lightning burst from behind. The trees trembled in the gusty wind. About a mile from town, about a minute from a torrent ...

"Except one thing," he said. "Something jus' wasn' right," halting to kick the rocks.

"What dude? Seriously we're about ta get dumped on here."

"The Bibles Randy!" desperately gazing into me. "In my dream you were holdin the black Bible, and *I* was holdin the white one."

I huffed a smirk. Everything around stopped — the lightning, the wind, the crickets, the fireflies, time. "Here," I handed him the Bible. "You can have it."

"No, I don' think ——

"Jus' take it dude, seriously."

"No, I don' want it."

Then why bring it up in the first place ...

It was always serious shit with him, all work and no play

because even play was work. I mean, fucking seriously, it's not like I didn't have fifty thousand other things I could've been doing right then instead of fucking walking on some country road miles from town with a huge-ass storm about to Baptize us all over again after we had just been cured of our eternal damnation! ...

As you can tell, the whole Bible saga really irritated me. As the summer wore on, I hated even possessing the damn book, but I hated more knowing that I could just give it to someone and then *they* would be possessed by the fucking curse. Nope, the damn thing needed to be destroyed forever, so one night when I was out camping with some disciples I threw it into the fire along with a twenty-dollar bill. Give the Devil his dues, right? And if I could've burned every damn Bible and every damn twenty-dollar bill on this planet I would have, because they're both fucking curses, but you gotta live with em because it's sure as hell impossible to get rid of em and anyone who thinks otherwise isn't a fool — he's straight-up delusional.

So yeah, that was me back in 2006. It gets better ...

Remember how Elmo freaked out about that silhouette of a man standing against my car? Well you see, I thought I was this 'Shadowman' character, so one night I painted myself all black preparing for a big bottle rocket war. Sarge and I had spent the day making rifles outta PVC pipes by filling one end with styrofoam and sawing three spiraling slits into the side: this would allow the projectile to spin on its way outta the barrel and maintain a straight trajectory. After testing the things on a couple stop signs, we marveled at their accuracy then proceeded to Biece's house up in Wembley where the war was scheduled to take place.

You see, Biece was shipping off to Iraq soon, so we figured to give him a farewell fanfare and maybe even a little practice. Well, there we were — about twenty of us all armed with bottle rockets, M-80s, Black Cats, smoke bombs, artillery shells, you name it — ready to fucking blow somebody up. We picked two teams and then picked our battle stations. Biece's team chose to entrench themselves in a ditch behind a makeshift fortress of plywood and sawhorses. My team took the open field, planning to make swift flank attacks and then draw back. Upon preparing our stations however, I came across an empty burn barrel which I turned on its side figuring to lie behind it and slowly push across the battlefield. It worked marvels. I put my spare ammunition in the barrel, ducked down to load then up to fire, and rolled forward a few feet — an efficient routine. Meanwhile, my teammates made charges on the flanks, tossing M-80s and Black Cats into the trenches.

We crept closer — a prolonged progression through the twilight hours. About one-hundred feet from their trench line, bottle rockets grazed the barrel left and right and exploded all around me as cherry bombs popped through the smoke cloud. I reached into the barrel and grabbed an entire roll of over three-hundred Black Cats then stood up — a dark silhouette in a fog of smoke — and I lit the wick, and hurled it over the wall.

... poppity-snoppity-nananoppity-loppity-crackity-crack-cra-ca-poppity! crack-cra-ca-pop! cra-cra-pop-pop-papapa-pop! ...

They scattered as the flankers came in to seize their ammunition, then they had nothing left to fight with/for so they fought to get back what they once had. Everyone was running around in a mad free-for-all, just grabbing explosives and throwing them from point-blank until Penny Biesterfeld, Biece's mom, came out and said, "Alright! Alright boys, that's enough! I think it's over now."

"See," I said. "We won!"

... wait wait wait you guys how could you have won if it just happened that winning happened because you didn't only if there wasn't but nobody to take it because it was bullshit stealing our fireworks but this is war man there aren't laws and regulations because fair and square and you ain't gotta right let's just ask a neutral party ...

"Penny! Who won?"

"I think they did," pointing to us.

"Oh! Obviously!"

"Yeah, you guys definitely won."

"Mom! What the fuck!"

"They came n stole all your explosives. You shouldn't've let em in there, you gotta protect your fort!"

"Yep! See, gotta protect your fort!"

"Jesus Christ! But yer my mother ——

"Fair n square, ya see?"

... ||| ... ||| ... |||

And now the moment you've all been waiting for ... the parting of the Red Sea ...

July 25, 2006 — hot and sticky; a light breeze stirs the sultriness; big puffy clouds roll across the sky; it might rain, but they've been saying that for days and still it hasn't in weeks; the Earth, dust.

I was scheduled to umpire the Little League regional championship baseball game between Hamilton and the Niemanville rivals. It was the final game of the year, and a big crowd would be on hand at the Hamilton Sports Complex. To say the least, I was looking forward to show off my mad strike-calling skills in front of a buncha rowdy moms.

Around five-thirty, I drive out to the complex. First pitch is scheduled for six o'clock. At five-fifty Niemanville folk discuss the two inches of rain they received before making the ten-mile trek east. I could feel it coming in the air that night, so we started early.

About the third inning, the clouds are all the way over the field; a cooling breeze out of the northwest turns still and eerie ... a long triple into the gap, and then to the west a bolt of lightning. I pull the players and coaches off the field and just stand there on the plate, hands on hips, staring up at the churning frontline coming right at me.

'you muthafucker'

It's not gonna rain.

'you ain't gonna rain on this here field as long as I'm

fuckin standin here you muthafucker!'

... out to the pitcher's mound to stand between six fifty-foot steel light polls; lightning striking to the west and north; the wind nearly blowing me over ...

'muthafuckin Mother-fucker!'
'muthafuckin Mother-fucker!'

... one foot forward and puffing my chest high so the wind gusts bounce back into the electrical spectacle cutting through the clouds all around; the dust billowing and swirling about me ...

'muthafuckin Mother-fucker!'
'muthafuckin Mother-fucker!'
'you ain't gonna fuckin reign YOU MOTHER-FUCKER!'

... a pit full of raging adrenaline opening inside of the electrical spectacle coursing through me so much energy without ...

'muthafuckin Mother-fucker!'
'muthafuckin Mother-fucker!'

... and then the Earth trembling an earthquake caused by my cell phone: it's Sarge.

"Dude."

"Randy are you watchin this storm?"

"Yeah. I'm at the sports complex. Where the fuck are you?"

"I'm down here by this big barn."

"Big barn?"

"Yeah, down by the prison south o' town — that big barn."

"Oh yeah! I know which barn you're talkin 'bout."

"I can' believe it hasn' rained yet."

"It's not *gonna* rain. I don' want it to."

"Well you know what Randy? I DO!"

"Fine then."

... godbye goodbye ... swirling wind and flashing lightning and crowd ooo and aaahhhing ...

'you're not gonna fuck n reign you MUTHAFUCKER!!'
'you're not ——

And sure enough, you wouldn't believe it and I don't

31

expect you to because sometimes truth is stranger than fiction, but the wind died down, and the lightning passed over, and the rain never came.

I reigned.

And I come off the field to mingle with the folk, everyone asking what I was doing out there, and just telling them real matter-of-fact and deadpan, "I was stopping the storm, didn' want it ta rain." And they just chuckle and stand around, and so we're all just standing around waiting for the lightning to completely pass when suddenly like only a kid could shout, "Look!" He's standing atop the bleachers pointing off to the south: huge flames shoot up over the tree line; the beeps and static voices from the pagers summon the volunteer firemen.

... what is it what could it be a house gotta be a buildin somethin real big gotta be a house pry got struck by lightnin ...

A woman on her cell phone announces the news, "It's the Mazzier barn, tha' big barn down by the prison. Got hit by lightnin!"

I felt like I had just won the World Series!

Calling Sarge ... "Randy!!"

"Dude what's goin on?"

"Randy," laughing hysterically, "you fuckin ——

"What the fuck dude? Did lightning hit that barn?" ... him cackling like a hyena ... "Sarge are you at the barn?"

"Yeah," inhaling, "I can see it right across the field." Finally composed, "It's gone! Burnin up!"

"Jesus *fucking CHRIST!*" This was heavy shit, and I didn't even know what-the-hell or what-the-fuck.

"Randy," laughing again, "*you* fuckin burnt down *that BARN!*"

"*I* burnt down the barn?!?!" ... '*yeah muthafucker I did burn down that barn*' ... "How did *I* burn down the barn?! *YOU* were the one down there!"

"But *YOU* were the one who didn' want it ta rain!" cackling again.

"And it didn' rain."

"Exactly. You won. And by winning, you sacrificed a barn."

"Yeah, alright. I burnt down the damn barn, so what? It's a *fucking* barn!" We both chuckle awkwardly. "But remember, I was out here *the whole time.*"

"Got it," he says.

We finished the baseball game: Hamilton won nine to four.

~~ *RW* ~~

That fall I returned to school and moved into my own apartment in Columbia. I had a lot of time to reflect on the summer and all of the glorious adventures. I would catch myself standing out on the second-story deck gazing back there to the east ... That little town was where my life began and where almost everything of significance I had ever experienced occurred.

I was still anticipating the Armageddon, but more than before, just wondering if it would ever come. Little did I understand that it had already passed, the Antichrist had come and gone, and I had already lived the Epic. Never again would I stop another storm; never again would I burn down another barn: that was all in the past. Now was the time to hide, if ever there was one: to hide from myself, the real Devil, and retreat into the woods and lie ...

Still though, I had fun. If I didn't I would've perished. I had a couple of girlfriends, smoked a buncha weed and got way too comfortable and yet completely miserable. For second semester, I had a roommate again — Mark Scherer, my roommate from the dorms freshman year. With someone to talk to, I grew more comfortable and still more miserable. I'd go back to Hamilton for winter break or spring break and everyone would flock to me like sheep ...

How are you? What are you up to? How's school? etc. ...

I was always fine, up to nothing, and school was just okay.

Sarge and I kept talking, but nothing really monumental happened. We reminisced and repeated the same conversations over and over until we had nothing to say to each other. Still though, I wanted to hang out and be friends with the poor bastard. We just needed something to do together, so we brainstormed and thought of taking a hitchhiking adventure to Canada sometime the following summer. It was bold and stupid. We had no idea what we were getting into.

We set a departure date for May 15, 2007, planning to make a documentary or even a movie about the journey, but more specifically about the state of the American social fabric. The night before we set off, Sarge and I met on his mother's porch, where so many of our philosophical broodings had begun the year before. Sarge grabbed the video camera; I sat down composing myself way-too-seriously, way-too-omnisciently, and way-too-comfortably. Thus, I began ...

"Today we prepared ourselves for our journey. We decided on how things would work here on our journey somewhat. We decided basic'lly where we are goin n what is the direction we will go. We'll actually see if this works out. I mean, we got a plan n ev'rything, but ya know plans don' actually unfold the way you expect them to, so whatever sortta idea that we have about how *this thing* is actually gonna work is prob'ly not gonna happen that way."

The character pauses. Yes, I say 'the character' for this was not I talking but a new personality emerging from within me. He sat there for a moment, struggling inside, completely motionless outside, as if calculating exactly what to say ...

"It's not gonna happen that way. So mentally, I think that we are prepared or so I hope, because I think we can handle whatever we get ourselves into. 'Fwe can't, well then, God help us."

And then he sings "Oh Canada!" in a rich baritone, backed by a chorus of barking dogs ...

"The most important thing you're gonna encounter is not necessar'ly gonna be like a Holy Grail. We're not in search of the Fountain o' Youth er anything like that. We may not be King Arthur er DeSoto, but we're in search of somethin. I'm not sure what. But for some reason, I sense it's somethin great. There's somethin we hope to find here, whether it be somethin we can hold in the palm of our hand er somethin greater, somethin ideal maybe, if there still is anything ideal left on this planet.

"Ev'ryday when we wake up, we have this sort of innate dream in our mind as Americans, as humans, wishing n hoping. Perhaps together, we can discover what is at the core o' these basic principles of human existence — ideas, feelings, perspectives. We are governed ev'ryday not by a congress er a president but by ourselves n what we treasure and value most. 'Fcourse there are natural laws n societal laws, but I believe in somethin greater, n I believe we all do. We decide what is morally right n wrong. We decide what we believe. This journey will encompass all o' those rights n wrongs, anything any religion has ever idolized, anything any government has ever governed, any righteousness to any ideology *ever!* We hold our values in our hearts as we try ta discover what it truly means *to be human.*"

But he pointed to his head, so he had to correct himself. And then the encore ...

"If we die, there's nothin we can do about it is there? HA! Yer dead yer dead, yer alive yer alive," staring off into the camera, a wink with a smile, "That's all."

IF YOU HAVEN'T TAKEN A BREAK YET, NOW'S THE TIME TO DO IT CUZ WE STILL GOT A LONG WAY TO GO, SO GRAB A BEER AND GRAB ME ONE TOO CUZ WE'RE GOIN AND WE AIN'T STOPPIN TIL WE GET THERE ...

It was just before ten a.m. when I set off. The destination was Cairo, Illinois. The purpose was to conduct an ethnographic case study on racial residential segregation. I had no idea what I was doing.

(You're probably wondering why we aren't on our way to Canada right now, and I'll get to that later, I promise.)

When I hit the road, I was armed with a half-dozen notepads, a tape recorder, and a computer. I had no idea what I was gonna encounter, but I'd heard stories, if you wanna call them that. Mostly it was just people saying, "Yer goin ta Cairo (pronounced CARE-oh)? Better be kerful, hear it's a buncha black people livin thur." Or my favorite, "Well don't get shot!"

Honestly though, I didn't really think I had anything to worry about. I mean, black people aren't scary unless you're playing basketball against them; otherwise they don't do anything but sit on their stoops drinking forties while passing a blunt ...

I'm just fucking with you, JESUS! It's not like white people don't do the same damn things: put on yer steel-toe boots n guzzle a case o' Natty Light then head down ta the bottoms fer sum good ol muddin in the Ford F-750 triple-duelly-wheeled-double-front-back-pull-behind, then later in the night pile in the back o' Ky-Bo's pickup fer a boony cruise throwin beer cans at mail boxes while "Free Bird" plays nine times on repeat.

See the similarities? Alcohol, lunacy, and what the Brits call 'anti social behavior.' This is America.

N ain't she jest a beaut!

From Hamilton I traveled south on Illinois Route 67 past two-story, frame farmhouses nestled amidst acres of knee-high corn and ready-to-cut wheat. To the west a hazy sky kept me wondering, but still it was a perfect day for driving: the sun wasn't too bright, the wind was calm, and the temp just right to keep the windows down. The date was Monday, June 18, 2007. I was to be in Cairo through Thursday then head back to Columbia with some interesting discoveries.

Hopefully ...

I tried not to think about the research part of this whole thing. You see, I hadn't planned very well for this endeavor, having only established two contacts and still waiting to hear back from Real Life Rehab, this nonprofit organization that allegedly provided a buncha services for poor drug addicts. I browsed their website, sent them my credentials and was just waiting for them to gimme approval or something. Fuck if I knew.

You see, back on April 27 when I was officially accepted into the fellowship program (the 'Undergraduate Research Fellowship' as they called it), I received a congratulatory e-mail full of bureaucratic jibberish, formal cordiality and cordial formality. I was so fucking excited to be accepted that I skipped class to go see Hideki who had received a similar e-mail, outlining tasks, submission statements and ass-fuckings I still needed to submit (to). Being that my research involved 'human subjects' I was required to fill out an application for approval by the Institutional Review Board which would make certain I wouldn't do anything that could get me, or more importantly the University, sued. It meant I couldn't take blood samples with dirty needles or subject anyone to water boarding interrogation. Most of the questions were expected:

"Do you have financial conflicts of interest in this project?"

"No."

"Are there any foreseeable risks imposed on subjects who participate in this research? And (if so) please describe them."

"There is no foreseeable risk imposed on subjects being that the nature of the research is strictly oral and conversational."

... etc. ... etc. ... official jibberitic bullshiterish ...

In Montgomery, thirty miles south of Hamilton, I stopped for gas, filled up at $3.02/gallon, then fought a demonic spirit for thirty more miles until I arrived in Breese and was finally 'aboard' sailing off into the wild blue yonder.

Of course I couldn't do this alone, so I picked up a hitchhiker at McDonald's in spite of his cutoff t-shirt of Confederate Rebel Flag print. He may have been a racist, but he was otherwise harmless I figured. I pulled up next to him and said, "Welcome aboard."

He said, "Thank ya," and climbed in.

"Where ya headin?"

"Oh I jes' live south o' town yonder," he said in that twiggish Midwestern twang.

"Well I'm headin south so that should work out for ya," I said, watching his hands.

"Where *you* headin?" he asked.

"Cairo."

"Nuttin but a buncha niggers down thur."

"Oh yeah! Sure as hell!" ... What else was I to say? ...

"So whudaya doin down in Cairo?"

"Oh, just visitin a friend o' mine."

"You got a friend down thur huh?"

"Yeah, he ain' black though."

"Naww, wouldna thought he wuz a nigger."

"Nope. Hates the niggers. Lives on the white side. Big ol nigger one time busted open the window of his dad's truck n stole a Hank Williams cee-dee. Nothin else. Now what a nigger wants with a Hank Williams cee-dee, I don' know."

"Su'prized he didn' steal the truck too."

"Hell no! Niggers don' like trucks!" ... this was too much fun ... "They want Cadillacs with big ol chrome wheels n shit."

"Fuckin right."

I just smiled real wide and stupid. After about five miles he said, "Ya gotta make a right up 'ere," so I slowed down.

"Here?"

"Yep."

... a gravel driveway, twisting down a hill and into the woods until terminating before a wide and muddy creek; there was no house ...

"Where d'ya live?"

"See that trailer over thur?" He pointed through the windshield.

"Ummm ——

"Way back in thur, ya kin barely see it."

... ??? ... "Oh yeah, across the creek there?"

"Yeah."

"Is it up on stilts er somethin?"

"Yeah, I put it up myself."

"Ah," thinking ... thinking ... sitting and looking; him still inside ... "So how ya get over there?"

"Oh that's easy!" He opened the door, climbed out, and jaunted over to a patch of head-high brush from which he drug an old johnboat ... "I jes' boat over!" he was excited to show somebody.

"Well that's cool," I said, kicked er in reverse, and shouted, "You have a good one now!"

"Alrighty! Be kerful down thur!"

I backed up and got the fuck outta there ...

... on down through Nashville and Pinckneyville — "The Friendly Little City" — and still further down and down past a few more towns whose names elude my memory and on into the capital of Southern Illinois, the not-Cairo Cairo of Little Egypt — Carbondale, home of the Southern Illinois University Salukis and strip malls, strip malls, strip malls — just one giant strip mall and one fast-food restaurant after another ... so on through Carbondale continuing down Rte. 67, winding up and around and back down through the dense deciduous foliage of the Shawnee National Forest, and then about twenty miles south of the capital, the forest opening into vast rolling prairie of vineyards, orchards, and cow pastures; the occasional line of trees separating the Earth from the sky: it looked like Southern Europe, but this was river country ...

And then on up and down past some more orchards and such, all the way into the little town of Alto Pass, population 400 — Main Street shops along a deserted dusty road featuring a dessert bar and a general store but no saloon and no people anywhere; the root beer shop was closed for the day and would reopen next Tuesday ... pressing on through the bluffs and forests and tops and bottoms and pastures and herds until cresting one last hill and then down to follow the winding strip of pavement through the bottoms again, and now there were no more hills — just the flatness of the flood plain and the foliage the darkest and brightest hues of green imaginable; the sky and everything looming over you as if you couldn't get any lower ...

Welcome to hell — plenty of rivers Styx over which to cross into the afterlife or ... Kentucky and Missouri ... same difference ...

Rte. 67 ended at a **T** with Illinois Route 5. I followed the sign that read "CAIRO 12" and continued through the bottomlands, past the town of Tamms — "A Good Place to Live" — nothing more than a massive trailer park, and on into Alexander County past rotting boarded-up houses: the only seemingly inhabitable dwellings were the mobile homes dotted along the highway every quarter-mile or so.

Outside one trailer, an 'African American' family seemed to be enjoying a Monday afternoon picnic: half-naked children ran in circles around bulbousing adults who gossiped in front of an old stone barbecue pit.

The trailers continued to line the highway until I passed under Interstate 57 which completely bypassed the town. You could drive down I-57 and never see Cairo, and if you weren't a sign reader, you would probably never even know the damn place existed.

But I knew.

And I knew it was on the other side of the levee gate behind the red railroad trestle that read in big bold letters, **CAIRO** ...

And passing under the gate and through the levee, it all hit me ...

I'm going into a place I've never been to talk with people about their lives and I don't know anyone except a local historian, a high school teacher and some bitch who works for a phony nonprofit agency. I needed to get my shit together.

Checking into the Belleview Motel, a brown-skinned not-African-American woman with a thick accent charged me $120 for three nights stay. She had this weird yellow creamy stuff on her face. While I was checking in, her husband (I assume) came into the office and started talking about me in an alien tongue. He then escorted me across the parking lot to my room.

"So how long you been in America?" I asked him.

"Oh no," he said with a wave of the hand, "I'm fine."

Funny ...

He showed me the room then left me to brood in the dark particleboard den ...

How was I ever gonna get an interview?

... ||| ... ||| ... |||

Just go for a walk and maybe I'd find somebody willing to talk, so I set out down the main drag, walking south along sidewalks that were more like rocky front lawns, past numerous abandoned houses caving in partially or completely, and some just simply lacking roofs. Those that were inhabitable were covered in moss and vines.

The business district began about ten blocks down the street, but most of those buildings too were beyond repair — crumbled bricks strewn upon the sidewalk, boarded up windows, and bars over doors to keep out ... somebody ... but who?

Young people, aged sixteen to twenty-five, idled in an empty parking lot drinking from brown paper bags and smoking cigarettes (maybe) while huddling around a black SUV blasting supersonic reverberations through subwoofers. Past them were the Tombstone Man and a restaurant proclaiming "The best hamburgers in So Il," a car wash where two teenage males were vacuuming the inside of an early-90s Ford Taurus, and then another block over, more bricks and cracks and crannies, followed by the liveliest business in town — a grocery store, and another lively joint — the Qik-Mart convenient liquor store, next door to a little walk-up-and-order fast-food joint called Dairy Shack. This was my stop — greasy cheeseburgers, thick milkshakes, and crispy fries, tastier and more fulsatisfilling than anything you can supersize. I ordered my food and waited graciously while others came and went. A mom with a baby waited next to me — the baby gazing perplexedly up from her mother's arms.

"Hey," I said. Its mother turned at me with her protective fire ... "Cute baby." Mom smiled.

After about seven minutes, I received my order and was just sipping my milkshake, moseying back up to the motel, when a large black woman caught my eye from in fronta the liquor store. She crossed in my direction while stuffing her boob back into her bra. I tried to play it cool, sucking on my shake ...

"Howdy," I said.

"Hi," she barked, still manipulating her boob inside her way-too-tight, cheap-n-trashy camouflage dress. She walked alongside me with an aggressive gate as I continued up the street. "Whuchu doin?" a temperamental glare and squinty eyes, head side-cocked ...

"Uhhh — nothin. How you doin?"

"Fine."

And then that descending silence — her still walking next to me ... this is a possible interview candidate ... but why did she come after me? ... probably for money ... gonna ask me eventually ... I couldn't take it any more ...

"So, ummm   ya see, I was wondering —— well lemme say I'm not from here and I'm doin research n shit on Cairo *annnnd* I need ta interview some people."

We each stopped simultaneously — the natural flow of human socialization rendered meaningless in this non-binding transaction.

"Mmmm-hmmm," she cocked and began walking again. I followed.

"Ummm — would you care ta be interviewed?"

"Naw," scratching her boob, "I'm good on that."

"Do you know anyone who would be willin ta be interviewed?"

"Naww. Th'ain' nobody."

"Ummm —— ... ?!?!?!?! ... 2+question = x-y-z = 5/0 = ?? ... "Well, how 'bout this: I give you my number n if you think of anyone you can have em call me," pulling the notepad from my pocket, then tearing a sheet ... "Here's my number n my name is Randolph Wolfram n I'm stayin down at the Belleview."

"Mmmm-hmmm. Wha' room you stayin in?"

"Uhhh — it's one-hundred something, like maybe — ummm — one-oh-six? Yeah, I think one-oh-six." ... It was really one-oh-seven ...

"One-oh-six?"

"Yeah, definitely."

"Alrigh', one-oh-six."

"Yeah, fo sho."

"One-oh-six," and she walked off mumbling to herself, "One-oh-six, one-oh-six, one-oh-six." ...

I continued back toward the Belleview. About ten blocks away I was stopped by an eager voice, "Hey man *yo!*" I turned around to find a lanky guy with a quick limping gate bouncing over to me.

"Sup dude?"

"Hey man, hey!" He came up to me, his big white hat cocked to the side, but not intentionally, more like he didn't care; it said 'USC Trojans, National Champions.'

"Hey man I need three dollas."

"Well," reaching into my pocket. "I got only some change," handing him about a buck in quarters, dimes, and nickels.

"That all you got?"

"Yeah man, sorry." He started walking off when I realized ... "Hey!"

"Yo," he stopped. I proceeded ...

"'Fyou do me a favor, I can help ya out."

"Yeah?"

"I'm in town workin on a story 'bout Cairo n I need ta interview people. Would you wanna be interviewed?"

"Wha' do I get?"

"Ten bucks," I blurted out ... wasn't really supposed to pay the interviewee — not academically ethical or something, but whatever.

The dude gave the proposal some thought, peering out over the street in search of his answer. Just when he found it ... "Yeah, I do it."

"Awesome! Well, we can do it now 'fyou want?"

"Naw man, tomorruh."

"Alright, well wha' time?"

"Ten o'clock tomorruh. See that house there?" He turned and pointed to a large Victorian with a wide veranda and boarded-up second-story windows situated at the end of a side street.

"Yeah, the big one?"

"Thaz right."

"Alright, well I'll see you there at ten o'clock tomorrow. I'm Randy by the way." I offered him my hand.

"Name's Steve," he said. We shook. I continued on. He crossed over and hollered something at a big guy sitting on the front porch of a small yellow house; the guy was drinking a forty. I wandered down a couple side streets back by the housing projects where a buncha teenage males huddled around a basketball court.

Continuing north toward the motel, house after house were in desperate need of various repairs; some were altogether wasted forever. The sheer extent of dilapidation is nothing that any series of words can do justice. This is America and it's breathtaking and mindboggling to think that people live in these impoverished conditions in this, the wealthiest nation in the history of humanity ...

But how can we possibly call ourselves blessed with riches when the have-nots still have so little? ...

44

But before I set off to write this, I vowed not to get political. Besides, the have-nots have enough to survive; obviously they're doing it. I didn't see one person keeling over in starvation. In fact, many people were fat and content. And why shouldn't they be? They got everything they need — beer, weed, water, food, and maybe someone to fuck every now and then.

~~ *RW* ~~

I woke up early on Tuesday morning for an interview I had scheduled with Barry Coldwell, the Dean of Students at Cairo High School. Two senior graduate students at the Schaumme Sociology Department who had once performed community service in Cairo referred me to Mister Coldwell, the man everyone in town called 'Coach.'

Cairo High School was located a few blocks north of the Belleview, just south of the levee floodgate. It was your typical American high school — football and baseball fields, a cinder track, and a huge empty parking lot. I proceeded through the main entrance into the office to be greeted by three ladies and an astute black man of an athletic constitution, dressed in a suit and tie and horn-rimmed glasses. He smiled brightly in a wise-American sortta way — neither black nor white nor anything really, just the good ol welcoming smile of a hearty ego.

"Barry Coldwell?"

"That's me," he said, rising. "You must be Randy."

"Yes sir."

We shook hands.

"Come into my office n we'll talk a little."

"Alrighty."

His office was a large room with a desk in one corner and a conference table in the center. Along the walls were old trophies and photographs of sports teams as well as various certificates of achievement.

Sitting across from Barry, my back to the open door, him

45

with legs crossed and a huge grin, I clicked on the tape recorder and began ...

So wha' d'you do?

"I'm the Dean o' Students 'ere at Cairo High School. My job entails handlin all the discipline. Basic'ly I make sure that kids all follow all rules n regulations and if somebody violates those rules I have ta deal with em."

If I were a student 'ere —

"You'd get your sermons. I'd preach to ya."

What kinds of discipline d'you typic'ly deal with?

"Your basic disruptions — playfulness in the hallways, silly things you know, and ever' now n then you get some defiant n disrespectful students, just your general type o' misbehavior."

Nothin you wouldn' find at any other school?

"Naw, nothin that wouldn' happen anywhere else. We're not hardcore. Our kids do a lotta those silly things, have fun, take things a little too far. That's it."

Never had any problems with hardcore violence then?

"We haven' had any what you would call 'inner-city' violence. Some o' the kids consider themselves tough n they find out they're not as tough as they think they are. It's jus' kids bein kids really. Mainly we have kids that are doin things like jus' bein tardy too of'en n disruptive in class n disrespectful: you have that a lot today — disrespectfulness. And we have kids that come ta school ever'day n do what they s'posed ta do. But I think disruption has been a major problem over the years. I don' see it gettin much better. I don' know 'fit's a society mentality now or not, but it seems ta be like a society thing ever'where."

How long did you say you've worked here?

"I've been back since ninety-fo'. This is my hometown. I grew up here, went ta high school here n lived over in the projects."

As far as the community and the school n ev'rything, how diff'rent is it now than it was when you were growin up or even in ninety-four?

"Well ninety-fo' was one o' those years where things had gotten bad. That was one o' the reasons that the principal — she's out there, she's the one that called me down in ninety-fo'. I was in Michigan workin for the department o' corrections. I had been there maybe five years, n they had hired her ta be principal here at the high school, n we had some cleanin up ta do. We had some problem kids; we had some gangs; we had some drug problems — typical problems that you have in any inner-city school or public school — and we dealt with it."

And it's better now?

"Yes, much better, yes. 'Fcourse we did have hardcore kids then. Kids had the gang mentality. Some people called them wannabes. I said, 'You call em whatchu want.' They were gang affiliated, n 'fyou gang affiliated you a gang member."

How has that changed then since ninety-four?

"Gotten better."

Why d'you think that is?

"Primarily because, at that particular time, you see there were a number of agencies in our community, n we still have those agencies today, along with the police department n those of us teachers n administrators n parents n we all collectively got together n jus' ——*

Said 'no more.'

"Yeah, we jus' did ever'thing ta put a stop to it, and it happened — all of us collectively workin together. Now we got — well it's jus' kinda mindset — kids jus' don' 'ave a whole lotta int'rest when it comes ta academics. School's more of a place ta go n hang out n have fun for some kids. For other kids, school's what it's s'posed ta be. Some come here ever'day and do exactly what they're told, n others are just here ta have fun."

And how is this diff'rent compared to — well when did you graduate from here?

"I graduated in nineteen-seventy. And you're — what now

47

you wanna know?"

How diff'rent, or what sortta ——

"Oh well the community is differ'nt, that's for certain, prob'ly because society is differ'nt. We didn' have rap music."

How was it diff'rent?

"Oh, well there were more jobs for people. The place was a village. Parents were very supportive of each other so you couldn' get away with too much in the community because ever'body had a sense of respect for the opinion of another adult. So if another adult saw you do somethin, you did it. It wasn' a question of whether you did it. You did it. That's jus' the way it was. They said it takes a village ta raise a child, n that's exactly where it's at. We were raised by the entire community, where today you tell on somebody's child, whatever the child say they just accept it."

D'you get much parent involvement in school?

"You get parent involvement. Some parents work with you n some don't. And most o' the time if they don' work with you, they gonna have some difficult times, the kid's gonna have some difficult times. As long as the kids know that he er she can convince someone that they didn' do anything, they're gonna continue ta do it. You and I did it too 'fwe thought we could get away with it. It's jus' normal. I don' think they're terrible kids because of it, n I don' think parents are terrible because of it. Jus' sometimes we do — today we're more easily manipulated because o' that. As parents, I think our kids — there are a lotta kids out there that manipulate n confuse their parents so it benefits em."

Why d'you think they do that?

"Well, ta get away with whatever they desire ta get away with. And I think they've become good at it. They do it because it works. If it stops workin they'll leave it alone, but as long as it works, why stop? Whatever works for em, they do it. And I've seen cases where we've had kids who've been doin it for years, n then all of a sudden the parents n the administration n the teachers, we do like a wrap-around session n there's no way out. In other words, parents are gonna work with those who are concerned aboutchu, so your excuses don' work anymo'. Your lies n your forms of manipulation jus' don' work no mo'. It doesn' matter whatchu say about the dean or the teacher: it's not about them, it's aboutchu doin whatchu s'pose ta do. When we stay focused on what the kids are s'pose ta be doin then ever'thing falls back in that individual's lap. When we all work together, the child's gonna win. He may not win where he *wants* ta win at, but he's gonna win where he *needs* ta win at."

You force an attitude of 'you gotta do what you gotta do.'

"Gotta get ta class on time, gotta do your discipline. If you've been given a detention you gotta do it. Momma can' getchu outta detention. The biggest problem is when they feel — kids like ta tell ya that, 'My momma gonna come up n snap! She gonna come up n turn this place upside down!' They like that."

Their mom is like their protector.

"Thaz right. But once mom n the administration start ta work togetha, it makes all the differ'nce in the world. And I think that's what's missin today: we don' have enough o' those circumstances."

Is it gettin better though?

"I think yes. I think parents are really startin ta see how kids can — well, we have a lotta young parents n they're a lot easier manipulated. I mean, grandmothers are thirty, thirty-five, thirty-six years old. It's not unusual ta have an under-forty-year-old grandmother anymo'. N think about it, that's awf'ly young. So it's pretty easy ta manipulate mom 'fshe's only twenty-seven, twenty-eight years old. Maybe, let's say she's fourteen years older than me, we're basic'ly in the same mindset 'fyou think about it."

Mom ain' had much time ta grow up without a kid.

"She can only give you what she's got. She only has so much inside, n she can only deal with so much. And today, a fourteen-year-old is pretty much on top o' things. There's so much exposure, so much exploitation, so much they see and indulge in, that he n mom are pretty much on the same level."

Let's talk a little about this phenomenon — younger parents, younger grandparents — I imagine a lot of it goes back to an increase in teen pregnancies over the years, and I mean, I think we all know 'why' people get pregnant, but what sortta things d'you think cause somethin like this?

"I jus' think personally, we up against a society that could care less. We claim we do, but we exploit. There's jus' so much sexuality on tee-vee n there's not very much ——

It's hard ta stop.

"It's very difficult ta stop cuz it's comin at em from all angles, n it's a natural thing for em, I noticed that. I can recall when we were kids, we danced with a girl, you couldn' hold her. You had ta hold her a certain way. She wasn' gonna allow you ta put your hand anywhere on her. I mean, we'd have ta hold her back and her shoulder. Where today, they can put their hands *anywhere!* There's no sacred place on a female anymo'. When they take pictures for prom, I've never *seen!!* — They are just so sexually explicit. Your hands can be anywhere — all over the girl's body, *butt,* anywhere! Normally, the photograph, when we took prom pictures, they tell you where ta put your hand. You put your hand on their shoulder n ya otha hand maybe in her hand, but your hand was not on her *be*hind or on her *hip* on the front o' her *thigh* or anywhere else near *down-there* parts. The photographer determined where your hands go. Now kids put their hands wherever they want. I think we've gotten too lax, think we're refusin ta challenge students ta do the right thing, and I think that's a society problem. I think we just allow our young people ta do anything they decide ta do, n then when it's gone too far we try ta correct it — too late. When it's corrected ever'time, ever'day, ever' minute we see it, then it becomes normal to ...

[end of tape, resume with Coach Coldwell]

"Kids are kids. I think sometimes when we become adults we forget that we were once that age n we didn' think like we do today. So I try ta think like them because I look back at some o' the things that I did in high school n I think, ya know, I blew it my junior year. I jus' tossed it. I got caught up with this girl n that girl n you jus' started ta grow up. You had other interests, n these things distracted you from whatchu shoulda been focused on. It's normal. Overall, I think our kids really try hard ta do their best n look forward to their futures. The outsiders may not see it cuz we have a lotta people condemn our little community: it's a predominat'ly black community n we struggle economic'lly."

But it's not necessarily the fault of the community that it struggles.

"No, you're right. You're right. I remember back in the day when they brought fifty-seven through here, it basically disrupted this little town."

Happens to a lotta towns.

"Thaz right. All the small towns. Hurts the local economy, n when you become economic'lly depressed then you have problem after problem after problem. Take a man who's got a fam'ly n all the sudden he loses his job. He can' find another one. His lifestyle will change."

Somethin I've been meanin ta touch on that I read a lot about before comin down 'ere are the riots. Were you ——

"Oh yeah! Oh yeah! I was parta all that shit — fourteen years old, fifteen, sixteen, seventeen."

What was it over?

"Oh jus' race riots. It started out jus' racial riots. We was doin the Martin Luther King marches n integration stuff, just a racial thing. We were protestin."

Was there somethin that triggered it?

"Well you know, it's always somethin. I think there were little things along the way, n then all of a sudden there was a black kid: his name was Robert Hunt. He was in service, n I don' know if he was AWOL or what, but anyway he was killed while he was in the possession of the police department. N Perry Ellis could give you a lot more information on that cuz he's got a lotta history on that, but he was a friend o' mine. We were all friends, n he was a couple years older than me, mainly a friend of one o' my brothas. I have seven brothas. But — uhhh — he was our — I think he was killed. They say he killed himself, but that ——

So was there a lot — what sortta — how many people were involved?

"Ever'body."

How long did it last?

"It last for — sixty-seven when it happened — sixty-seven, sixty-eight, sixty-nine, seventy, seventy-one, seventy-two."

And what would happen during these days?

"Race riots, burnin, shootin, ever' night."

Like a little civil war.

"It was. Predominat'ly the black area, the project area down in the southern part o' town, southwest part o' town. There was the projects down there we all lived in. That area was surrounded by National Guards, so that itself wasn' a good thing from the mindset of black people cuz you jus' surrounded us n that was the mentality. So they put all the National Guards around the projects n we couldn' leave unless we had permission."

So I imagine that was fairly traumatic ta be involved in?

"Yes, it was your typical Chicago, Detroit, Memphis, the other big cities that had serious racial riots like the ones down south; Cairo was no diff'ernt. It was little Chicago as they called it, so whatever happened in Detroit, whatever happened in Chicago, whatever happened in Mississippi, happened right here in this little community. Cairo was one o' the headquarters tryin ta get equality, fightin for equality: thaz what it was all about durin the sixties — jobs, respect, bein accepted."

After the riots, did a lotta people move out?

"A lotta people did move out. Some people stayed. The opinion of a lot of us was — those of us who lived through it, we sortta realized things never really gonna get back ta where they once were. Jobs left the area. The division continued. They never could sit down n work things out. 'Fcourse the schools integrated. It took a while."

So it wasn' integrated before?

"No."

There were two high schools?

"Segregated, yeah. There was Sumner High School n black grade schools n white grade schools."

And this was durin the sixties, after ——

"We integrated in sixty-eight, sixty-seven — the year of sixty-seven, sixty-eight."

And that's about when the race riots started?

"Ever'thing, yeah. Because so much was goin on all over the country — Chicago, Detroit, Little Rock, Martin Luther King was killed. There was jus' so much goin on, episode after episode, incident after incident, jus' turmoil all over the country. That's when songwriter Marvin Gaye came out with "What's Goin On?" He was talkin 'bout *what-the-hell is goin on!* N in the song he spelled it out. That's why I've always admired musicians: they can reach out n put a song together."

Capture an emotion.

"Capture it. It's amazing. Gotta be a gift. Thank God for those people durin that time cuz those songs would calm ever'body's emotions, whereas these songs today that these rappers are singin ——

Fire em up.

"Thaz right. Fire em up. And people wonderin what's wrong with the kids. Well look at what they listenin to. They listenin to this twenty-fo', twenty-fo' we don' hear the blue moon! This is a kid's lifestyle. I remember listenin ta James Brown n Marvin Gaye n Smokie Robinson n The Temptations but they weren' ——

Peaceful music all around.

"Thaz right. They was sayin, 'I love you.'"

Ev'ryone.

"Yeah! The way you do the thing you do. You smile so bright, it wasn' 'bout the fight; it wasn' 'bout the pigs; it wasn' 'bout the shootin. You know, it was 'bout how good you look

53

n how much I love you. That's what was instilled in us. But today the biggest thing bein instilled in these kids is shootin the cops, crack cocaine, the drugs, ever'thing. And the blink-blink all gold n all that. N we wonder why our kids are the way they are. They can' help it! All we can do is be as big of an influence as the bling-bling as the rapper with the gun. We have ta *be an influence!* We have ta try ta compete with that image. I have ta let them know where I come from too. We're dealin with here, in my opinion, I've seen the change in the mindset o' kids all the way back since I started workin with kids in corrections in seventy-seven n it has ta do with society. We wanna blame it on parents, young parents; we wanna blame it on race; we wanna blame it on a variety o' things. But in reality it's the music; it's whutchu see on tee-vee; it's whatever is puttin things into yo' head that would not normally be in yo' head. It's a war goin on, n the good book says that. The evil is very strong; wickedness is very strong. So you gotta be powerful n put as much good out as possible n hopefully kids will weigh the differ'nce n make the right decision."

Our interview didn't exactly end there. We talked about sports, then he gave me a tour of the school, making certain to point out the graffiti.

"This is our graffiti." ... 'JN loves NK,' in faint pencil above a water fountain ...

"There was more graffiti in *my* high school."

"See," he said. "It's all jus' goofy stuff."

Barry showed me several classrooms, specifically those for students deemed 'learning disabled.' Cairo has a lot of 'LD' students. "In a town that's depressed n has financial difficulties, you'll have those types o' students," he said. "Local economics has a lot ta do with the ability ta prepare ta learn."

As Barry pointed out, many of Cairo's citizens are unemployed and dependent on government aid. If mom and/or dad don't have to get up and work in the morning, then they don't have a daily routine and neither do their children. People sleep when they want and eat when they can afford to. Contrast that with the typical blocked regiment of an American high school, and it's no wonder certain students have difficulty completing assignments on time and focusing in the classroom. Coldwell noted that only the best teachers are selected for positions instructing the 'learning disabled' because the district must put forth its best effort to provide everyone with the opportunity to do whatever they want with their lives.

Easier said than done ...

After our tour, Coach led me back to the office, where we thanked one-and-other and bid each other adieu.

... ||| ... ||| ... |||

Back at the motel, having missed my scheduled interview with Steve, I was sitting outside smoking a cigarette when a woman caught my glance from the convenience store across the street. She too was afflicted with oversized mammary glands.

She crossed ... "Hey, how you doin?"

"Good. How are you?"

"Man, I don' gaw any money."

"Awww, that sucks."

"I jes' needs sum money ta get me sum weed."

"Well I can help ya out there."

"Really?" her eyes got real big.

"Yeah," I said. "You wanna smoke?"

"Yeah," she said bluntly.

"I'm Randy," offering her my hand.

"I'm Angela."

"Nice ta meet you."

"You too."

We went inside. I loaded a bowl. She asked for a glass of water then took a plastic cup from the bed table, filled it herself, and sat down on the edge of the bed. I took a hit and passed her the bowl; she choked and passed it back ...

We get to talking and I reveal myself — a journalist. She thinks I have money — lots of it ...

"You gaw aleas' ten bucks."

"I got a dollar," and I hand it to her.

"You gaw more'n that."

"No I don't."

"Whyz you lyin? Howz you managin?"

"I got a credit card they gimme ta work with."

"Why donchu go ta the bank n gimme sum money?"

"I don' think so," a chuckle.

"Man, I needs ta gimme sum blaze," another hit of the free weed, then ... "This 'ere town's where drug dealers have cum n taken over."

"So there's a lotta drug dealers here?"

"When I say — I don' mean like fuckin Scarface. Not a'ythang like that. Real basic. Know what Ize sayin? Ain' even covered up. Ya see, I don' even know why ——

... abrupt pause, vacant brooding ... "I came here cuz they shot up my house when my kids came up short on money. Ya see the guvament ——

... marijuana meanderings roundabout something to do with something or something ... "They wuz stashin the drugs n this money in the holes in the wall. N wha' happened wuz the rats wuz stashin it so people were gettin butted down n beat up cuz they thought people wuz stealin the money. I wuz standin there n hear something go POP!" an imitative clap ... "I wuz like, 'Whu' the fuck is that?'"

... me passing the bowl, her lighting it sideways like a crack pipe ...

"There's a carb there."

... smoking and choking ... "I don' wanna be smokin none mo' o' that!"

"This is good shit."

"Uh huh. Anyway, ta make a long story short — so they got a big jack hammer n all the money n fuckin drugs fell outta the wall. The *rats* had made a *nest!*"

"Outta the money n drugs?"

... imagine a cracked out rat ...

"Yes."

"So did the dealers get it back?"

"Yeah."

"So that happened 'ere in Cairo."

"NO! Thaz in Baltimore."

"Well what are you — are you stayin with a relative here?"

"Ize stayin with Mister —— ... eyes to ceiling and all around then back down ... "You see thaz why I wuz tryin ta get sum money cuz I need ta get im sum food cuz I jes' got the light bill yesterday n I wuz tryin ta stay at Reality House ——

... Reality House is a division of the aforementioned non-profit agency, Real Life Rehab. Before embarking for Cairo, I attempted to contact Real Life, left umpteen voicemails, sent e-mails, all to no avail. One day I called and was put through to a woman who will only be referenced as L___ T_____ — assistant to the executive director, whom I will only refer to as F_____ G_____. This was sometime in early June, so I told L___ of my intentions to perform research on racial residential segregation and what I planned to do — interview people, etc. She told me to e-mail her my credentials, so I sent her my IRB (Institutional Review Board) approval and research proposal. She said she would review my credentials and contact me at a later date to schedule a time when we could meet in person.

A week passed and I hadn't heard from her, so I called Real Life and was put through to a woman who I will call W____ I__, head of the organization's Assertive Treatment Program which deals with "psychosocial and intensive case management services," according to their website. W____ told me she would be happy to work with me after I explained my research proposal and plans. I informed her that L___ was in possession of my credentials, so she said she would talk to L___ and call me back in a few days. She never called.

On Thursday, June 7, I called again and asked for either L___ or W____, was directed to W____ who told me that she had reviewed my credentials and was "interested" in working with me; however, she wasn't certain whether that would be in the organization's "best interest."

... Somewhere a bell tolled but all wasn't quiet on this front ...

On Friday, June 15, three days prior to my arrival, I telephoned Real Life. The executive director, F_____ G_____, spoke with me ...

"Hello, this is F_____ G_____, how can I help you?"

"Hi, I'm Randolph Wolfram, a sociologist with Schaumme University, and I'm coming to Cairo next week to perform research on racial resid ——

"What are you researching?"

"Racial residential segregation. And since your organization is such an important part of the commun ——

"What is it that you are doing for your research?"

"I was gonna get to that. I'm interviewing people, compiling oral histories, n tryin ta paint a picture of this community as it is today. Being an influential organization in the commun ——

"What do you want from us?"

"Well, I'm attempting to establish some contacts so I can get some interviews."

"Sir, we cannot give you the names of our clients."

"I'm not asking you to. I would just like to work with your organization in order to better understand what you do for the community."

"Well, do you got a pen? Cuz I can tell you right now what we do. We are an organization that caters to ——

"I can't base my research on your word, ma'am. That's just not how ——

"Well in order for you to work with us and do research with us, we need a number of things from you."

"I sent you my creden ——

"We need documentation of what it is that you plan to study and how it is that you are going to go about that. We also need documentation that your research has been approved by

58

your institution's review board."

"*Yesss*, and I sent all of that in an e-mail to L___ about two weeks ago."

"L___'s not in charge here. I am."

... bitch ... "I'll e-mail you then."

"You certainly *can* do that, but before we begin any correspondence I must have your application reviewed and approved by the board of directors."

"I'm comin ta Cairo on Monday."

"That's fine. Our board meets Monday night. We'll look over it at the meeting and I will call you and let you know."

"Alright, well I'll send that to you n attach ——

"Good day sir." She hung up.

... the fucking dry cunted bitch was so fucking corporatey formal and cold and rude that I already *hated* her and her fucking sketchy organization ...

"Real Life is a *racket*," Angela said. "It's a very big racket. It literally *owns* this town. I lived in Real'ty House n I lived in an apartment n the apartment was *ruled* by it. When they got me thur I wuz tryin ta tell em I wuz usin crack, right? N I wanted ta go to a treatment center. Thaz what you do when you get into one o' those kinda, uhhh ——

"Organizations."

"Yeah. You tell em, but those muthafuckas put me out in an apartment."

"They put you out on your own?"

She nodded.

"D'you think they're incompetent?"

Her eyes got huge and locked real intense on mine ... "Oh yes! Oh yes! E'rything is a big *ra*cket. One psychiatrist, one nurse — how the fuck can ya have only one?"

"Did it cost ya money ta go there?"

"They take my money. They take yer check. Yer rent is three-hunderd bucks."

"Wait, what check do they take?"

"Yer aid check from the state: rig it up ta where Real Life

59

n yer name n you can' cash your check 'thout Real Life staff."

"Yet they put you on your own?"

"They put me out cuz I had a drug addiction n I wuz tryin ta get help. They couldn' get me in a treatment center between here n fuckin Chicago. N I know I could ——

"They couldn' put you in one in Sain' Louis er somethin?"

"Sain' Louis is in Missouri. My Medicaid n Medicaid cards only cover the state of Illinoise."

"So you come 'ere ta Real Life for treatment, or what? Why did you come 'ere?"

"Because they do — or I thought — well, listen ta what they do: at first, they have me in transitional housing, right. And I kep' tellin em, 'Look I'm havin flashbacks n I'm havin cravings,' right. Ta make it short, with my addiction, three days wuz not enough. So they wanted me ta go ta this town that the name of it is — how d'you say it? TWO-SHEA. N it's by Eas' Sain' Louis."

"Sauget?"

She spelled it out, "T-O-C-H-E-T-T, TWO-SHEA."

"Okay."

"And — ummm — they — ummm, only gave me three days."

"Ta get clean?"

"Ta get clean thaz right. NO!" realizing ... "Cuz they medicate you. But when you get medicated there n you try ta get in a treatment center yer dirty n if yer dirty ya can' get in."

"Uh huh."

"Iz like this," Angela said. "Instead o' yer energy goin like this ta try ta get help," pointing to the ceiling ... "Iz like chchph-chchph-chchph-klapo*woooosh!*" and spiraling down to the floor ... "Iz jes' fucked."

... ||| ... ||| ... |||

Yep, fucked. At least that's what Perry Ellis thought. I met with the local historian and former chair of the Cairo chapter of the NAACP on Tuesday afternoon at the municipal building. Perry was a tall, lean man with a few grays flaring from his dark sponge top. He wasn't the blackest man in town; in fact he was one of the lighter-skinned black people I had seen. Nevertheless, he was the self-proclaimed and community-recognized local historian.

Perry laid out a series of documents denoting Cairo's historic population numbers. He explained that Cairo was originally a transport hub for people and products traveling up or down the Mississippi and Ohio Rivers. That was, of course, back when people traveled by ferries and steamboats. When the automobile was invented, Cairo was just fucked.

The city's population peaked in 1920 at around 16,000, then steadily fell off right around the time the first automobile bridge over the Mississippi was built (1927): traffic bypassed the town and barge and ferry companies lost more customers in addition to what they had already lost to the burgeoning railroad industry. In 1960 the population dipped below 10,000 for the first time since 1880. Then came 1967 ...

The riots.

"We don' use the word 'riots,'" he said. "There were no 'riots' here. What there were was confrontations between blacks n whites doin marches n then at night there was exchange of gunfire between blacks n whites."

Call it what you want, Mister Ellis. You were the head of the NAACP at the time and probably had a hand in the goings-on. Perhaps that's why you are the present-day Omniscient One. Afterall, your camera captured the only images we have of this historic and tumultuous affair. Now I'm not pointing any fingers here or accusing anyone of propagandizing an historical movement ... NO! NO! ... You can think whatever you want.

I'm just saying that people like Perry (a lesser known leader) as well as people like Martin Luther King Junior are historically glorified both by the media and academics because they fought for perceived illusions of 'righteousness' and 'equality.' While now here we are, over half a century after Rosa Parks refused to give up her seat and places like Cairo still exist ... and East Saint Louis, West Philadelphia, the entire city of Detroit, Gary, Indiana — all of these places and many more festering cesspools of violence, substance abuse, and millions of wasted lives. And what color is the skin of most of these people who live in these rotten places?

It's black.

But what does that mean? And does it really matter?

Does it matter if everyone over the age of eighteen can legally vote, pending registration and other X-factors like citizenship and criminal history? Does it matter if discrimination based on skin color, hair color, ethnicity (whatever that means), place of birth, sex, sexual orientation, etc. is illegal? Does it matter if we Americans have elected a semi-half-black-man-with-a-Muslim-name President? Does any of this shit matter if I'm lucky enough to have been born into a caring and nurturing family of comfortable fortune?

Really it doesn't.

Because the most obvious and most despicably gut-wrenching and contemptible form of discrimination in the history of mankind has yet to be addressed.

It's not race or any of those things, because race and sex and sexual orientation and all of that shit only matter to shallow, narrow-minded, emotionally-void opportunists who are too afraid *not* to care. Nope. This great form of discrimination isn't social or economic and certainly not faith-based. It has something to do with everything, but nothing to do with me OR you, rather everything to do with Us — not as persons but as people, not as blacks or whites, men or women, but as Humanity.

Yes, in this, the twenty-first century, the greatest form of discrimination that we have yet to address, let alone conquer, is the discrimination of Humanity against Itself. We divide ourselves into groups and clusters based on fickle physical appearances and/or ideological constructs associated with linear, hierarchical orders and a-personal, disaffecting moral beliefs. We rally around one cause only to set ourselves against another. We violently fight for peace against those who idle peacefully and create war. And we say, 'YOU YOU YOU' and point our fingers ...

Oh, shame shame shame! ... not on THEM at whom you point your finger but on YOU for pointing your finger and on ME for pointing my sword at YOU and cursing SHAME.

These simple acts are discriminatory — one verses another singular one; and it is because of these singular acts on the most mundane level, that we will always be divided.

Now, by no means am I saying that there is something inherently *wrong* with this form of discrimination. It *must* be because it is. If it didn't exist, if we didn't have anything to fight against or for, if we didn't behold differences between various individuals, groups of individuals, and other individual groups, then the universe would implode upon itself and Everything would be the same to Everyone. We would all share the same perspective; we would all look the same, act the same, think the same ...

Nothing would be original.

But this thought is fucking insane, so pardon my rant. Seriously, I don't mean anything by it and I don't want to cause any pain or suffering in any sortta way unless that's what you want, then you can have it.

I was talking about Perry Ellis and the Civil Rights Movement. He was one of the local leaders who followed Martin Luther King Junior away from the spinning merry-go-round and into the dark forest leaving everyone else back on the merry-go-round as it whirled and whirled, until one day it stopped and they all vomited everywhere ...

"So we come up ta Cairo, ta the late sixties movin on toward seventy almost, n the Civil Rights Movement started here," Perry said. "It was over in the South before it ever came ta Southern Illinois."

"Why did it take so long?"

"Well there was resistance here. See, this community felt that the Civil Rights Movement had passed its back. The white leadership didn't 'ave any foresight ta see what had happened in the South. Segregation in Illinois had been prohibited by the Illinois Constitution since eighteen-seventy. But the State of Illinois was not into enforcin. There was sep'rit n segregated schools in Springfield, Peoria, here — they wouldn' do anything about it. In nineteen-sixty-two the sit-ins took place here in Cairo in places like restaurants, swimmin pool, movie theaters. Then that died down," staring through the table ... "Things were quiet until we got ta the late sixties n the death o' the soldier in the jail is what kick started the full-blown confrontation between the blacks n whites."

... the merry-go-round off its axle rolling into the dark valley of chaos ...

"What's the story behind that guy?"

"Well — uhh — he was a nineteen-year-old soldier who died while in police custody. The belief was, well — they said he committed suicide. They said they had stopped him on a traffic violation and he didn' cooperate with police, so they placed him under arrest n took him ta jail on a Saturday night. He was arrested at about eleven o'clock, and at about three the report was out in the community that he was dead. The next day the blacks converged on the police stations. They had rallies n marches n decided ta form an economic boycott agains' white-owned businesses. So in my book *[insert title]*, all that is set forth throughout the book, with photographs n stuff, includin the American Nazi Party which came here ta picket agains' blacks, and all guns n the shootins between blacks n whites n all that kinda stuff." ...

There were too many things to think about; my brain was clogged, so I left Mister Ellis at City Hall and went for a little walk, meandering down side streets, passing one dilapidated building after another and the occasional porch-sitter, stoop-watcher, or basketballer. I decided to cut up east toward Commercial Avenue — an old cobblestoned street that runs parallel to the ten-foot-high retaining wall keeping back the Ohio River.

64

Standing atop the levee, I gazed west on the descending sun and all the houses and old brick buildings competing with the trees in the great race to heaven. Below me, Commercial Avenue was lifeless like Main Street of an old Western ghost town. Up the street, a ten-story-high, project-style housing-complex loomed over the pristine blue waters of the majestic Ohio; a singular fat, white wife-beater stood on an upper-level balcony sipping a beer; children rode tricycles in the deserted street.

Behind me, down by the river, three younger lads, shirtless except for one, dreadlocks except for none, sat with poles waiting for supper. About fifty feet south of them, a fat woman sat on a cooler talking on her cell phone while smoking a cigarette. Tugboats towed barges up and down; waves lapped against large boulders; cars and trucks and trains whooshed and roared over the bridges to the north and south.

I made an about-face back into the crumbling town. There were no church bells ...

~~ *RW* ~~

Day three — Wednesday, June 20, 2007 ...

There was an old white woman sitting inside of a bubble behind a desk facing an old white man, who dawned a blue mesh hat with some military logo on the front. He had bright blue eyes peering through wide lenses of old-man glasses, scrutinizing anything he looked at, calculating a judgment before deciding how and whether-or-not to proceed. His build was lean but hard, like that of a lifelong farmer. For a flash-in-the-pan we beheld one-and-other as separate-but-equal.

Then I introduced myself ...

"Howdy."

He looked me over with those scrutinizing eyes, lips pursed flat in neither a smile nor a frown.

"I'm Randy," I said, extending my hand.

"This young man's a writer," the old woman spoke

pleasantly. He remained silent and scrutinized.

Then, "Tom," grabbing my hand, shaking it coarsely and firmly, his lips ever so slightly curving into a vague smile.

"I'm doin a case study on this town," I said. "Would you be willin ta talk with me?"

"Sure," he said. "Wha' do you wanna talk 'bout?"

"Well, it looks ta me that this town used ta be a pretty — ummm — *happ'*nin place, and now — well obviously it's not."

"Well, ya know this *was* a *good* town."

"You lived here your whole life?"

"Huh?" offering me his ear.

"You lived here your *whole LIFE?*"

"Naw. I was in the military thirty years."

"But you were born n raised here?"

"Naw. I was born in Kentucky. We moved over in *nineteen thirty-nine,*" aggressively emphasizing the year. "But there was a grocery store 'bout ev'ry corner back then."

He spoke slowly, reclined back all crossed over himself, each syllable twisting from his knotted lips, his icy blue eyes focused distantly inward on the game plan: he was the quarterback not the receiver ...

"I remember this was a boom town 'bout twen'y-five, thirty thousan' people. There was a li'l grocery store jus' 'bout ev'ry street. We've got two grocery stores in Alexander County now. One's here in Cairo. One's up in Olive Branch. So it makes things high. Most people go ta Wal-Mart — Sikeston, Paducah, er Cape Girarduh — and do their shoppin. There was a Main Street — Eighth Street, over there on Commercial — those where all the bis'nisis used ta be. Couldn' make it cuz they couldn' sell nothin. Nobody shoppin."

"Why was nobody shoppin there?"

"Uhhh — well," pausing and tilting his head back, untying himself, then retying the knot left-handed. "It started off, ev'rybody started movin outta Cairo. They didn' want the whites goin ta school with the blacks. Knocked out the swimmin pool right out fast n that started. We had three

66

theaters here — one uptown n two downtown," an indignant sigh ... "That didn' work out either. Those people — white people — weren' goin ta the movies n started movin outta town. If they all movin outta town, you ain' got no tax money."

Pride crept beneath his skin like a demon, coaching him through every word, every syllable; his body all twisted in an effort to disguise his strategy. He didn't come off as hateful or bigoted, just superior — basking in the blinding light that radiated out from within him. Nevertheless, he had to be dealt with delicately.

"D'you think the exodus outta town, so ta speak, happened because o' the race riots or it happened because there weren't any jobs?"

... Please wait while we process — "It's like any other big town, n small town — Benton Harbor, Eas' Sain' Louis," glancing down then up and right at me with those sharp daggers ... "It'll kill a town. It's jus' like anything else. You're gonna have good people n bad people. Black guy told me one time, 'Put em all in a paper bag, shake em up n roll em out n they'll all look the same. But some of ems bad, some of ems good.' That's true. I'm talkin 'bout white people n black people n all other nash'nalities. So — but the school started flounderin with white students cuz 'fyou ain' got enough kids goin, people payin money with taxes, they're gonna cl-cl-close up," sputtering as he shifted.

"So all the white people started ta leave town?"

"Now we're 'bout eighty percent black er maybe more righ' now. So then the dope problem came along."

"After the shootings n stuff?"

"Yeah. Now then they had — you notice outside that buildin you see the bullet holes are? ... Hit the buildin."

"Oh you can?"

"Yes ya can."

"I'll have ta look at that. On the wall?"

"N a couple o' them guys got shot 'ere. N there was farr stations. There was a downtown farr station. Down here, this is one uh their newer farr stations. Used ta be a farr station right across there, 'ats an auxiliar' now. But — uhhh — summa the farr men got shot. The black project was over there, n of course they was armed ta the tee, n the bullets was flyin this way. N then the Nash'nul Guard was down there, State Police, n ev'rybody else."

"So you were in town during all o' the shootings n that stuff?"

"I came thru one night, but I was on my way — see I was stationed in Utah, n I was on my way ta Germany. Was comin out on leave, n I read about the trouble here. I know. I've worked over on the grocery store on Walnut one time. So I started ta go over there ta see a friend o' mine, n I was drivin the boat n turned down the street n 'bout fifteen black boys got me. Stopped me. Held their guns. I was lucky I knew a few of em. N I heard one of em say, 'I know him. He use' ta work at that grocery store n he's in the service. Let eem go.' So I got out of it, see. But they were shootin. My heart was a pumpin."

"So they were shootin ev'ryday?"

"Yeah. Mostly night, though."

"D'you remember what set it all off?"

"Well — they was arguin fer differ'nt rights like goin to the restrooms. See that used ta be segergated. N 'fcourse back in the day they did have it segergated. N they had back rooms — back rooms fer the cuhlerds, front rooms fer whites," like a General remembering his enemy ... "But they wanted more." ... an arctic gale ... "N they got more." ... lightning illuminating the darkest hollow ... "So you don' see no white people walkin the streets at night 'round 'ere."

... wait a second, don't ... "I was walkin the streets the other night."

"You were?"

"Yeah. I've been ta Eas' Sain' Louis before, though."

"Well okay, once ya git used to it. I wouldn' be 'fraid o' doin it no place else. I wouldn' be 'fraid o' walkin down the street cuz I know ev'rybody, black n white. O' course I taught school up here one year n you meet a lot of em. I taught one year," chuckling ... "but it was a madhouse, I'll tell ya. But — ummm — we didn' have very many white kids gradjeeatin. But like I say, we got sum good blacks, we got sum good whites ... we got some bad whites."

"So wha' d'you — ummm ——

"They keep thinkin we're gonna come back, ya know. 'Fyou ever get any bis'nis in here. They're talkin 'bout buildin an ethanol plant located outside the city limits, out by the airport n buy up all the ground, buy up ev'rybody's property. Well that might be so, but how many years it gonna be?"

"When's it gonna be built yer askin?"

"They ain' started yet. This is what we keep gettin said in the paper n ev'rything else. N once this big plant cums in, we're gonna start growin again. Well, they're hopin people'll start movin in, ya see. But we really don' have anything ta draw anybody in. N I know this myself, even our rest'runts, wha' few we got left, their clientele is gittin smaller n smaller. How long can they stay in bis'nis? Not for long," forebodingly, stopping to soak ... "N our light bills have gotten so high."

"I think that's across the state — that new state law."

"It is. It is."

"They're a lot higher in Missouri," the woman clucked. "N Missouri's squawkin."

"Here wha' we got righ' now is mostly welfare, disabled, retired, like me — retired. So these people on welfare n stuff, they're not payin no taxes. 'Fyou got a low income, you git yer license plate fer twenty-figh dollars. We pay 'bout eighty. But a'yway, I noticed my insherns went up three-hunderd dollars jus' the other day from eleven ta fourteen hunderd," a wry laugh ... "n I'm thru AARP, thru Hartford, n I'm fixin with em. I called em. They ain' got back with me yet. N I told em, ''Fyou don' do better'n that!' N I've got a two-thousand-n-three vehicle — a truck *and* a car. I tell em, ''Fyou don' widdle that down, I'm fixin ta buy me a hunderd-dollar car, put liability on it n that's it.' Hell, bein seventy-figh years old, n

I've only got a-hunderd thousan' on it. I don' hardly even do anything. Oh, I take my wife ta the doctor — Paducah n Cape, but that ain' ——

"So d'you live in town?"

"Naw. I live 'bout five miles outta town. Urbandale."

"D'ya live on a farm errr ——

"Naw, it's a li'l village out there. I'm honorary mayor out there. I get ev'rything done — the houses tore down."

"Is it north on highway three?"

"Naw, fifty-one."

"So yer the honorary mayor there?"

"Yeah, honorary mayor."

"Whacher name again?"

"Tom. Tom *Frer-ann.*"

"So one last question. How d'you think this community, that the people that still live here, that were here before the riots — how have they taken ta integration?"

"That has finally settled down," loosening the knot, uncrossing, and spreading open ... "Ya see, we jus' got a new mayor n he's black. The other guy, when he got elected, as soon as he was elected, he wen' right over there n fired ev'rybody. That caused some big problems. So you know what happened ev'ry board meetin doncha? ... Nothin. A big spot nothin. When this happens you don' git nothin done in a town. I see now, since the new mayor's been 'ere few months, things are settlin down. I see em startin ta tear down houses. N evenchly they'll start tearin down all on Commercial er whatever. 'Fwe kin git that cleaned up, 'fwe kin ever git a big bis'nis in here we might grow but it's gonna be a while. This hurts people who gotta work ta make a livin cuz they gotta drive outta town. Fine fer us retired people. I don' like traffic n we don' have a lot of it."

Tom kept talking about something to do with him having an aneurism and having to go to Saint Louis and almost dying on the way there. He wasn't trying to get sympathy or anything, just anecdotally highlighting why he doesn't like Saint Louis — the traffic.

So bye-bye Miss American Pie,
Drove my Chevy to the levee,
But the levee was dry.
And them good ol boys were drinkin whiskey and rye,
Singin, "this'll be the day that I die,
This'll be the day that I die."

      —— Don McLean
      "American Pie" (1971)

You should listen to that whole song. It's prophetic I tell ya, but maybe even more than that, like how the Bible is more than just a book: it's a damn tool for ideological indoctrination. When is (was) that day the music dies(d)?

Not a word was spoken,
The church bells all were broken.

Have you seen these new churches that all these new-age, coming-of-Christ's-harvest Evangelists attend? They don't have spires or altars or steeples or bells; they don't have organs or statues or Eucharists or priests.

They have some schmarmy muthafucker that stands up there in front of all the begotten pigs and piglets and screams into his wireless microphone to "Repent! And ye shall be healed! For the Lord is at your footstep but He's gonna step on you 'fyou don' come on down 'ere n stand before me n get the Devil knocked out o' ya! The Devil's around, I can feel him amongst us, but I also feel the power of *JESUS* amongst us! And you can too. *Yes you can!* For a one-time donation into the baskets that we are sendin 'round right now, you *too* can have the *power!* And for weekly donations hereafter, we'll even letcha *keep* the power!" ...

No need to confess your sins to some creep in a box or eat a stale wafer manufactured in some Eucharist factory in Poland (that's where the Catholics have Jesus' body on ice for an eternity). Nome. Alls ya gotta do is accept the power of Jesus

71

in yer heart n yer saved forever — that's it! Don't worry 'bout the rest o' yer life. Might as well fold up n keel over righ' now, so ya don' lose it n 'tleast ya know yull git inta heaven. Ain' tha' righ'?

Amen.

Father, Son, Holy Spirit — but wait!

> They caught the last train for the coast,
> The day the music died!

So there I was late in the afternoon of my third day down in Little Egypt with not a word to be spoken, the music dead, and my spiritual brethren already gone to hide away.

I was all alone, wandering aimlessly over the crumbling sidewalks when I happened to come across a flock of sheep guided by some big white lady with a perm haircut dressed like she was from one of Chicago's everything/everyone-looks-the-same burbs. They were coming down the sidewalk right at me, not really single-file or anything, just huddled together. I stopped and watched them like a lion, and of course like the idiot sheep they were, they didn't seem to notice me until it was too late.

"Howdy," I said to the overweight mom.

"Hi," she said cautiously.

"May I ask if y'all are with some sortta organization?"

"Yes," she said. "We're with Service Angels."

I was aware of this organization as a nonprofit, missionary-type churchey thing whose members were the recently-converted and financially-coveted children of Waspy Northern Suburbanites.

"Really," I said with enthusiasm. "I've heard o' y'all before. I'm here doin research on the community. I would love ta look at what you guys do 'fyou don' mind."

The teenagers huddled behind her — about twenty of them giggling dumbly. She glared protective and pensive.

"Is there a way I could come see you guys sometime tomorrow?"

"I'm not in charge here," she snapped like a Lake Michigan breeze.

"Oh."

"We're helpin just build houses n stuff here, but if you go down Cross Street here to the Harvest Life building, the Service Angels people are there."

"Alrighty," I said, turning down the side street from where they came.

One block later, I stood in a parking lot in front of what-looked-like a small elementary school building. All the rooms opened into a covered walkway exposed to the elements. I entered through the door (one of nine) marked 'Service Angels.' Within the dark chamber were three older young people — not high school but college-aged — sprawled on an array of beanbag chairs. They all turned and gazed at me as if looking at stars. They must've been saved.

"What's up?" one dude approached me.

"Actually, I jus' ran into some o' your people up the street. They told me ta come here n talk ta you. You see, I'm researching the social dynamics o' this community, and I've heard of your organization n all the great things you do, so I jus' thought it might be worth a gander."

He nodded and smirked slightly. "Yeah," he said. "I'm with Service Angels, n we're working on some houses n stuff."

"Would you guys mind if I came n observed what you do?"

"Of course not, not at all. Sherry," he called. Sherry came over. "Sherry, do you have the addresses of the places we're working at tomorrow?"

"Sherry," I said, offering her my hand and a big genuine smile, "I'm Randy."

"Nice to meet you." We shook.

"Randy I'm Josh," and I shook the alpha's hand.

Sherry gave me the addresses and we all stood and chitchatted while a doe-eyed boy watched from a beanbag ...

Sherry and Josh were college students from Ohio and Minnesota employed through Service Angels for the summer.

Josh was the boss of Service Angels, but not the head missionary. Service Angels, he explained, utilizes the facilities of the Harvest Life Missionary during the summer, working alongside the Harvest Life staff members, cleaning up houses, summer camps for kids, safe place for teens to hang out, etc. ... Plus Christian indoctrination and free internet access (no MySpace or porn).

I bid them adieu, promising to see them tomorrow, and then proceeded back to the motel. It was a little after six o'clock. I was walking past the liquor store when I heard, "Hey," loud and barking. It was USC Steve!

"Hey man, hey," he stumbled over to me from across the street. "Can I borrow a lighta from you?"

"Hold on," I said. "Before I do anything, you gotta promise me you'll do an interview with me."

"Alright, when you wanna do it?"

"Tomorrow."

"Naw, how 'bout Friday?"

"I'm gone Friday."

"Well, tomor' then. Uhhh — let's see here, wha' time?"

"One o'clock."

"Alrighty, one o'clock. Now can I borrow a lighta from you?" He was trembling and tossing his head about trying to be patient.

I reached into my pocket for the lighter and then, "Wait," pulling back, "Where at?"

"My house right up 'ere. Cumon," he cut quickly up the side street before turning into a walkway between two large houses. His was a shanty house occupying the backyards of two bigger homes across the street from the big Victorian where he told me to meet him the other day. Steve said to wait outside while he went in, so I plopped down on the moldy, rotten couch next to the front door, holding an unlit cigarette until he returned ...

"I had a rough life," he said impromptu.

"Would ya like ta do the interview now?"

74

"No. Tomoruh. I gotta go." He glanced around to make sure nothing was watching then went back in.

I walked back to the motel then solicited some slut to buy me a forty. She said she'd do it if I bought her a chicken sandwich, so I said alright, and we cut over to the gas station. She went in with ten of my dollars; I told her she could keep the change from my forty which would leave her with about seven for a sandwich — more than enough.

As I was standing outside waiting, a cool cat in a doo-rag pouring a beer into a styrofoam (not Styrofoam™ — see Wikipedia: *s(S)tyrofoam*) cup came up to me and said, "Tha' girl youz jus' talkin to — shih dude!" This wasn't a good 'shih.'

"What's her deal?"

"Dude, tha' bitch is crazy. She a mooch." He shook his head then looked away when she came out and shook his head even more when she handed me my forty before hopping in the back of a black car with fully tinted windows. There was no chicken sandwich.

"I'll come by n see you later," she said.

"I'll be sleepin." But the car sped off ...

I was lying in bed, playing with my dick when someone knocked on the door ... "Yo dude!"

The knocking turned to pounding, "Yo dude ya in there?"

I pulled on some shorts and jerked the door open.

"Wuz you sleepin?" She seemed a bit on edge.

"Yeah I was," lighting up a cigarette. "You wanna smoke?"

"Sure." We sat on the ledge smoking ...

"Dude, you got anymore money? I need ta get a chicken sandwich."

"I jus' gave you money."

"Yeah, man, but my friend took it." She was getting a bit upset ... Maybe that guy driving the black car was her pimp and she owed him money because she fucked some nigger and failed to collect ...

But —— "That's your problem, not mine."

75

She stood up glaring at me helplessly. "Man alls I need is five bucks fer a chicken sandwich!" barking ...

I flicked out my cig. "Good night. I'm outta money," I said cooly.

"You ain' got any?" begging now ...

"Nope." ... slammed the door in her face, took care of unfinished business, and slept like a baby ...

... ||| ... ||| ... |||

I was in a garden of naked sugarplum fairies when suddenly I saw nothing but felt everything shaking like I was inside a grumbling monster. The alarm clock flashed 12:00. My cell phone said it was 7:52.

I stretched, showered, then walked down to a diner for breakfast with all the great white elephants watching *Montel*. I ate, paid, and dug out, ventured back to the motel to check out, and set off for my dates with the sheep and Steve the Congressman (vodka that is).

After drudging through five decaying blocks, I found an old frame house surrounded by pale faces. Some stood on the roof, others on the ground. One guy, Mike, seemed to be in charge ...

"It seriously looks like a hurricane came through n destroyed this place," he said. Mike was another paid intern for Service Angels.

"So why are you guys fixin up this house?"

"It's gonna be a children's home."

"So like an orphanage or somethin?"

"No, not really."

"Well, then what is it?"

"Ummm —— ... looking around for the answer to appear ... Then, "There she is, talk to Karen, she'll tell you more." Mike climbed up on the roof to hammer away with the monkeys.

Karen was seated on a stack of shingles just watching. She looked like a Karen ... I introduced myself, told her what I was doing/researching; she responded with an elongated smile crossing her jolly red face. She was enthusiastic but painfully comforting — her eyes innocent, virginal and nice. She laid out the facts really well, but spoke very dull and very boring. Here's pretty much what she told me:

... Service Angels is a national organization that helps people in downtrodden neighborhoods clean up their communities. They get a lotta their money from donations, but they also charge $200 per-person to *perform* a week of missionary labor and whitewash Aunt Polly's fence. The Cairo Service Angels chapter was working on about twenty-five houses over the whole summer — three or four per week. Karen wasn't directly associated with Service Angels but was the director of the Harvest Life Missionary that partners with Service Angels during the summer months. According to her, Harvest Life is a faith-based community that involves "being with God" and "doing what He tells you."

Ironically (and you'll understand why this is ironic a bit later), all of the people that run Harvest Life are white and none of them are actually FROM Cairo. "Most of our staff right now are from out-of-state," Karen said.

She continued in a depressingly slow, dispassionate humbum, "When I first came here it made me really sad. My first impression was of extreme depression and extreme poverty."

Sometime around 2003, Karen came to Cairo on a missionary trip with Service Angels. The place left such an impression on her that she later moved from the buckle of the Bible belt (Springfield, Missouri) into a house on Washington Avenue right in the heart of Cairo. She felt that was where (how) God wanted her. She never planned to start a ministry, just be a really good neighbor, so she baked cookies for the children and read them the Bible. She didn't start the ministry until after she had established her goodness ...

Karen kept yapping rather dully about the organization and its goals which, of course, all led into various vagueries about *God* and what *He's* doing and how Cairo is *His* beacon of hope for the future of America and the world.

"This may seem a little far-fetched based on where you are in the spiritual world, but this town has been so oppressed because God has a plan for it and the enemies don't like that plan, so they try to break our spirits, but God will prevail as He always does. I think it will happen as a result of a disaster."

But what I've always wondered is, how does God have any enemies? If God doesn't like something can't He just make it non-existent?

Based on where Karen was in the spiritual world, I knew she wouldn't understand so I didn't ask her. She just kept talking ...

"Thousands of people come to Cairo because they believe there will be a natural disaster here that will spawn a revival and give rebirth to the whole nation!"

The spirits are alive and they are dancing on civilization's decaying corpse ...

"We have a promise from God," she said. "And it's been confirmed several times, that God is gonna make a place of refuge here for those who believe in him."

"That's very interesting," I said. "How have you confirmed this?"

"Through prayer and prophecy."

"Awesome! Awesome!" I jotted ferociously. I mean, this was great stuff! God and prophecy and spirits and beacons ...

I bid her adieu and kept writing as I walked away. Then, putting my notepad in my pocket, I crossed back over to her, still on those shingles.

"Thank you," I said. "I appreciate you talkin with me."

"You're very welcome!"

Somehow or other we kept talking. I got around to telling her about how I stayed down at the Belleview, and she stopped me mid-sentence and said that if I ever needed a place to stay, I should just call her and she would help me out. I thanked her graciously, took down some contact information, and ventured back up the street where another battalion of Service Angels was busy on a house about three blocks past Sycamore Avenue.

When I arrived at the scene, I found the crew painting the pillars on the front porch of a two-story, frame stucco surrounded by a chain-link fence. The place belonged to an old black man who was squatting on the stoop — Bermuda shorts and a button-up shirt over a heavy, bulbousing frame; thick plastic brim glasses and a low rumbling voice like that of a bullfrog. He was jivin the shih with some neighbors, puffing on a blunt while the white Christian kids slaved ...

I introduced myself, thoroughly explaining that I was an independent researcher with no affiliation to anyone or anything what-so-ever. I asked him if he would "mind clarifying a few things about the sixties n seventies here."

In a deep, yet friendly bellow, he said, "I'll talk to ya, but you can' use my name or a tape recorder."

"Understandable," I said, arming myself with my notepad. From here on, this man will be known as Bullfrog Bill ...

"It was bad. There ain' nothin you can say now thaz gonna change anythang." ... the tape recorder was on, hidden in the palm of my clenched hand beneath the notepad on which I furiously jotted ... "I come out on the police force in sixty-eight, sixty-nine — the people thaz runnin the town now, many wuz runnin it back then."

To be here during the protests ...

"I'm not wha' black people call a h_____ *[inaudible]*. I see a pi'ture for what it is n speak on out for what it is. Back in the olden days, there were a lotta prejudice white people, but they would help black people if the black people showed they wuz worthy. As blacks got an education, the element between blacks n whites growin up togetha — the element changed. Back when ev'rything wuz segregated, a lotta young white kids didn' know 'bout how blacks lived. Blacks got educated, then they start seein the wrongs imposed on em. They start complainin n doin things about it."

Justifying arousal ...

"I would say they were justified in risin up n demandin better treatment, but we had some black leaders that were prejudice n selfish n used they own people fer they own selfish gain."

Bullfrog Bill spoke differently about the movement than either Perry or Coach. There was no intellectual morality or Romantic righteousness in his tone; rather he was very down-to-Earth, closer in perspective to Tom (the old white guy) because he didn't seem to associate or disassociate persons or people with various rights and wrongs just because of skin color.

In his narrative, he pointed out that the conflict began when white organizations — namely Illinois State Police and the Ku Klux Klan — fired automatic weapons into the Pyramid Court housing complex. This was later confirmed by Ellis, yet directly contrasts Tom's story in which the blacks began the shootings. Still though, Bullfrog had a twist: the black militants kept the battle going even after the State Police and KKK backed off, terrorizing white business owners and local residents.

Why keep fighting?

Money.

Charles Koen was the leader of the United Front. Perry Ellis was his second in command as head of the NAACP which partnered with the United Front — a conglomeration of local Civil Rights organizations.

"The leadership turned down ev'rything the guvament offered because the leadership didn' want it ta stop."

The United Front received funds to keep fighting from national militant organizations including the Black Panthers and the Nation of Islam. The Pyramid Court housing complex became a fortress for the militants. Most of the locals wanted the fighting to stop, but the leaders had more to gain than the people they claimed to be fighting for.

"We didn' get nothin outta the movement that they wuz askin for because o' the crookedness o' the black leadership. The downtown area became a ghos' town."

After Koen horded hundreds of thousands of dollars

through his string of nonprofit organizations, the fighting stopped. Koen had the money he wanted, so he purchased the old Security Bank Building and sold over a million dollars in shares to open up the first black bank in Cairo.

But, "It was a scam," Bullfrog said.

According to the Wikipedia entry *Charles Koen,* Koen was "convicted and sentenced on May 21, 1991, to 12 years imprisonment, ordered to pay $636,000 in restitution, and $5,000 in penalties. His sentence stems from a conviction on charges of embezzlement, misapplication of Federal Program Funds, theft of public money, false statements, arson, and mail fraud."

The arson charge was for the 1985 conflagration of the Security Bank Building into which he moved his United Front 'front.' The jury (Wikipedia makes special consideration to note its all-white make up) found that the fire was an "act in a scheme to collect $550,000 from an insurance policy and a means by which Koen attempted to conceal his alleged theft of Government grant funds."

The article goes on to note that Koen was further charged with other fraud-related schemings and plottings in 2008. As of January 1, 2010, Koen was 64 years old.

In 2007, when I spoke with Bullfrog Bill, Koen owned and operated the Heavenly Gates Funeral Home in Cairo; however, Bullfrog said that he doesn't live in Cairo anymore, just stays at the funeral home sometimes. A subsequent phone call to the funeral home resulted in no answer and no voicemail or answering service; Bullfrog didn't think Koen would talk to me anyway.

Bullfrog continued describing selfish and greedy acts that took place during the tumult: white business owners burned their own buildings "to take advantage of the opportunity," collecting on insurance by blaming the fires on the black militants.

Of course now, in the twenty-first century, everything's pretty much calmed down and "things are pretty well normal."

That's right. Normal ...

Go with the flow and trickle slowly downstream, away and away from your origins until you spill into the salty sea ...

... ||| ... ||| ... |||

After listening to Bullfrog Bill, I had had enough of Cairo for a while. I dug out of there as fast as I could, then slowed down when I got into Missouri and realized I had to cross a big black spot on the map — the Ozarks — and a map I didn't have, so I bought one and examined it thoroughly, planning to cut through little towns like Park Hill, Steeleville, and Saint James, all the way back across the Osage River, through Jefferson City and finally to Columbia. I know, not quite the promise land, but hey, I was excited to get back to being a normal college kid with normal college-kid fun-things-to-do and no more conspiracies, Christians, and crap to care about.

I popped in the Grateful Dead while passing through Sikeston, Missouri, just across the river from Cairo, and on up Interstate 55 to Cape Girardeau and then Jackson where I exited on to State Highway 72 to wind up and down and around hills and valleys, through cow pastures and farms. I would describe this route with more aesthetic and linguistic vigor, but it wasn't really all that exciting: I listened to Simon and Garfunkel (after The Dead) and smoked cigarettes, just cruising along back into the trees, twisting knots outta the cardinal directions ...

Ba-da-ding-ding-ding-ding-ding-ding-a-ling ...

Banjos and log cabins and Confederate Flags and firewood for sale and Busch Light camo cans; time slipping away; the sun steadily arching across the sky, always ahead and always behind — eight minutes old: it's already burnt out and we're all screwed, so quit thinking about it because it's over, done, and so are you.

This is the future ...

Then I reached Fredericktown somewhere out in the middle of those dark woods. There was a massive steel building constructed of huge, vertical panels of corrugated, rippling siding painted a poopy tan color — no windows, just a huge set of quadruple doors underneath a drive-up valet-parking awning, above which was a huge spire, at the apex of which was golden glimmering sunlight; Calvary Temple of Christ the Martyr right on the edge of Fredericktown which was, of course, "A nice place to live" ...

A cute little puppy running around your backyard while your children play on an arsenic-tainted jungle gym and your neighbor yells at his whore-wife for stinking up the trailer with her meth stew ...

So nice ...

I kept going, thank the Lord, Christ the Martyr, all the way through Park Hill where Mount Sinai rose from the Earth as if man with all his might had put it there. He had: a 900-foot-tall mountain of dust in the middle of the town — "tailins from the strip minin," a woman named Agnes told me. Four-wheelers rode up and down its steeply graded slope, some points practically perpendicular to the ground. The mound was composed of a dust "finer than play sand," again thank you Agnes ...

On to Potosi and Steeleville and the Meramec River and Saint James, and stopping now and then and here and there to take in the scenery and listen to the folk talk about their kin and the rivers ...

up stream, down stream, away to and fro

go go go, back from whence you didn't come to the same place and all of the little places you've never been before

go go go

the seed you sow

the harvest you reap

the key you don't have you will always keep

go go go

And I went through all of the little towns past all of the little boxes, racing that sun as it descended closer and closer to the asymptote ...

getting lower and lower and lower

And then to Jefferson City and the domed capitol —
civilization's silhouette against the promise of the distant ever-
reaching, never-to-be-reached horizon ...

go go go ...

will you ever get there? will it ever be done?

go go go ...

follow the setting sun.

you can hide but can you run?

which is more fun?

bewitched until the job is done ...

I went until I was almost sick, following that burning orb
until it burned out forever only to rise again for another never.
I sped along the highway all the way back to Columbia because
I felt it up ahead closer and closer, coming and going past all
the familiar places and unfamiliar faces, through the valley and
over the mountain then back to level again, the rays parting the
curtain and curving around the spires reaching for the stars ...

And as I turned on to College Avenue and into my
driveway, it all disappeared behind the curtain, beyond the
horizon.

Home Sweet Home

The hiding place from which you roam

Not as homely as the road

To brood in your comfortable, miserable abode

Back to fear and to conspire

To disappear into your mire

The adventure over for Now

From it questions to inquire

Who What When Where How

Next?

2

Who, What, When, Where, How ... but Why?

The Devil

I grew up in a traditional white, middle-class American family — one dad, one mom, and a little sister. There were also grandparents who were all still married and aunts and uncles who were all married and a buncha cousins and faraway relatives that everyone always missed and a buncha other people I would only ever see at reunions, weddings, and funerals. Most of my relatives resided in Montdale County, Illinois, and most of them will die there and be buried there because they've never lived anywhere else.

You see, my mom, Denise, was the oldest of four children begotten by Joe and Charlene (Mramor) Mueller. She had two younger brothers and a little sister, and they all grew up in Hamilton in the Sherwood subdivision where everything was perfect — the houses, the lawns, the conservative families, the dark forest surrounding ...

It was the nineteen-sixties. Love was in the air and especially in this quaint neighborhood of Baby Boomers. Everyone had kids — lots of them. The Rosensteins who lived across the street from the Muellers had like fourteen or something ridiculous, and now they have like thirty grandkids and like ten great-grandkids or something absolutely absurd: Catholics, that's what they were. But so were we, running around in the woods and the neighborhood — my mother that is — playing and fighting and beating up her little sister all the while keeping care of everything in and around the house while her parents were at work or something of the sort: she never really tells that many stories.

My dad, August, on the other hand, can ramble on and on

and tell story after story after story about growing up in Rutherford, Illinois — this li'l ol coal-mining town about sixteen miles east of Hamilton on Illinois Route 18. My grandparents, Adolf and Sylvia (D'Angelo) Wolfram, owned a tavern in this little town of about six-hundred people: Wolf's Tavern it was called because that's what everyone called my grandpa. The place was world-renowned for his (Wolf's) cheeseburgers that he made fresh everyday ... drive into town (Chatawpa, population two thousand, bordered Rutherford) to the local IGA for ground chuck then come back to the tavern/house (they were all the same building, connected with a shared kitchen) and roll the chuck into balls then smash the balls into patties and presto! — Ready to throw on the grill! So what was Wolf's secret ingredient?

Well you see, Wolf ate garlic five times a day, and I'm talking *raw* here — just peel a clove and pop it in like a breathe mint — so when he rolled those beef patties with his bare hands, they absorbed the aroma of decades of garlic that emanated from his pores. Seriously! You could smell him coming from miles away — this wrinkled old man all hunched over, his knees bowed out to the sides from standing up his whole life. Anyway, that's Adolf 'Wolf.'

Now my grandma — she's a-whole-nother story — always had her hair tied up in a layered beehive-like thing and smiled and fawned all the men at the bar. When she wasn't out flirting (yeah, she flirted all the way up to the day they closed the place: Wolf's Tavern, fifty-four years in business — 1946 to 2000) she was in the kitchen stirring the chili that she made from scratch everyday — her secret recipe. She never wrote down the recipe, and years later when she was in her eighties spiraling into dementia and my mother tried to get it out of her, she told my mother, "Well I'm not telling *YOU!*" like a witch protecting her secret potion ...

So those are my grandparents on my dad's side — colorful individuals, I do say. But that's not all: my dad has two older sisters, Margaret and Isabel, and to this day they always fight and yell and scream about bullshit, usually when my dad's telling a story about almost blowing off his mother's head with a bottle rocket, or the time one of the Beckett boys told him he was getting ready to go fuck his mother (the Beckett boy fucking the Beckett mother) — dead serious. This was Rutherford, Illinois. I don't know how else to describe it. I feel like I could talk forever about everything but then we wouldn't get to the meat of the issue which is, right now, my family — WHO, ya see?

Here's the rundown, continuing with my father's side ...

Alfred Aloicius Wolfram III was an Austrian noble who immigrated to America after World War I in order to escape the socialists. Wolfram married Matilda and they begot Adolf 'Wolf' and Ernest 'Ernie'. Alfred died in a coal-mining accident in Rutherford in 1930. Wolf was just ten years old.

Salvatore Agosto D'Angelo was the father of my grandmother, Sylvia who was the youngest of seven. D'Angelo immigrated to America in 1906, sending money from his labors as a coal miner back to his wife, Lila, who resided with children in Bologna, Italy. Salvatore returned to Italy in 1908, and in 1910, he and Lila immigrated their entire family to America permanently. They came through Ellis Island and resided in New York until he found a job with a coal-mining company. In 1911 Salvatore, his wife, and his children (Sylvia was yet to be born) moved to Ten Sleep, Illinois — the newly formed mining suburb of Hamilton — where he built the house in which he and his family lived until Lila died in 1973 and possession of the property reverted to Sylvia who gave it to my father, August, in 1982, who lived in it and began his law practice in the living room then married Denise in 1986, who gave birth to me in 1987 and my sister, Bella Elise, in 1988, who were both reared and raised in the house that has been in the family for an entire century.

Back to my mother's side ...

I remember my great-grandmother and her brothers and sister all sitting under the big Sycamore Tree at Nona's house (that's what we called her, my great-grandmother, mother of my grandmother Charlene, a.k.a. Noni). Nona was drinking Old Milwaukee with her brother Paul Salvani, a.k.a. Pow-wow, a.k.a. Uncle Pauly, who was pretty much just a round ball of fleshy goo with a toothless orifice into which he would pour beer and outta which would emit the syllables, "Pow wow wow wow!" — loud barks descending into muffled ughs. At dinner, everyone huddled around the picnic tables and all tried not to look at Uncle Pauly. I could never help but notice how the jowls of fat beneath his chin would jiggle in tune to the smacking of his gobbling-groveling so that he looked and sounded like a big turkey.

After dinner, all the adults — Nona Gianna, Pauly, Aunt Mimi, Uncle Reno, Uncle Marco, even Pauly's mistress Dorris — would sit around drinking their cheap light beer and tossing their empty cans into the yard where us kids were running around barefoot, so that it always happened that somebody stepped on a can and cut themselves, hobbling back with a bloody foot to the adults in their hotchpotch. They were always just laughing and laughing, having a dandy ol time, and so were we — usually myself, my sister Bell, my cousins, and some of the neighbor kids.

So that's Nona — the matriarch on my mother's side, my mother's mother's mother. There was also great-grandma Peggy, my grandpa Joe's mother. When I was much younger, Peggy would babysit me during the day so my mom could get some shit done around the house. I remember going over to Peggy's house and her smoking those long Capri cigarettes as we sat around and watched *Mister Rogers' Neighborhood* and *Sesame Street*. My grandma loved Mister Rogers ...

Grandma Peggy would feed me bologna sandwiches, and we would play with the floor fans with which I had an obsession as a child. When I was three, I asked my parents for a green garden fan — the kind that are supposed to scare away moles — for Christmas. My dad found a white one and painted it green. I was a simple child, easily pleased ...

Anyway, Peggy descended into dementia and spent the last five years of her life babbling away in the nursing home. Everyone thought she was incoherent, but I thought it all meant something, so it scared the living piss outta me. I remember when she died, and I remember when Nona died, they played "On Eagles' Wings" ...

> And He will raise you up, on Eagles' wings,
> Bear you on the breathe of dawn,
> Make you to shine like the sun,
> And hold you in the palm of His hand.

And so that's where they are, sitting in some dude's hand somewhere out there up above, shining down on us.

Watching ...

... ||| ... ||| ... |||

Years later after the State of Illinois required that 'they' remove the merry-go-round for the safety of the children, Randy happened to find himself on the old playground hiding in a fog of light beneath the autumn moon ...

Atty lit it and passed it to him and he puffed it and passed it to Vinnie who puffed it and passed it back to Nate and so on and so on ...

Randy gazed out upon all of the trees and all of the new plastic playground equipment and he heard *their* screams echoing beyond the stony whitewash of reverence ...

~~ *RW* ~~

When people ask me where I'm from, I say, "Oh, just a small town."

Then they ask, "Really? Where?"

"Oh, south central Illinois."

"That's awesome! I'm from a small town too!"

And I ask, "Really? Where?"

"Springfield."

And I inform them that *Springfield* is not a *small* town. And they are like, "Oh?!" all shocked and violated, "How big was *your* town?"

"Six thousand," I say proudly, "but that includes the prisoners, so really only like four thousand."

And they look at me in gaping befuddlement and say, "Wow!" because there's no way anyone actually lives in places that size, let alone someone enrolled in a major state university because everyone who comes from places like Hamilton all must be idiot hicks or farmers or something. Of course, after revealing the population of my hometown, some ask, "Wha' d'you guys do there?"

And I say, "Oh not much, ya know, jus' go drive aroun' n get high n park in cornfields, drink beer, go down ta the creek with our four-wheelers n go muddin, tear up some farmer's field, ya know? Things like that."

And then they laugh as if they had never heard of anyone doing such things. I continue, telling stories of black panthers living in the woods behind Fillmore, or the old lady who lived across the street and grew poison hemlock, or the time me and some friends drove down to Sorento along the winding gravel roads to torment Mister Miyagi ...

"Like the karate kid?!"

"Yeah. He was jus' this old guy — pry just a white guy but he looked jap — n he lived in a li'l ol house — one-story, bungalow-lookin thing — on the outskirts o' Sorento facin the woods," and the more I talk, the more the country accent comes out ...

"We would jus' drive by n honk r horn, flyin fas' down this straightaway, cuz ya see the road was really long n straight n you could build up good speed n git a good head start on im 'fore the first turn, n you needed a good head start on im cuz he drove — get this! — a li'l blue Ford Festiva, but it wuz souped up: I tell ya that thing could fly! Anyway, ya go back aroun' n do it agin, three times, n on the third time ya better watch out cuz he'd be sittin there in his front yard — there was no driveway — in the car waitin for ya with his lights turned off n as soon as you pass he'd swoop out n start goin real slow, n we'd be cruisin over these three li'l dips n rises n there he'd be back there. You could see his headlights comin real slow, n then ya get over the secon' rise n now he's closer! n then by the time yer over the third rise, he's right up on yer ass! I mean seriously, ON YOUR ASS!! You can' even see his headlights! N then ya hit the first stop sign, n fuck! ya don' fuckin stop! I mean ya got fuckin Mister Miyagi chasin ya n he pry wants ta kill ya, n not with a gun, pry a fuckin MACHETE!" ...

So now you're picturing this fantastic mystical place like something out of a movie, but it's all real. Seriously, we did this sortta shit all the time when I was in high school ...

"Well, one time — lis'n-uh-this — he chased us. It was me n four friends o' mine n I wuz drivin the Focus n we wen' down n did the whole loop-dee-loop three times aroun' n he —— well, I told em, I told the guys with me, I said, 'I wanna git this fucker back on our turf. We're gonna git im back in the Ham, see what 'appens.' So lo-n-behold, the third time around 'ere 'e comes slow n then fast n now he's RIGHT ON OUR ASSES!! N I ain' playin *no* games this time! UH UH! I whip 'roun' the corner n start zig-zaggin 'roun' these sharp hairpin curves on this country road, but I'm headin straight for the highway. We're gonna see if this guy's got any BALLS right?! See 'f'ee can take a high-speed chase on the highway — the li'l two-lane thoroughfare that cuts right through the center o' the county. Well thankfully it's late, like ten o'clock er somethin, n after ten in the cunt'ry e'rybody's at home sittin 'roun' the fire cookin chestnuts jus' like in the movies so we pretty much had the whole road t'ourselves. I *floored* the sun-uv-a-bitch, n he wuz still right there! RIGHT *ON MY ASS!!* Five minutes — that's all it took ta go ten miles — we were back in Hamilton, so I turn off the road n inta this residential neighborhood, n he's still back there followin us, so I take im 'roun' the block a couple o' times — nice neighborhood, old cobblestone streets n fancy houses where all the doctors n lawyers lived. But anyway, he realizes we *fucked* im after we took im 'roun' the block a few times n now he ain' up on our ass no more. NOPE! Jus' slowly creepin behind us always one turn back, so we stop n he stops a block back n then he moves for'd n gets close to us but not right up on us like before, jus' followin us like normal. He's fuckin lost! We bring im on our turf n the ol bastard gits lost! Don' know which way's home, poor muthafucker.

"Well anyway, I figure what-the-fuck, why not fuck with im a little more right? So I'm drivin real cautious but headed for the main road — MAIN STREET! N I turn left on Main Street n now we're *headin for the courthouse,* n Miyagi, this local legend —— seriously, ev'rybody, ev'ry kid at Hamilton High School knew exactly who this guy was n exactly what his car looked like n they all knew the stories of im chasin people off the road n *slittin their throats!*

"So lemme explain somethin real quick: Main Street is where ev'rybody hangs out on a Friday night, ev'ry high school kid in Hamilton either wantin ta go to a farm party er jus' sittin in the back o' parked trucks, lawn chairs propped up in the bed n drinkin beer outta coozies, smokin dope n cigarettes, a big ol hunka chaw in their lips ... So there's e'rybody up thur, n here I cum, Miyagi right behin' me n we're headin fer the courthouse n we pass the firs' group o' kids parked in fronta the Bank n we start honkin n leanin out the window, pointin back, screamin 'MIYAGI! MIYAGI! IT'S MISTER MIYAGI!' n ev'ryone hops in their big ef-five-fiddy pickups n files in! Now we got *a p'rade!* N e'rybody's honkin, even the cops, n we're all p'radin 'roun' the courthouse — me in front, Miyagi secon' n about twenty trucks n beat-up corvettes behind, the cop bringin up the rear. We swing 'roun' the courthouse, 'roun' the square goin 'bout five miles an hour: it's a bigger p'rade than when the football team went ta the Final Four! Miyagi in Hamilton?! It's fuckin *unheard of!*

"So we swing 'roun' the courthouse n then courteously 'fcourse, I keep goin south back to'rd Sorento, n I lead im back ta the road that'll take im back, n then I slow down n pull ta the side, still movin but jus' creepin along ya know ta let im pass, show im the courtesy. N you know what he does? You know what this *freak face DOES!?!?!?* ...

"He cums up along side us ... n he stops ... n I look over ... n it's the only time I ever got a good look at im ... n he smiles n waves ...

"Then he cruises off, speedin away in his li'l blue Ford Festiva into the black forest, back ta Sorento."

... and there's the silence ... the entire room of city kids stunned in disbelief ... This doesn't happen! Not in the twenty-first century! Not in America!

But it does. I assure you, it did. You can ask anyone — Atty, Vinnie, Cam, Devin, Jess, Nate, anyone! They all know. They all remember. But you know where they are?

Back in Hamilton.

Of course there are other legends ...

Like the story of the two twin girls who died at birth and were buried next to each other in Clear Springs Cemetery down south of Ten Sleep next to the abandoned church at the top of the steep wooded ravine, overlooking the rippling creek.

According to legend, at midnight on a full moon, two greenish-yellowish orbs appear above the respective graves of the twin girls. It may be a stupid ne'er-do-well who fucks with Mister Miyagi, but only the brave and adventurous make the trip to Clear Springs Cemetery, and even once there, few ever get outta the car, and those that do, well even fewer of them actually go into the damn cemetery. In fact I'm willing to bet that a grand total of less than ten people in the history of humanity have ever been in that cemetery at midnight of any given full moon, and of those ten, maybe five of them are still alive, and of those five, maybe two of them are Rachel Byrne and Ashley Provence.

So why the twin girls? Well, each of their tombstones features an engraving of a hand shaped like one of those foam finger thingies you get at baseball games. One of the hands is pointing up to heaven and all of God's angels; the other points down to the Devil's fiery furnaces and salt baths in the bowels of the Earth ...

There's another legendary place just a mile or so from the cemetery, back in the woods down in the bottomlands where three creeks all converge into a swamp and vicious dogs roam in wild packs. In fact it is common for adventurous youth to explore the cemetery and then drive on down the road, through the ravine, twisting around the looming hardwoods and into the muddy bottoms. At night, you park your car down at the bottom of the hill, turn it off and get out and just listen to the crickets, the frogs, and all of the swamp creatures alive and invisible ... the bugs sticking to your skin, something splashing in the muddy water just off the side of the barely elevated trail ... somewhere out there a coyote howls and wild dogs bark — one yelp and then dozens more ... no streetlights, only the moon, billions of stars, and fireflies in the trees flickering like stage lights synched with the croaking bullfrogs ...

It all fits together like a scripted play — the entire spectacle far more breathtaking than any Eiffel Tower or Great Wall or World Trade Center ...

Everyone wants to see all of man's creations before they die — the Taj Mahal, the Golden Gate Bridge, Red Square, the pyramids of Giza, or even the ruins at Machu Picchu. At least they're fucking ruins! As if they were once *better* but somehow, something ruined them ...

Yeah, nature did. And it will one day ruin our civilization too.

But our ruins will look different than those at Machu Picchu. We build huge ginormous cities with ginormous buildings the equivalent of mountains. Imagine! — thousands of years into the future, there will be great concentrations of metallic ores in places like Manhattan and Los Angeles, and all sorts of strange monkey-like animals living in the nooks and crannies swinging around on weird viny plants from building to building, outlandish trees growing from the tops of skyscrapers and schools of rats roaming floor to floor ...

... But back down in those bottoms, remember? There you are ...

You stand around for a little bit and smoke a bowl maybe or a cigarette for sure and maybe crack open a can of Natty Light from a thirty-rack that you're buddy's older brother purchased for you three days ago and you've been keeping it in the trunk of your car and now it's hot and stale but you drink it anyway because this is what you're supposed to do. Just like crickets have been chirping, frogs croaking, and fireflies flickering for centuries, teenagers will always drink warm, cheap beer, smoke weed, and drive around looking for places to perform such activities. The Shoal Creek Bottoms, as they are geographically known, happen to be such a place.

So here you stand, beer in hand, cigarette in the other, Led Zeppelin, probably album <u>IV</u>, playing over the car stereo, or The Grateful Dead, usually <u>American Beauty</u>, and maybe Pink Floyd, <u>Dark Side of the Moon</u> (one of *those* albums) ... and you and your beer and the music and the crickets and the frogs and the howling dogs and the trees and the muskrats and the stars and the moon and the red lights flashing on the plane thirty-thousand feet overhead and the car and the gasoline in the tank and the lighter fuel in your Bic and the aluminum can you'll probably throw into the water and the turtle that will get its head caught inside the tab and the tadpole that will die from alcohol poisoning and all the little microbes that live up your ass and around the corner: ALL OF YOU, animate and inanimate, are coexisting. Whether you litter or not — COEXISTING ... eat organic food or not — COEXISTING.

So you're down there in the bottomlands and you're getting drunk on warm beer and smoking Marlboro's while "Going to California" plays in the background. Your friends are silent, all doing the same shit as you — just wiggin out — when one of y'all decides to get back in the car, so everyone else follows, and y'all proceed on, twisting through the swampy bottoms until up ahead you see a railroad crossing atop a steep incline. Slowly, you climb the hill, watching out for trains chugging through the trees (there are no flashing red lights in the swamp). You don't see or hear any so you pull forward and park right in the middle of the tracks.

The moment you've all been waiting for ...

You and the guy sitting shotgun get outta the car and proceed to the trunk where there is a big bag of flour (yes, the stuff in bread) that you've been saving for just this occasion. You open the bag and each of you reaches in and grabs a big handful and then you proceed to the front and dust it over the hood and across the windshield, just enough so that you can't see through it. When it's all dusted nicely, you get back in the car, lock your doors, shift 'er into neutral, turn off the headlights and the radio and thus commence the sequence ...

LIGHTS BACK ON
HONK ONCE
LIGHTS OFF
LIGHTS BACK ON
HONK AGAIN
LIGHTS OFF
LIGHTS BACK ON
HONK AGAIN
LIGHTS OFF

... now sit patiently ... quietly ... tell your friends laughing in the back seat to shut the fuck up ...

... if you listen closely you can hear their little raspy voices whispering quiet ... and if you look closely through the flour-coated windshield you can see their cherubic faces ... and if you did everything right you'll see their hands on the windshield and you'll feel them slowly pushing you back ...

... back ...

... down the hill ...

... and off the tracks ...

This is the legend of Third Arch — the third and last railroad crossing south of Ten Sleep, and the only one that isn't a crossing at all, just a road ascending an embankment, dead-ending on the tracks.

The story goes ...

One time long long ago, back when the road actually crossed over the tracks and continued on the other side, a bus full of children got stuck on the crossing ...

Yadi-yadi-yada ... a train hit the bus.

Yadi-yadi-yada ... all the children died.

Allegedly if you perform the aforementioned launch sequence correctly, the porthole will open and you will be transported to the dimension of dead, ghostly children where they will find you, see that you are on their turf and subsequently push you back into your little three-dimensional comfort zone.

And the entire car full of people will be freaking out: one guy trembling, one guy pale white, two others laughing, and you're playing it cool like I-told-you-so, but you're really stunned in disbelief because you never thought it would happen in the first place.

And you know what?

It never does.

~~ *RW* ~~

But there were real legends too ...

... Imagine a little dollhouse — not one of those big Barbie mansions, but just a plain ol dollhouse, four to five rooms, pseudo-de-facto antique furniture, flowery wallpaper, etc. ...

... Imagine a little white picket fence around the little dollhouse and inside the white picket fence, imagine little gardens and flower beds ...

... Imagine a doll, pale and grim and sexless with the innocent smile of a child, sitting there in a little rocking chair in the little living room of the little dollhouse and just smiling oh-so-serenely-eerily ...

Now blow it up! Seriously, destroy the little dollhouse, then build it up again out of the ashes of the previously imagined perfection, so that what you now imagine is a *real* house in a *real* neighborhood with a *real* picket fence, *real* gardens, and a *real* doll who lives inside, except this doll is no toy, no innocent child, but a witch! ...

And now imagine the little house and its lone, singular porch light illuminated on a dark, windy autumn evening: dry leaves skitter about the dimly lit street and come to rest against the little picket fence surrounding the only house on the block without a tree in its midst ...

... ||| ... ||| ... |||

May 2006 — the day after Giby resided over what-so-ever was celebrated ...

"D'you remember Rose McCoy?"

Up and over from his pensive position, eyes swirling bloodshot, "Wha' d'you mean do I 'member Rose McCoy? 'Fcourse I 'member Rose McCoy."

We're stoned.

"Huh! Yeah dude! D'you 'member the time she came out with a fuckin shotgun!?"

... a high-pitched cackle, then over again — that light flitting ...

... have to look to have to look to ——

"Yes!" he exclaims, facing shy back into his supportive palm.

... crouching in the bushes behind the little yellow house and the television in the basement flashing real close could almost hear it and the cops circling the block and then their spotlight but they couldn't find you and then the footsteps trampling-trampsing-traipsing then Jess coming and you whispering loud and him diving in before they could sweep him with the light ...

"She came outside n had that thing," the shadows dancing behind time's curtain ... "We tee-peed her like four or five times in two weeks, you remember?"

"Yeah, yeah," smiling back at the reflections.

"And YOU!" I snap. "*You* had your little code!" ... his smile fading ... "Remember? It wuz like seasons or somethin,

101

like we had those walkie-talkies, each of us with the walkie-talkies — this was a hell-uv-an operation we had set up 'ere — n you were on lookout in the street."

"I was in the tree across the street," his corpse like a viscous blob sprawled out in the chair, motionless except the lips.

"That's right!"

"Winter," vacantly dour, "it was winter."

"Yes! That was the cue ta fuckin RUN!"

"Yep," fossilized.

"N d'you remember her comin out? Oh my *God!* I saw her in the kitchen window talkin on the phone! What a witch!"

"Yep."

... the lens the camera your face glancing up from the driveway off to the side the porch light yellowish-orange covering the toilet paper covering the bushes and the knick-knacks and Halloween decorations and the banisters and the poles in the light no cars coming or going just the dead silent waiting and the door swinging open and then outta the walkie-talkie 'winter! winter! winter!' like 'boo' and then running away away away faster faster faster until the legs work harder than gravity and the ceaseless chatter over the radio like 'I saw her! I saw her!' — 'run! run! run!' — 'Zeek's house! Zeek's house!' — 'Beckemeyer!' — 'no Kenny! don't go into Beckemeyer!' — and through the backyards of little dollhouses a giant a shadow a superman and all the dogs barking and motion lights flashing then the tension in your shins and quadriceps the houses and garages and trees and bushes all filling up bigger and bigger down down down like an anvil on your shoulders so that each step is heavier and louder stomps echoing and the listeners and watchers all in the little boxes so you hide in the alley a dumpster shrouded by a wall and the crouching and panting and sitting and the sounds without all around of scattering footsteps and dogs ...

"D'you remember later when we went back — WAIT A SECOND!" ... him looking up, expressionless again ... "Were

102

you with me?" thinking into the white streetlight flickering behind the tree branches ... "No. I think it was Cam — it was! After 'bout an hour er somethin like that — a long time later — the cops were gone n he n I snuck across the playground ——

　　... little gnomes in the big oak trees ...

"We had ta crawl on our hands n knees because o' that one streetlight by the big rock there," me gesturing; him looking away back into that thinking palm ... "Anyway, we army crawled n got ta the edge o' the playground behind the house across the street from her n then stood up n the houses were dark — there never was anyone alive in any o' those other houses, ya know?"

Chuckling to himself ...

"I mean seriously! Doesn' it seem ta you like all the houses we never tee-peed were always dark n empty?"

Another chuckle, then up with a grin, "Maybe they were jus' sleeping."

"Who sleeps at nine o'clock on a Saturday night?"

"Lots o' people."

"No!"

　　... corpses waiting to turn to dust ...

"Anyway, you alright?"

"Jus' tell the story."

"Where was I?" ... ||| ... "Oh yeah! Well Cam n I army-crawled n then there she was on the porch with a shotgun, n then we saw 'er grab 'er kid n throw im in the back o' the big truck n drive away like she was comin ta look fer us er somethin."

　　... the truck pulling out and revving then driving right past you and Cam hiding behind that house waiting then seeing it coming back into the parking lot to corner you with those searchlights sweeping across the open and you thinking 'she saw us' and him saying it real slow but you 'no she didn't' as the truck comes back so you run her turning down the street you running right in front of her house accelerating fast and then screeching to a stop back there over the fence and through the shrubs past the vicious dogs around the searchlights pants and shirts ripping on thorns and barbs and then the door slamming so you stop and crouch behind a burn barrel to peep at the truck staring you down a predator with two big bright eyes locked on dinner and then the shadow leaps into the back of it idling and the slow clickity-clank of gears and slowly swinging backwards to idle some more and him saying 'is she giving up' and then slamming the door flickering the headlights and ———————————————————————————

——————————————— 'she gave up' so you walk in the serene stillness back through the alleys and behind the houses careful and stealthy and finally pounding on the back door and Zeek coming inside greeted by Sarge and Kenny and Jess and Latty and Atty and Whitey all waiting for the story — 'she had a gun' — 'she chased us in the truck' — 'she was sittin on her front porch with a gun waitin for us ta come back' — 'and she chased us' — 'n we had ta duck under branches n hop fences n stuff' — 'and she might've seen us' — 'but I don' think so cuz then she would've got out n come after us' — 'she had ta see us dude' — 'but I don' think so cuz she woulda shot us' — 'Randy! she's not gonna shoot us for tee-peein her house!' — 'she had a gun dude' — 'we jus' tee-ped her house' — 'she's crazy dude she had a gun' — 'she saw us!' — 'I don' think so' — 'whatever it doesn't matter' — 'she had a fuckin gun!' — 'it's over' — 'she wanted ta kill us!' — him looking down and fading away 'she's nuts' everyone silent with gaping mouths then wondering where Giby is and Sarge shrugging and Latty saying he saw him sprint up the street after she came out but nobody's seen him since so the cops probably got him but nobody knows ...

Turning to Sarge sitting there blank-staring out into the darkness, he catches my gaze and glances back, "D'you remember what 'appened ta Giby that night?"

Tying his face into knots trying to squeeze a memory from his scrunching forehead, holding it like that for a while, then relaxing real slow and dramatic, his eyes real wide, he raises an index finger and says, "Hambone!"

"What?"

"Remember?" and now all excited, leaning into it.

"Tell me."

"We all went back ta Zeek's."

"But me n Cam didn' get back until ——

"No NO! Before that!" and now animated ... "We all reconvened at Zeek's n we were standin in his living room — I remember this! — and ev'ryone was there, all of us!" sitting up to put on his golden mask ... "All of us that is — except Giby."

And then really remembering and realizing that everything is wrong, and shivering like cold hands on my shoulders ... "That's right" ... him staring at me ... "so what 'appened next?"

"Well, we were sittin there in the living room, all of us. It was me, you, Jess, Kenny ——

"Zeek."

"Zeek, Cameron, n Latty n Atty n we were ——

"Wait. You forgot Whitey."

"Was he there?"

"I'm pretty sure he was there dude."

"I don' think Whitey was there."

"Really?"

We tried to remember ...

"No," he shook his head, "he wasn' there."

"Alright, anyway ——

"So we were sittin there, wonderin where Giby was, and then —— (KNOCK, KNOCK, KNOCK)," onomatopoetically knocking on the wall behind us ... "Somebody (KNOCK) was at (KNOCK, KNOCK) the DOOR! Ev'rybody froze! I happened ta be sitting closest ta the door, so I got up n looked through the peephole ——

"There was *no* peephole!"

"Alright, alright. There was no peephole. But I opened the door, just enough ta peak through the glass, and *who* did I see?"

Shrugging.

"Kenny Leach."

"Oh yeah! The cops came!"

"The cops came. So I slammed the door n locked it, n Latty," pointing now ... "Latty was standin by the window! And he runs over ta the couch n falls down," barely able to contain his laughter ... "and he looks like a fuckin ghost. 'Latty, are you alright?' and he says, 'I jus' saw the scariest fuckin thing in that window!' — 'What Latty? What is it?' and he looks at each of us, face ta face ta face, 'Rose McCoy,' he says, 'was fuckin starin at me in the damn window!'"

... 'she's fuckin lookin in the damn window!' — 'she was in the window?' — 'we gotta get the fuck outta here!' — 'where are we s'posed ta go? we got the cops outside n Rose McCoy starin in here!' ...

"That was hilarious dude. She fuckin came up n peeped in that window!" ... will never forget her staring through that window ... "Ya know dude, we had some fuckin crazy times with that damn bitch!"

"Yeah we did," smiling off ...

"Ya know dude, it's these stories like this that we'll carry with us forever."

"Forever?"

"Well, not forever, I mean ——

"Randy, *forever* is a really long time."

"Yeah I know, but I mean ——

"Randy, I don' think you *do* know."

"No, you're right, pry not, but I mean, you know they ——

"Randy, *forever* ... is an ETERNITY."

... crickets, a big gulp ...

We brooded a while, then working up the courage, I asked him, "Wha' d'you think of memories?"

A slight twitch, "Wha' d'you mean?"

"I mean, d'you think that what we remember is actually what happened or do we only remember what we want ta *think* happened?"

Knotting and squeezing, then a head cock ... "Does it really matter?"

"I don' know — I mean — I guess not. You're right. I shouldn't've even asked."

"No Randy!" ... you should know better ... "Does it matter *whether or not* it actually happened?"

"Oh!" realizing, "I guess not." Chills up my spine and cold hands on my shoulders ... "I mean 'fcourse, I'm only gonna remember somethin because somethin would've had ta happen in order for me ta remember it, but what exactly happened ta trigger that memory doesn' matter because the memory has been morphed n warped by my own mind from the moment I started ta remember it."

A nod, "Memories are in your head."

"No debating that."

"I wrote a poem the other day."

"Really?"

"Do you wanna hear how it goes?"

"'Fcourse."

"The darkest place in the universe is the space between our ears, the home of all our memories, the place of all our fears."

Thus it ended — me shivering into the white light, him gaping into the chasm ...

... ||| ... ||| ... |||

"So whatever happened ta Giby?"

Sparking the bowl then bursting smoky coughs and cackles ... "Ahem! — Ahem!" pounding his chest, his droopy gaze turns into a goofy smile that flickers into another exploding cackle ... then emerging feet first, "Yer still on that?"

"Sure," grabbing the bowl, puffing without a cough. "So we were sittin in the living room at Zeek's house n Rosey girl came up and ——

Again that cackle ... "Rosey girl," subsiding, "I like that."

"Yeah. Anyway she came up n looked in the window, but Giby wasn' there. Where was he?"

"I don' know."

"Did we see him again?"

"We jus' saw im yesterday!"

"Fuck you, I know that. I'm talkin 'bout that night."

"That was years ago."

"So? You don' remember?"

"I do, but wha' does it matter, it's all in the past. You think on the past too much Randy n you'll get stuck there."

... mommy with the silver-bound book ...

> ba ba black sheep have you any wool?
> yes sir yes sir three bags full
> one for my master one for the dame
> and one for the little boy *who lives down the lane*

... the little boy who lives down the lane ...

"You know the nursery rhyme, 'Ba Ba Black Sheep?'"

Twisting into a tension ... "Maybe. How does it go?"

"Okay," real slow, "ba ba black sheep — have you any wool? — Yes sir yes sir — three bags full — One for my master — one for the dame — and one for the little boy — who lives down the lane" ... brooding ... "I mean, what the fuck?"

"Say it again."

Again ...

Him repeating, "the little boy who lives down the lane?" trailing off like what-the-fuck.

"Yeah, seriously. Wha' does that mean?"

"I *don't know*," bewildered

"Okay okay. Let's think about this, break this thing down."

He turns to his darkness, me to my light ... then settling in, "Ba ba black sheep."

Staring into our respective portholes ...

Then him, "A black sheep? Aren't they uncommon?"

"I think so. I mean I've only ever seen white ones."

"So a black sheep — is it fair ta say that this black sheep is a little bit diff'rent than all the other white sheep?"

"Yes, but," away from the porthole ... "He's not a wolf."

"No. He's still a member of the herd."

"Maybe."

"Well, let's say he *is* a member o' the herd."

"Okay."

"'Fall the sheep are white n there is one black sheep then not only is he going ta be diff'rent but he is going ta be noticed more because he *is* diff'rent."

"Yes yes!"

"Okay," molding his thoughts with his hands ... "So we got a black sheep, diff'rent than all the others — how does the rest of it go?"

"Ba ba black sheep — have you any wool."

"So the nursery rhymer is talkin to him asking him for wool."

"Yes! This wool — is it a symbol of wealth? Money maybe?"

Pursing his lips, furrowing his brow, "Something of value, yes. I think wool is valu'ble."

"Definitely. Okay, so we got this black sheep; he's diff'rent than ev'ryone or at least seems ——

"Yes! He only *seems* diff'rent, but doesn' that mean he *is* diff'rent?"

Well ... "Aren't we all the same on the inside though?"

"Wha' d'you mean?"

"Well, ya know, we all have organs, the same ones, n blood n stuff and it's all pretty much made up o' the same stuff, so when we see somethin that's diff'rent isn' that jus' because we're lookin for it? You know, comparing it ta stuff around us — fickle stuff?"

"No, no. Yer right, yer right. But what I was —— ... a gust of wind rattles the leaves; the light flickering behind the applause ... —— thinking is that comparisons only matter 'fwe — comparisons only matter 'fwe think — I don't ——

"Yeah, yeah dude. I get what yer sayin. If somethin looks diff'rent than somethin else, it looks that way only because that's what we see."

"Yes! But that's all that matters, because it's our

perception!"

"Okay." Another gust ... "Feels like a storm's comin."

"Yep." Then a flicker, a flash, splattering drops becoming intermittent plop-plops then plop-didily-plops then plop-de-plop-de-didily-plops then, "Cats n dogs, Randy. Cats n dogs."

"Oh no! Not another one! We still haven' figured out the black sheep!"

"What's there ta figure out?"

"Ev'rything!"

"Randy it's just an expression. It doesn' mean anything."

"Yes it does! These are the metaphors of our culture, of our lives! EV'RYTHING!!"

"NOTHING!" ...

The light now a hazy orb behind the sheets ... Sarge staring silently into the curtain ...

... but he's sprinting up and then down underneath the deck behind Lawson's house just crouching like a cat watching her standing there on the porch and everyone else scattering and then the cop swerving into the street and cruising past Kenny sprinting into the school yard and disappearing into the trees and getting out yelling 'stop! police! hey!' but you already hiding in the bushes down the block and around the corner while he's still under that deck back there waiting for Hambone swinging around in her dad's big red truck just scoping cuz they almost killed Kenny and Jess in the bushes before the rendezvous at Zeek's house and no Giby still no Giby and then sneaking out the back door and behind the houses through the gardens and then across the streets and across the playground to meet her with the shotgun on the porch before riding in the big truck around the corner into the parking lot to blind you against the wall exposed and ready to confess but not quite then over the fences and through the yards about to kill you idling in front of her homestead leaving just enough light for the shadow to hop into the back of the truck ——

the shadow hopping in the back of the truck ——

the shadow ——

110

backing into the driveway and the garage then back at Zeek's house still no Giby ...

"Giby got in her house."

"What are you talkin about?"

Into the murky light ... "He jumped in the back of her truck right before she backed into the garage."

Fiddling, "Are you sure?"

"She saw Cam n I spyin on her. We were behind the house across the street, peakin 'roun' the side — the perfect view of the porch. She was sittin there with a shotgun for a long time."

Him gaping ...

"And then she walked down off the porch n jus' stood there in her front yard, the toilet paper all around her, n she jus' looked around n then off into the distance n out n around. We were in the shadows across the street. There's no way she saw us — it was pitch black. Her house was the only one lit up on the whole block so me n him jus' stood there watchin her. But it was weird dude, almost like she knew we were standin there or at least knew someone was out there watchin her."

A gulp.

"She took her shotgun n got in the truck — it was parked in the driveway in fronta the g'rage — turned it on, revved it up, n came aroun' the block, so we posted up agains' the house but she came all the way around n pulled inta the parking lot at the school — the way the back o' that house was facin, so her lights caught us n she saw us. She saw us crouchin there behind that house, so she turned around n jus' started cruisin back our direction. We were about a-hunderd feet from her at least. She couldn't've caught us on foot, so she drove back n tried ta catch us from the other side. I mean, it was an awful effort on her part tryin ta get us: we jus' ran behind the houses n hid by these burn barrels down the block. We could see the truck parked in the street but not her house."

The rain falling slower now, the light clearer, the air cooler and lighter.

"N I saw this shadow come runnin down the street from

behind her n leap inta the back o' the truck. The truck was jus' sittin there idlin the whole time, like she was waitin for us ta come out er somethin — but ya know what? Now that I think about it, I don' think she was even in the truck. I think she wen' inside n came back out n backed up the truck. I figured it would jus' be in the driveway, but when Cam n I scoped out the house on the way back ta Zeek's, there was no truck. We thought maybe she had left er somethin cuz we took a roundabout way ta get back and she could've left while we were walkin aroun', but I remember all the lights were out in the house. It was late, like at least eleven."

Freaking ...

"She fuckin parked that thing in the g'rage with him layin in the back! He was waitin ta get in that house the *whole time!* But she was guardin it like a hawk."

His face opening into gaping bewilderment, then puckering again into skepticism, he shakes his head, "No —— wait a second, wait a second, yer sayin —— Oh my GOD!! —— but how come we never found out about this? Why didn' Giby ever say somethin?"

... a witch with a shotgun ... "Somethin *happened* to him."

It's so heavy Sarge cracks, laughs-guffaws-hacks-chokes, and morphs into a beet ... "That's pretty out there, Randy. What would she have done to im? N why didn' he ever say anything?"

"Don' you remember?! We never *saw* him for the rest of the NIGHT! At school on Monday he jus' said he went home."

"Yeah so? Maybe he did."

"I don' know dude. That woman's fuckin nuts."

"We could just ask him."

"Are you *kidding ME!?* Like he's gonna remember that! Somethin real traumatic happens ta someone, they block it outta their brains! He pry wouldn' wanna remember what 'appened that night."

"What would it hurt?"

... everything ... "It doesn' matter dude."

112

"But don't you wanna know?"

"Not really, no." ... still you could go look ... "Hey you wanna go for a ride?"

"Where to?"

"Jus' come on."

"Randy, you know we're not allowed on that ——

"It was five years ago! We can drive down her damn street. Besides, she's prob'ly asleep anyway."

We tee-peed Rosey's house again a week after Giby's disappearance, but she was ready — fishing wire across the sidewalk and between the bushes, all of us tripping and choking. She had installed a motion-detector floodlight over her front yard, so as soon as we set foot on her property, she came out and got a good look at us. She knew who we were and so did the police. Nobody ever caught us in the act, but the cops called our parents and told them that we were never allowed to be on Russell Street ever again. Rosey had won the war.

"Why are we goin here again?" Sarge asks, crouching into the passenger seat of the Focus.

"I gotta see somethin."

The rain had all but stopped except for a very light drizzle. The lightning had moved on to the east. It was late, definitely after midnight. The traffic light at the intersection of Claremore Avenue and Lincoln Road flashed red.

I crossed the deserted highway heading west on Claremore, jostling over the jagged cobblestones. Five short blocks later, I signaled for a left turn on Russell Street and slowly swung on to the narrow road. All the little houses were dark, curtains drawn. Rosey's house was second on the left — dark too, curtains drawn, no porch light, still the same white picket fence.

As we crept by, I noticed the garage — pretty much a shed with a door, nestled right up against the house, but I could see light coming between it and the house. There was about a one-foot gap between the two structures ...

"Damn it! They're not connected."

"Did this trip satisfy your curiosity Randy?"

Reaching for a cig from the pack in the cup holder ... "Nope." Sarge strikes a match, bringing his light to the end of my stick ... "I still don' know 'bout that damn shadow."

$$\sim\sim RW \sim\sim$$

"So Randy, wha' d'you think of the Devil?"

"I don' know dude" ... sweat dripping down my face; I was shaking on the inside inside inside deep deep down ... Nobody knew.

"You know who wears a white tie Randy?" He did, shielding himself with sunglasses ...

"No."

"Lucifer."

Puss oozing from a volcano ... "Really?"

"Yes," standing to introduce, "the story of the fall of Satan ...

"Once upon a time there was an angel named Lucifer. Lucifer was known as the light bearer and sat next to God in Heaven. He was God's favorite of the twelve Arc Angels. But Lucifer grew more n more powerful, eventually rivaling God and His ultimate authority over All. One day, when God grew tired of Lucifer's pride n arrogance, He banished him from Heaven," peering into my window then raising an affirmative finger ... "*FOREVER!!* — 'Be gone! For dust thou art, and to dust thou shalt return.' And Lucifer disappeared."

Stroking my beard and then realizing, "God said that t'Adam, dude."

A maniacal-proud-smirk-laugh ... "Yes Randy. I altered the stories a little. Creative element, right?"

"Yeah, you can do that, but really Satan, Lucifer, whoever-the-hell was banished ta Earth, right?"

The snide know-it-all chuckling ... "Yes Randy." Then humbly, "You're right. I was jus' tryin ta make a point."

Looking over everything really up close split into millions upon billions upon trillions of little ones and littler little ones and littler littler little ones ... "Oh!! — Cuz the Earth is made o' dust dude!"

The smile fading ... "Yeah dude. Of course."

... ||| ... ||| ... |||

Then one day, later that summer, I wake up and just have to tell him because it seemed so real. We meet on the porch and before we even sit down ... "Dude I had a dream las' night."

"Me too," he says.

"You go."

"No you."

Me sitting on the edge, him leaning back serenely comfortable ... "Dude, so — you're not gonna believe this but this is fuckin crazy."

"Go ahead, Randy," coaxing me with his omniscient smile.

"I had this dream — you were in it. I had this long mangley beard and you were kind of — well you looked like you except not really cuz you were wearin these tattered clothes, we were both wearin tattered clothes," the images flashing back faster than the words ... "I mean ——

"Go on, go on," little giggles ...

"N we were standin abreast, me on the right n you on the left."

Giggleackling ...

"What dude?"

"Keep goin, keep goin," a sadistic grin ...

"N so there we are standin next ta each other n we're standin on top o' Monk's Mound lookin out over Sain' Louis n behind us there's ——

... ack-ack-ack-ack-icka-icka-icka-icka ...

"What dude?"

"DON'T STOP! DON'T STOP!"

"Okay, so there we are all in tattered clothes n like holdin up these weird flag things, like somethin outta Braveheart right? N behind, there's this army o' people all the way back n they're all in tattered clothes n we're up there lookin out over Sain' Louis n the city is like ——

"GONE!" ... leaping into the fire ... "GONE! GONE!" ... rising before me ... "Randy, lemme ask you something."

"Okay."

"Was the arch?" ... holding up his hands vertically in front of him as if to bring them together to pray but keeping them just apart because that's exactly how it looked ...

"Yeah, like the top had been blown off."

"Yes!" ... silent hysteria ... "Randy, we had the *same dream!*"

"Okay, okay, okay, so lemme ask YOU something."

"Shoot."

"Who were those people standin next ta us?" ... into the Mystery ... "Cuz I remember one person on my right, but I never saw a face, n there was another person on your left n then us in the middle."

"I *don't know,*" falling back melodramatically ...

"Yeah, me neither dude."

Brooding still ...

"In your dream, was Saint Louis like ——

"Like it'd jus' been bombed er somethin."

"Yeah! It was like smoldering n ev'rything destroyed."

"Yeah! Wha' d'you think it means?"

"I don' know. Maybe like apocalypse now, the end is near er somethin."

"Maybe. But why were we ——

"I don' know."

"And those people —— why were they ——

"No idea."

Brooding brooding brooding then an intruder ... "I thought," I did, "that maybe since we each have one sibling, maybe it's Belle n Sage standin next ta us."

"Maybe."

"Or it could be Latty —— or Whitey."

"Latty maybe."

"I don' know dude —— maybe Atty?"

"Could be Atty."

Rambling down the spiral ... "Who else could it be?"

"I don' know."

... Could be him her you or me ... exactly Who — the most mysterious character of All ...

~~ *RW* ~~

So what do YOU think of the Devil? Yes, YOU dear reader, go to hell, because this is neither for you or about you, it's about me and it's for me, so I'm going to eat it all up and devour myself whole in one big gulp, just like way back on that playground when I turned inside out and became a total asshole. This is my shit, and this I give to you. In return I ask for nothing, because I don't wanna be a greedy Devil — the Devil doesn't give, he takes. Who gives. But what is there to give anyway? Perhaps a present wrapped in a little box full of _____ ...

Mmmm-hmmmm, gadoomaloom-batookaroo-anellazajou, maybe poo-poo? ...

No it's not bullshit, it's real. Everything I've told you thus far is a *real* story, the truth I tell ya, the truth. Why would I lie? What motivation have I to conjure up something so amazing, so profound and so laced with enigmas? What sick and sadistic person would sit on his ass all day scheming plots and conflicts and characters for a story he intends to put on paper and sell to the world in order to turn a profit, thus justifying his material consumption? I have, therefore I must exchange for more more more ...

Maybe buy a house in Fort Lauderdale and flip it for a couple extra grand.

Or maybe, how about this ...

I give you a piece of paper and on another piece of paper I write down that you owe me one piece of paper; therefore, you are in debt to me. And then I call you night and day everyday asking for payment of debt, and you say you'll get it to me as soon as you can. Then after a few days, I still don't have that piece of paper so I start mailing out notices on pieces of paper, reminding you that you owe me one piece of paper and if you don't pay up soon why I'm gonna ... I'm gonna ... I'M GONNA SEND YOUR DEBT TO A THIRD-PARTY COLLECTION AGENCY! AND THEY'RE GONNA CHARGE YOU AN EXTRA 33.333333333333333% INTEREST PLUS PROCESSING FEES ON TOP OF THE DEBT ALREADY OWED, SO YOU BETTER PAY ME NOW BECAUSE IF YOU DON'T THEN YOU'LL OWE THEM NOT JUST *ONE* PIECE OF PAPER, BUT *ONE AND ONE-THIRD* PIECES OF PAPER!!

And every week, once a week, I send you a piece of paper that says you owe me one piece of paper and you better fucking pay me or else, and I do that for eight weeks, utilizing eight pieces of paper plus the copies for my own filing purposes, thus amounting to sixteen pieces of paper in total, eight envelopes in total, 44¢ multiplied by eight times for a total of $3.52 in postage, as well as one manila folder which contains the copies of the notices I sent you for my own legal protection, etc. etc. etc. ... all because you owe me one piece of paper and haven't paid ... PAY UP! ... So when the eight weeks of written notices are complete, I sell the debt that you owe me of ONE PIECE OF PAPER (specifically 8.5" x 11" 20 lb. bleached) to the Big Bad Debt Collection Agency for the price of three-quarters of one piece of paper, and now I never have to worry about you owing me anything ever again. You just owe the Agency one and one-third of a piece of paper ...

So you'll always owe the Devil something, and I tell ya what, you better pay him his due cuz he's got a fiddle o' gold against your soul cuz he thinks he's better than you so what ya gonna do? what ya gonna do when he comes for you? you gonna cry in the corner like li'l Jack Horner eatin your curds-n-whey? maybe you'll fall asleep in this place where the shadows run from themselves and no strings can secure you oh tired starling! oh darling please believe me! I'll never make it — oh but yes yes yes you will! as long as you're just in it for the thrill and you drink your daily apportionment of swill, everything will turn out just swell in the long run if you keep running but not too fast or too slow just enough to continue to go and when you encounter a demon of might and he gives you a perplexing intoxicating fright, well then you better show him how strong is your fight cuz it don't matter if he's wrong or if he's right — Just beat it! Just beat it! No one wants to be defeated — But surely somebody does ...

    ... ||| ... ||| ... |||

Back in high school when I was too important to do fun things, Sarge and his buddies (pretty much everyone else who's already been featured) staged the most sophisticated student uprising in history. They were twenty-first century, home-grown terrorists, but not indiscriminately, not because they didn't like freedom or hated democracy, rather because they believe not in anyone, everyone, or anything other than an individual and his intelligence and cognizance to make choices for himself. It's when others start making choices for us, when someone tries to take away something you've always taken for granted or when some asshole is being a real conniving prick trying to Hitlerize everything because he's insecure about his own ability to possess, utilize, and delegate power: that's when social tumult and upheaval occur.

When we were in high school something of this magnitude happened overnight, and we all suddenly found ourselves living under a fascist regime. I'm not just talking about 9/11 here, I'm talking about Hamilton High School. And I'm talking about a specific man, a man who will only be known as Yessir.

You see, Sarge never 'hated' Yessir, and Yessir never 'hated' Sarge. Their personalities just clashed — one a middle-aged, ex-marine high-school principal, the other a cunning kung fu artist with intuitive sage-like abilities; one possessed the certificate of power granted him by the Hamilton Board of Education, the other the owner of a vast fortune of spiritual capital handed to him with a silver spoon on a chain. The stars were aligned for a clash of epic proportions.

Our senior year of high school, Yessir decided it would be good for all if the annual traditional homecoming festivities were canceled. In an attempt to protect the weak underclassmen who would resist the initiation rites of passage, Yessir canceled all festivities thus rendering our existence meaningless.

Sarge couldn't bring himself to simply accept this nothingness, so he formed a committee of various esteemed members of the Class of 2005 in order to map out a course of action in response to this sordid executive order. Among a number of fuck-withings decided upon was to indiscriminately borrow lawn ornaments — gnomes, deer, those statues of boys with lamps, stupid glass balls, etc. — from unsuspecting civilians and place them in Yessir's front yard one night so that the ornaments all faced his door and he would find them upon waking for school in the morning and probably wonder 'what-the-fuck!' (no lawn gnomes were harmed in this endeavor and all were returned to their respective owners). Sarge and his gang executed this scheme flawlessly, including with it a typewritten list of demands taped to the head of a particularly goofy but disturbing-looking gnome that they placed directly before Yessir's front door.

Still, Yessir wouldn't budge. So the terrorists decided to take it a step further, stealing his cardboard cut-out of Clint Eastwood from his office one afternoon during lunch hour when nobody was around to see anyone sneaking around. They knew Yessir would not be in his office based on intelligence received from anonymous faculty members who could attest to the times of his daily routine. The kidnapping of Clint Eastwood was executed miraculously, without flaw.

Whereas the lawn ornaments may have seemed more like a practical joke, this prank was personal, and it greatly disturbed Yessir, so much so, in fact, that he eventually paid the ransom. Yessir and Sarge agreed that if Yessir executed a particular demand, Clint Eastwood would be returned and the horrific madness would cease. Of course, Yessir also had to agree to total immunity for all parties involved, and that he did: nobody was ever charged with a crime, nor openly persecuted. In fact, Sarge and the members of his gang became folk heroes, even though they ultimately failed to reverse any of Yessir's policies. The sheer fact that they stood up to him without being punished or submitting to threats of suspension, torture, and humiliation indicated to us, the general populace, that they had won!

They had defeated The Man.

After the graduation of the Class of 2005, Yessir was never the same. Because of the entire debacle, he lost political muscle with the school district hierarchy as well as respect from students and faculty members. He could no longer govern effectively, so he retired in 2008.

... ||| ... ||| ... |||

Thursday, March 20, 2008 — telephone conversation with Sarge explaining everything ...

SARGE: They took it away from us. Junior year was the last time we had a homecoming parade but it wasn't student oriented. But they still wouldn't allow anybody to come to the high school at night and decorate. It wasn't patrolled and Yessir just assumed that nobody was going to go do anything because he said so, but Shea Nieman and Sonny Smith all met at Shea's house and from there about twenty to thirty of them went out decorating. These characters of the senior class were pretty good friends of the police force and they had the cops chase off any juniors that would come around to mess up their decorations. That year, we were being chased by cops who actually helped the seniors get on the roof of the building. Leach pulled up his SUV to where they just built that addition next to the gym and they jumped up on top of his car and went on top of the buildings. Nobody cared.

ME: We were kind of ——

SARGE: The guinea pig class for some reason — the first

class to be denied all of that freedom and all of those rights. You lost something that you knew. When we were freshmen and sophomores we were initiated, we experienced the homecoming tradition that had been going on forever! I remember kids coming up and writing on my face, just their year — their graduation year — and their name, like tagging you because they could, because they were older and had already gone through all of that. We just took it for granted that we would get the same freedoms that they did when we were older.

ME: Do you remember why he decided to take away all of the traditions?

SARGE: I think a permanent marker busted open in some fat kid's mouth. He was pry resisting. If you don't resist, nothing bad's gonna happen: that's what they told us and nothing bad ever did. I had senior girls writing all over my arm how cute they thought I was and the junior and senior guys coming up and writing on my face — this was just one day a year! That's it. It made you feel good when someone would write on you. It was like a bonding experience, and they were always good sports about it, and if you were a good sport too they weren't gonna tackle you and throw you into a trash can and shove a marker down your throat. If that happened, you probably deserved it.

ME: It's this political correctness bullshit everywhere: you gotta be nice to everyone. But the problem is when people look at things like this, for example — a tradition that's been going on for generations. My mother did this stuff when she was in school! But these people decree that something isn't 'right' or something isn't 'fair.' You're never gonna please everybody. There's always gonna be somebody who's upset about something and some idiot who doesn't wanna partake in the festivities. It's just bullshit really, and it's got us all afraid of upsetting or offending someone. Well you know what? I DON'T FUCKING CARE! FUCK YOU! Not YOU of course, but whoever's offended by me — FUCK YOU!

SARGE: It's funny how you tie this in with political correctness because I just thought about how bullies have always been around, and this homecoming thing and the traditions that we took for granted really highlighted positions of superiority and positions of inferiority, but that was the purpose of them. It was *natural*. And throughout the rest of the year, I never — did you ——

ME: Nope.

SARGE: Yeah, I can't think of one time when somebody was being a bully to someone — legitimately hateful. Sure, people would get in fights, but that was always personal and a lot of the times it was a friend you'd be fighting. There was no random, legitimately spiteful bullying, just playful stuff.

ME: Yeah, you're right. The haters were the ones who got all pissed off about the traditions and resisted it — the little fat kids with glasses who play role-playing games on the weekends.

SARGE: Hey, I've played role-playing games.

ME: See, my point exactly.

SARGE: Alright, alright. I get what you're saying. It's a no wonder ——

ME: Kids bring guns to school? Yeah, totally. And it's always the kid that doesn't fit in or conform to the greater social conditions and conditionings.

SARGE: Yes! The kid on the outside looking in.

ME: Exactly. He isn't comfortable inside — *wait! wait!* Listen to this, I just remembered something.

SARGE: Okay.

ME: Do you remember in like kindergarten getting ready to walk down to the cafeteria and the whole class had to line up, single-file exactly three blocks away from the wall, you know? Like those floor tiles?

SARGE: Yes! Yes! It's a big paradox. You wanna give kids and people the ability to ——

ME: Not just kids dude.

SARGE: I said people.

ME: Oh, my bad. Anyway ——

SARGE: We're taught how we're supposed to make our own choices and set our own goals and sticks and stones can break my bones but words will never hurt me unless you call me a faggot and then I'm gonna have you fired from your job because you offended me. So on one hand we're supposed to have freedom to think, freedom of speech — these principles are what our society is founded upon. But if you're caught thinking outside the block three blocks away from the wall ——

ME: They martyr you.

SARGE: (that cackle) *Yes!*

ME: Okay, so we got this school shooter standing outside the box looking in and watching all of his classmates having just a good ol time inside of their boxes, and they're looking at him calling him a 'freak' because it's like 'why don't you just be normal like the rest of us?' Talk about peer pressure.

SARGE: Yeah, but sometimes that peer pressure is against the system and people get tired of all the rules and regulations, especially new rules that change something they took for granted for a long time.

ME: Like our class.

SARGE: Exactly. Remember our freshmen year? We saw the towers come down, and now we have to decide: are you a patriot or a terrorist. When you do something against the system, you're a terrorist no matter how many people support you. They'll spin it all against you.

ME: The system has the resources to spin itself however it wants.

SARGE: Yep.

ME: So in order to beat it, you have to spin faster than it.

SARGE: Yeah, but I'm pretty sure we're going to be fighting Big Brother as long as there is a Big Brother to fight.

ME: But you gotta remember something Sarge: you and I have younger siblings. Who are we fighting?

SARGE: Who.

ME: What an enemy.

The Box

Home sweet home on the range,
  Where the ghosts and the rats are estranged,
  Where seldom is heard an encouraging word ——————
... and the starry sky can't be seen because the streetlights
keep that guy with the black mask from robbing your house or
raping your daughter. The neighborhood is always watching
itself — you and me and they peering from behind our vinyl
blinds to see why they/we are mowing the lawn that way ...
  ... Perpendicular to the sidewalk! Doesn't he have any
taste?! Somebody oughtta tell him — diagonals, diagonals!
  ... Why don't you tell him darling if it upsets you so?
  ... It's none o' *my* business. He can mow his lawn how he
wants. Why should *I* concern myself with how *his* lawn looks?
  ... I don't know, why do you?
  ... Huffity-puffity ...
But they're just little pigs in straw houses along twisting
spaghetti roads that dead-end deep in the forsaken annals of
American suburbs ...
  Meanwhile, deep in the woods down in that valley next to
the spring, a family of wolves (Wolframs that is) barked and
howled for reasons beyond the comprehension of startlesome
piggies. Yes, yes, these wolves, including Randy, would bark
into mirrors and closets and at Master Wolf sitting in the living
room with the television turned up way too loud, and Momma
Wolf would bark at Master Wolf and the little wolves when
they tracked in mud on her pristinely shining kitchen floor. You
see, Momma Wolf was a passionate homemaker who spent her
days perfecting the exotic gardens that surrounded the castle

and her evenings spicing simmering, savory feasts of pork chops and ribeyes and baby-back ribs. Papa Wolf would wash down his evening feast with the intoxicating blood of the lamb while the children begged for more bread, or sometimes sweets if Momma had made cookies to fatten up her Hanzel and Gretel.

Later, they would bark and howl at-and-with each other before settling down in front of the tube/tunnel for the hypnosis/vision. After the moon had risen, Momma and Papa Wolf would retire to the consecrated bed of glass, while the little wolves slept in their respective dens ...

Sometimes, late at night, Randolph would awaken to find the accordion doors of his closet cracked open. He would stare into the tiny crack of pitch-black nothingness because he knew It was in there. Like a frightened dog, the sprouts of hair stood up on the back of young Randolph's neck, but he couldn't/wouldn't scream. The sheer thought of It knowing that he knew that It was in there scared him more than the presence of It Itself. On and on, every night they went like that, staring each other down, but It never came out and Randolph never opened the door ...

Then one day It went away, and Randolph stopped waking in the middle of the night. Years later, when he was much too old to be afraid of Its lurking in closets, he awoke in the night to find the doors cracked open just enough for something to peer out ...

His logic-complex would have nothing of this! Randolph threw off the covers, hopped from the bed, and proceeded directly to the doors, coldly determined to put an end to this saga once and for all ...

He jerked open the door ...

And found ...

Exactly what he had been looking for ...

... _____ ...

... What's inside the box. Not?

If you wrap the box in gold and plant flowers all around it

and build a big wall to keep it protected, will anyone ever open it to find What inside? If you don't wrap it and throw it outside your trailer with all the rusty car parts and empty beer cans, will anyone ever notice it and think maybe _____ is inside? ...

The box could be empty or full of dust,
The Holy Grail or nothing,
Be a secret it must ...

~~ RW ~~

After the trip to Cairo, I returned to my 'responsibilities' in Columbia. You see, I had this job at a local coffeehouse that was fun because it didn't require too much thought, and I got to hang out with a lot of really interesting people. That summer, I was either researching racial residential segregation or working there: those were my responsibilities by day.

At night me and my roommate Mark and some other friends would just get stoned, drink beer, and play video games. We would've gone out to one of the hundreds of bars, but we were all just twenty years old, in between our sophomore and junior years of college. For most of us it was our first summer living away from the places we all still called 'home.' We were free! But it wasn't all that special.

Anyway, I returned to Columbia on the evening of Thursday, June 21, 2007. I immediately e-mailed my mentor, Hideki, telling him briefly of my safe return. After a couple plings and pongs we scheduled a time to meet on Monday morning in order to cover a few basics — just check in, catch up, you know, standard operating procedure.

I spent the weekend working at the coffee shop and/or brooding intensely about what I was going to say to Hideki. What had I discovered thus far? He was pry gonna ask me if I interviewed people and recorded 'oral histories.' I did interview people. I did record oral histories. I didn't ask them about racial residential segregation or anything like that. I

128

didn't ask them how or why they thought their skin color affected their lives or socioeconomic status. I didn't ask them if race actually meant anything to them because, honestly, it didn't mean a damn thing to me ...

We have these eyes that perceive light and brains that interpret it as an image, which consists of various wavelengths of visible light, which are what we define to be 'colors,' because you see, from a very early age, we are taught that *what we perceive* actually has a name. As soon as a word is introduced to our consciousness, we behold _____ not as *what it is* but rather whatever word defines it. But you see, we're not really that good at defining things. Light is the perfect example: wavelengths elongate and shorten at infinite ratios, not integers, yet we define specific tones of color — wavelengths of light — as if they were integers to be counted 1-2-3-4-5, forgetting that there are an infinite number of numbers between one-and-two-and-three-and-four-and-five, just as there are infinite possible wavelengths and thus tones of color between red-and-orange-and-yellow-and-green-and-blue and so on. And we haven't even talked about the color of people yet! The aforementioned is just an example of our perceptive prejudice.

Yes, people have skin tones of various colors, but they also have thoughts and feelings, which are expressed and/or suppressed in ways that vary from person to person, so that often we can perceive one expression on one person's face (for example) and a similar expression on another person's face (perhaps a grimace) and we associate this with a feeling or a thought (in this case, disgust, though we really don't know).

Still though, we *love* definitions. We love to know that 'green' is 'green' and everything that's pretty-damn-close-looking is 'green' too, but some people call it 'blue' and others may say 'teal' or 'turquoise' and cause a big huff. And just as we strive to define our visual environment, we strive to define our emotional one, thinking that we know what *they* may be feeling because *they* look like *that*, and from what we've

129

experienced, most people that look like *that* feel like *this*, so *they* must have _____ sorts of problems going on, because *they* look like *that* and *this place* looks like *this*, and since all *these* people in *this* place have a common feature that isn't really that common we assume ...

... that black skin must have something to do with being poor, right? Or is it just a *coincidence?* Perhaps even the result of an infinite array of coincidences, lined up from the beginning of time all the way to now ...

Something stinks here, but I can't smell it cuz its way way deep down below the surface, like that big turd at the bottom of the pool ...

You see, that's what I thought, and I wanted to figure out who shit it out and what they ate for breakfast yesterday. I wasn't looking for a causal explanation anymore. I was looking for a story, specifically a story about (not explaining) humanity's great flaw; a story about the Fall from the Garden of Eden or the core of Adam's apple: it was there rotting in that damn town and underneath all the rot were seeds, and if those seeds weren't rotten after all of these years, they would grow into a beautiful story about people and their plight. I had to find the damn story. Fuck the reason why!

But I couldn't tell Hideki that: he wouldn't understand. So I freaked and wigged-the-fuck-out until ten a.m. on Monday morning when I knocked on the door to his office. He was in there reading from academic journals and textbooks of jargon. He answered with a smirk ...

"Hideki," I said, offering him my hand.

"Randy." We shook. "How are you?" His voice was tranquilizing.

"I'm," I paused to think then chuckled and glanced around at all his books ... "I'm good." ... the papers piled on his desk and on a chair next to it and the radiator below the window ...

There was one empty chair next to his desk, surrounded by walls of books stacked cover to cover, unshelved, floor to ceiling ... "Have a seat," he said.

We each sat down, him crossing his legs at his desk, me fiddling with sweaty palms. He reclined in the ergonomic chair, positioning his right index finger on his temple, leaning on his elbow into the armrest.

"So," he said. Despite being Japanese, he was very easy to understand, academically fluent in English. He spoke very soft and humble like a samurai from some Hollywood movie. "How is your research coming?"

I bowed my head, exhaled then sucked it all back in, "Good. Really good," nodding back and forth. He sat there, motionless, eyeing me curiously, indicating by inaction that I had to go into further detail ...

"I went ta Cairo, and well, I met a lot o' int'resting people, made some contacts," glancing up, smiling and nodding; my heart might have stopped beating: I was dealing totally outta my head, like a calculator computing every detail which I could and couldn't tell him ... just tell him what he wants to hear ...

"Did you record oral histories?"

"I interviewed people."

"Do you have these on tape recorder?"

"Yes. I've been working on transcribing some o' these this past week. It's really time consuming."

"Yes it is," he said, leaning back, uncrossing his legs then crossing them the other way. "You will spend hours and hours getting *each* sentence and *each* word recorded on paper."

"Yeah, it takes a lotta time."

"So how many people did you interview?"

"Oh, quite a few actually" ... be honest ... "But I only recorded on tape a couple of em, like three or four, but I talked to a lot o' diff'rent people n took notes during my interviews."

"Did you get oral histories or did you *interview* people?"

... gulpity-gulpity ... sit up straight and tell him; this is your project not his, besides you already got the fucking money ...

"Both," I said. "I interviewed a lotta people who hadn' lived there forever. Many o' the people I encountered had jus' moved there recently, n a lotta people who are born there end

131

up movin away, so there's a very high turnover rate in the population."

I smiled up at him, his face contorting into an inquisitive sage-like squint before returning to its symmetrical, skeptical countenance ... "So are you finding the reasons for *racial residential segregation?*"

"I'm not quite sure. I mean, I understand *why* all these people live there: their families are there er relatives are there and a lot of em jus' can' afford ta leave. They 'ave nowhere else ta go."

"I see. I see."

"But then there are some of em who come there from other places. For example, I met this woman named Angela who was all —— ... (searching for a word other than 'fuck') ... —— mmmmessed up on drugs, n she said she came there from Baltimore ta live at Real Life."

"Real Life?"

"Yeah. There's this place in town called Real Life Rehab that deals with drug rehabilitation n mentally retarded people. It helps them, or at leas' that's wha' they *say* they do. I don' know," shaking my head, looking away ... "I don' know what I think about them. I've tried ta call them n talk ta them ta set up an interview with somebody n *no*body will return my phone calls er e-mails — nothin. It's kinda sketchy. N then Angela — she told me all about how they take your gover'ment check n won' give you any money er anything, *and* how they don' treat you fer your addiction n don' medicate you er anything like that, and how it's not really run well er anything, n it jus' *seems* like somethin's not right, ya know?"

"I see. I see," he nodded.

"I jus' wonder what-the-hell that place is all about, I guess."

"Yes. Yes. But what does that have to do with *racial residential segregation?*"

Sighing, looking away then back, but the voice coming really fast ... "I don' think it has anything ta do with *why* that town is the way it is n *why* it can' get any better than it is n *why* the people are so poor n all so fucked up 'specially if they're gettin taken advantage of by them."

"I see. I see. But remember," speaking slowly and methodically, "you are looking for reasons for *racial residential segregation.*" ...

Those damn three words! I *hated* those fucking words!! What do they mean anyway? ... NOTHING! Not if race doesn't matter, doesn't even fucking exist! ...

It was all just bullshit really. I just used that proposal to get the damn grant money so I could do something different with my summer other than sitting on my ass at 'home' back in Hamilton again. I didn't actually care whether or not I discovered the reason for *racial residential segregation;* it just sounded like fun, plus maybe I could do something great and be someone great cuz not only was I looking for (insert three fucking words) I was looking for 'the truth.' That's what I told people whenever they asked me what I was doing for the summer — I was looking for 'the truth' about an impoverished community of black people.

'Why?'

Why not!? I don't fucking know! Who the fuck knows anything anyway! Or even some things. Maybe only what you want to think is true, and hell maybe it's all a damn illusion, all a giant acid trip, or maybe an acid trip is the only thing that's fucking true, and when you're drunk and stoned that's true too, but reality isn't true because it isn't even real, just a giant lie, and what you think you know is a giant lie, and none of it — knowing or not knowing it or thinking that you don't know it or even knowing that you aren't thinking that you don't know it — really matters.

But how can I know? ... And what if I can't? ...

"I know," I told him. "But I don' think that race is really the issue here."

Reversing back to his original pose ... "That's very interesting. If that's what you find in your research then you can say that in your final report. If you discover that race is not the issue then that is what you should say. But you must indicate *why* race is not the issue and provide data and information that support your claim."

I sat there nodding, staring at a picture of Don Mattingly perched on one of Hideki's shelves ...

"Yeah," I said. "I don' know. I jus' feel like there's somethin else there beyond race, beyond skin color. The town has been corrupted by greedy people in the past. That's what led to the race riots.

"Greedy white people didn' wanna give up wha' they had always known — the white people that were in power I mean. I guess I don' know 'f they were greedy. We're all greedy sometimes, I guess. But maybe we're not, I don' know. It jus' seems like there's somethin else here. Like, for example, why won' Real Life return my calls n e-mails? It's like they're tryin ta hide somethin. And then there are all o' these people — all o' these people that've been affected by the things that've happened in this town by the greedy people like Charlie Koen — *oh! — Charlie Koen!* — So lis'n ta this okay ——

He shifted forward ...

"Charlie Koen was this black guy back during the race riots who was the leader of the coalition of civil rights organizations workin ta end discrimination n oppression in the town, n he got all this grant money from the gover'ment and donations from across the country ta fight for civil rights. Well, ya see, white people — the white police — started the violence n riots n pretty much the war that 'appened down there when they used tear gas n stuff ta break up a crowd of black demonstrators who were protestin the death of — of — ummm," up to the ceiling searching ...

"Well, I don' remember his name — but this guy that was beat ta death by the police allegedly. I mean, nobody really knows if the police killed him but they prob'ly did. He was stopped by a white cop for speeding er somethin n the cop took him ta jail one night n the next morning he was dead — hung

134

himself, they said. But why would anyone hang themselves over a speeding ticket, ya know? I mean," chuckling ... "Seriously! So anyway, the next day all o' these black people take ta the streets — only a few of em like fifty er a hunderd er so, not too many — but they're protestin the death o' this guy, n then the next day the protest gets bigger n turns into a protest for civil rights n then a protest agains' segregation, n then the gov'nor orders the state police ta go down there n patrol things, n the state police — listen ta what the state police do — start firin tear gas n shootin at people with rubber bullets n beatin people for *no reason!* I mean, *come on!* This was a peaceful protest right? *Bullshit!*

"Anyway, the blacks form a coalition called the United Front, n Charlie Koen, who happens ta be a local minister, takes control o' the coalition, n they organize more protests, n the police fire more tear gas n kill more people, *and then*, one night, some white guys, maybe state policemen, maybe local business owners er somethin, fire shots into the Pyramid Court housing complex where a buncha black people live. Some people are killed, so Koen organizes a militia, so now there's fightin goin on at the complex every night n they — the blacks — turn the damn place into a fortress. The schools close, so nobody's goin ta school, n nobody's leavin the housing complex, n at night there are shootings and exchanges of gunfire. But get this, okay?

"So the white people started all the violence, but even after the state police decide ta call it quits, ta have a truce n ev'rything, Koen's guys keep shootin n keep firin, n the looting of all the stores continues, *and why?* Because Koen is gettin money for his organization, so his organization is making money off all this, n he's pocketin some of it 'fcourse. Well finally, when he's got all the money he needs n the town is practic'ly destroyed, he calls a quits to the shooting n decides ta open up the town's first all-black bank. He gets a buncha black people to invest in the bank, *and then* the building mysteriously burns one day n Koen escapes with all the money.

The bank never opened, but here he is with all o' this money, and 'e finally goes to court n gets convicted of money laundering er somethin, spends twelve years in prison, n now he's out but he doesn' even live there anymore, jus' owns the funeral home but lives in like Eas' Sain' Louis er somethin — I don' remember — But d'you see what's goin on 'ere?"

Hideki sat there, nodding into his cupped hand, staring at the toe of the shoe of his crossed leg ... "That is very interesting," directly at me ... "It seems like you have a story."

"Yeah," bowing because I was blushing.

"What do you plan to do with this story?"

"I don' know. Maybe write it er somethin —— I don' know."

"Maybe use it in your book."

"A book?! ... I think I'm a long ways off from writin a book."

"I think you can do it. You're a very good writer, Randy."

... and there it was ...

"Yeah."

... ||| ... ||| ... |||

After the whole debacle with Hideki, I hurried to the coffee shop for my twelve-o'clock shift. I was working with the most intimidating employee of the entire Nakota Coffee Company — Ian Woodburn. Now, Ian wasn't like huge or anything, not a boxer or a UFC fighter, and I had never seen him get mad at anyone. You see, he was actually really skinny and nice and he spoke very pleasantly and always smiled and everyone always loved him and thought he was just the greatest thing. I wondered if he was gay, and if so, well fine, that would explain everything. But if he wasn't, Jesus Christ, what a fucking creeper ...

Way way way way way way way way way way NICE! And legitimately so! And he wasn't an idiot either, not like some airhead, ditsy muthafucker — no! He was smart and cunning and understood aesthetics and liked to talk about how everything you do, whether you're doing the dishes or making a latte for someone, you have to do it with love.

So I thought maybe — and this was another possibility — maybe he had tripped acid too many times and it reversed his aging chromosomes or something, so that his personality was reverted to his child-within ...

Anyway, the shift went fine except I had to clean up a buncha messes that Ian made. He was a disaster and liked to just stand around and talk to people the whole time. It really irritated me when the place got all messy and outta hand, but he would just write it off and say, "It's a coffee shop. It'll be okay," like coffee shops are supposed to be dirty or something. Well the owner didn't think that, and since Ian loved everything and everyone loved him, guess who would have gotten in trouble had the owner come outta his office and seen the place in utter shambles ...

So I toiled and sweated and heaved and hoed but not really heaving — I mean, it doesn't take that much effort to lift a dish rag — and then when I was done I grabbed my backpack and walked home just puffing a cigarette as the sun was setting. I had a few things to think about, that's for sure, like how weird Ian was and how effeminate he acted, but then I realized that it didn't really matter because his actions and mannerisms were only part of his outward appearance, and I had already determined that outward appearances like hair color and skin color don't really matter so why should someone's perceived effeminate behavior elicit a judgment from me? I determined that it shouldn't until something told me that behavior and appearance are two different things and that behaviors *do* matter and I *can* judge them if I damn well please, because afterall I am a sociologist and all of my 'training' or 'studies' what-have-you, have been based on observing peoples' behaviors. But then I thought about it some more and I wondered where-in-the-hell do we draw the line between behavior and appearance because they're kinda the same thing, because people can appear to behave a certain way whether or not they are intending to, so is behavior somehow linked with intent because obviously appearances — or more specifically, physical attributes — aren't because nobody can intend to appear black except somebody like Michael Jackson who intended to *not* appear black, but then again the more I thought about it, girls intend to be blondes even if they're naturally brunettes, but most of the time you can tell if their hair is fake or not, unless it's really good and they spend a lotta money on some professional stylist then you may not be able to tell the difference; so at that point, I determined that appearance and behavior don't really matter because you can change both if you want, and if you have money you can get a stylist or a personal trainer or a speech pathologist and be whatever-the-hell, whoever-the-hell you want; so really, the only thing that matters is money.

I checked my pocket, pulled out a twenty-dollar bill and realized I was thirty short of a bag o' weed, so I would either have to go by the ATM or split a sack with Mark, that is, assuming he was home and also willing to spend money on marijuana.

Entering the darkened box — all the shades were pulled and the air conditioner roaring — I found Mark sprawled out on the couch reading some art history book while CNN flashed silently behind him.

"What's up," I said. It wasn't a question.

"Yo dude."

I plopped down in the recliner across from him and grabbed the remote off the coffee table strewn with two heaping ashtrays, a couple of art books, two glass pipes, and a book of Ziggies (rolling papers). I flipped the tee-vee to *Sports Center* transitioning into *Monday Night Baseball* — A's at Twins.

"American League bullshit."

"Yeah, fuck that dude."

The Cards and Pirates were on FSN, so I watched that boring shit for a few innings before Pujols finally hit a homer in the fourth to put the Birds on the board, and so I ventured out on the deck to smoke a cigarette beneath the streaking orange sky. A couple of faint stars had already appeared above the dark eastern horizon, dominated by the flashing red lights of radio towers. Gazing off into the murky beyond, I felt antsy, like I needed to go out and do/get something somewhere out there beyond the towers past the twinkling stars. My heart was filling/emptying with anxiety/dread, dead fear and worry about whatever-the-hell-didn't-matter like what would be done or should be done with all this Cairo bullshit and everything else with my life because something was very very very wrong and felt very very very bad.

I wasn't stoned. Obviously that was the problem, so I went back inside to inquire ... "Dude, ya got any weed?"

Mark was still sprawled out on the couch reading that book, the tee-vee still flashing its hypnosis ... "Naw dude," he said staring at the page. "I was just about ta ask you 'fyou had any."

"Nope," I said, eyes fixed on the tube and some commercial for Taco Bell ...

I pulled out my cell phone and plopped back into the e-z chair, perusing through numbers to decide which sketchy muthafucker to call first. There were a number of options for marijuana at eight o'clock on a Monday night, but I wanted an immediate pick-up guarantee — no fucking around or I'll-call-you-in-an-hour bullshit or my-connect-is-just-getting-in-town-with-it ...

The first guy I called was some schmarmy, doe-eyed Saint Louis Jew. He didn't answer. So I called my main man — a chill buddy of me and Mark who always hooked us up with deals on primo shizzle — nugs with glistening fibers and bluish-white crystals, furry little seedless beauties ...

He came through but said the shih he had wudn' tha' great so he'd go down for me ta forty an eighth. I told Mark; he confirmed willingness to partake in adventure to procure elicit drugs.

We jaunted out to the car and cruised over to Rosemary Street. Teek lived on the second story of an old brick house.

We entered via the balcony in back, traversing the slippery-slimy wooden stairs to the screen door and walked right in. He was in there watching the Cards game.

"Losin huh," I noticed.

"Yeah, we suck this year," Teek said maintaining focus on the screen.

Mark crossed over and plopped on the couch, lighting a smoke. Teek glanced away from the screen for just the amount of time required to reach under the couch, pull out a shoebox and set it down on the coffee table. Returning focus to the tee-vee, Teek opened the shoebox and pulled out two bags of pre-apportioned eighths. He handed me one and Mark the other.

"These are the two best nugs I got."

Each bag contained a single, symmetrically-trimmed nugget with a knockout whiff.

"I know it smells great," he said. "But it's kinda deceiving."

"Really? Doesn' seem like ——

"Yeah, seems like it'd be great, but it's jus' alright."

... he was pry burnt out ...

I looked at Mark who looked at Teek who looked at me ... "Seems good 'nough for me," I said.

"Yeah? You guys wanna smoke a little? Courtesy bowl?"

"Sure." I handed Teek my sack. Mark took out his nug and started breaking it up.

"We're gonna split one."

"Whatever."

Mark and I each pulled out a twenty and handed them to him. Mark then sparked the bowl which went around about four times before kicking. We vegged into the tee-vee, puffing on slowly burning cigarettes, watching walk after walk and ball after ball — the announcer silent between pitches only to say, "the three-oh," and then, "another walk" ... and it went on and on like that, an endless high and endless game of baseball back and forth and back and forth ... "the three-oh" ... "another walk" ... and the occasional "That's a gonner!" or ...

"Line drive ta left, will it get down?! *YES!* Two runs will score n here comes Wolfram —— we're gonna have a *play at the plate!!* HE IS .... !!!!!!!!!!!! ....
... In. Not out ...

God is in His heart. The shelves are all stocked, overflowing with gifts of love, still wrapped, and the presents still in their little boxes.

"He got a gift," they all say in their wise, nigger drawl. "A gift God give im."

But only one of em ever said, "Don' get caugh' on tha' shit!"

"What shit?"

"You know."

... spreading your arms open and flooding the world with your God-given powers of seduction and manipulation ...

"Oh that."

"Yeah. Don' be doin nothin foolish foolin 'roun' with them there thangs. Leave em 'lone!"

"Leave what alone?"

"I ain' gonna spell it out to ya! Jes' don' be messin that all I'm sayin. Ya keep on messin, ya keep on makin the mess bigga thaz why! Don' need no big mess, ya gotta clean up the li'l messes fust. Ya know!" a cackle of intoxicating(ed) omniscience ... "You do fine. I kin see it in ya. Ain' nothin gonna get in yer way butchu!"

"Yeah, we're all our own worst enemies."

"Thaz *right!* But that why we got God on our side. He he'p us when we needs it. Jes' ask im. Say, 'Lord! *Gimme he'p!*' n he give it to ya." ...

~~ *RW* ~~

One afternoon I was working at the coffee shop when a random know-it-all came in and said, "So these Mormons came up ta me on the street n asked me if they could talk ta me about

141

Jesus Christ's salvation."

Mister Brown was a self-proclaimed atheist who knew he was overtly loud and didn't really care. He had graduated from college and perused potential future careers in medicine but abandoned his efforts in order to focus on something that gave him more satisfaction: he was training to be an airline pilot. But when he wasn't training, he sat around the coffee shop reading *The Economist* or *The Scientific American*. Nobody paid him any attention.

... So I said, "And?"

"I asked them 'salvation from what?' And here's what they said — listen ta this!" He looked around to see if anyone was listening; I was the only one.

"I'm listening," I said.

"They said," he leaned over the bar, "'Salvation from all o' your sins.' And I asked em, 'Well how d'you know I've ever sinned?' And they said, 'Ev'rybody sins,' and then I asked em, 'Well what about Jesus? He never sinned.' And they said, 'No, because he was the savior.' And then I said, 'Well how d'you know I'm not Jesus n I'm jus' here ta ——

"You're Jesus?"

"Well no. Jus' listen ta what I'm sayin here," softly hammering his fist into the bar, thinking into the marble countertop ... "Okay. So here's the thing. Christians believe that Jesus came ta save them from hell n you have ta accept him into your heart *if* you wanna keep from going ta hell because he's gonna come back n save everyone again. That's what they *fucking believe!*"

"I know that."

"Well how are Christians supposed ta *know* what Jesus looks like when he comes back?"

"I don' know," wiping the bar with a damp rag ... "They prob'ly *won't* know what he looks like, at least the majority of em because hell, we don' even know what he looked like back then. We think that Jesus was this Caucasian guy with long hair when really he was prob'ly shorter n stockier with darker skin

142

n curly black hair. So if Jesus really would come back n save us all, he prob'ly wouldn' save them anyway cuz Christians think they know ev'rything about Jesus n they think they're so right about shit that he'd pry send em all ta hell fer bein idol worshippers anyway."

"Yeah, but I don' believe in Jesus or hell or anything like that. Their argument for salvation is completely ridiculous n totally flawed — that's what I'm sayin. They can't *prove* to me that salvation ever happens, so I don't believe them. I don't believe that *any* o' them have been saved because wha' does that mean?" ... imitating an idiot ... "Oh, so I'm walkin down the sidewalk and, like a giant meteorite falling from the sky hits me on the head. Well, these Christians would probably think that's because I'm an atheist and that was my judgment er something, but if it was one o' *them* that it happened to, they would prob'ly jus' think that God was up in heaven calling them to his service. I would think it's just a fucking *freak* accident but if ——

"You wouldn' think SHIT!"

"Why not?"

"You'd be dead!" ... Some freakishly skinny hipster at the other end of the bar laughed into his shitty novel ...

"Okay, no! Yeah yeah yeah, yer right. But still, listen ta this — okay, let's say that meteorite falls from the sky ——

"*Let's* say it!"

"Yeah. Okay — so it falls from the sky ——

"That guy!"

"Jus' lemme finish for a second."

"Okay okay, sorry. Go ahead. I'm lis'nin."

"So let's say this meteorite falls from the sky n lands two feet in fronta me, and I about die but I don't. I would *think* it's just a coincidence because I was jus' seconds away from walking right under that thing n gettin smashed, but I didn't because it all just *happened* ta come down a split second after I would've crossed that point on the sidewalk. But if it's a *Christian* walking along and the thing lands in fronta them, they're gonna think it was like the hand of God saving them. But they can't prove ——

"And you can prove it's just a coincidence?"

"Yes I can," crossing his arms then stepping back on the rubber to throw another pitch ...

"How?" I asked.

"It *just is*. I just happened ta be right there when it happened, that's it. The only reason it happened was because somewhere out in space, a piece of rock broke off an asteroid at a specific trajectory and came in the path of the Earth's orbit n then was caught up in our gravity, so it came down at a specific angle n trajectory that it *happened* ta land right behind me while I was walkin down the street."

"I thought it landed in fronta you."

"Whatever. You get what I'm sayin."

"I do," wiping the slate clean ... "Now lemme ask *you* something."

"Okay."

"What caused that rock ta break from that asteroid in the first place?"

"Maybe that asteroid slammed into another asteroid and a chunk broke off."

"Maybe," towel into bucket ... "But if that's true, then why did that asteroid, as you say, 'slam' into the other asteroid?"

"Because their paths were intersecting with each other n they collided and ——

"I understand that, but why were they intersecting?"

"Maybe because a long time ago whenever the comet, or whatever it is that they were a part of, broke apart, these asteroids got trapped in diff'rent orbits around the sun ——

"But why dude?"

Shaking his head, stepping back, then quick and flustered, "Now you're jus' bein ridiculous. You're tryin to ——

"I'm not *trying* anything. I'm just asking you some questions."

Shaking his head again, lips locked down and out, "Yeah,

but you're asking questions without even *thinking* about what I'm tryin ta say here — that there is ——

"What are you tryin ta say?"

"I'm goin ta tell you — Christians would jus' say that God made it happen when they can't *prove* that, but you can prove all of these other reas ——

"To an extent. After a while, 'fyou keep askin 'why,' there's only so far you go before ya don't know the answer."

"Yeah, but if you research n do experiments n analyze and hypothesize according to the scientific method, then ——

"The scientific method is just a buncha bullshit though."

Laughing and leaning ... "How is the scientific method bullshit?"

"It's just another formulated way of thinking, no diff'rent than religion er anything like that."

"Except scientists try ta *prove* what they're saying and scientists aren't afraid ta say that they're wrong. They're not afraid ta see another side of the argument or conclude that their theory is incorrect. Try ta get a Christian ta say that they're wrong. I dare you," pointing hard at me. "You can't."

This was way too ironic ... "Well Mister Scientist, it seems that *you're* no different than any of those Christians."

"Wha' d'you mean?"

"I *can't* get you ta say that you're wrong either."

Twisting into a squint, and convulsing reverently ... "But what am I *wrong* about?"

... okay okay, just breath and ... "Okay." ...

"Tell me what I'm wrong about."

"Okay," wiping the bar ... "You won' admit that not ev'rything can be explained through science n that there are some things that science *doesn't* know and *can't* explain. Sure, you can *try* ta gimme all these little fickle answers as ta *why* that meteorite landed in fronta you, but if I keep askin 'why,' eventually yer not gonna be able ta gimme an answer."

"That's because the answer has not yet been discovered!"

"*Exactly!* But that doesn' mean there isn't an answer."

145

"I never said there *wasn't* an answer. Somebody can go out n find the answer and someday they will."

"Maybe," applying grease to a smudge ... "but there will always be more answers ta find because we could explain things n ask 'why' forever because the universe is infinite ——

"Actually, they think they might've found the end o' the universe."

... Lord ... "Then what's on the other side?"

Crossing smugly, "Scientists think that the universe is finite."

"Yeah, that's what they *think* not what they *know.*" ...

Thank God! Salvation in the form of a customer who wanted a double latte. I turned around to make the drink. He kept talking ... "But they *know* because they can use these high-powered telescopes ta watch the universe expand. It's all about technology that helps us see faraway n discover more n more things about the universe, givin us so much more knowledge n information."

Shouting above the roar of steaming milk, "But you still don't ever know that final answer!"

"No. But maybe someday we will 'fwe ——

"NO! NO!" shutting off the steam wand, "We *never* will! The answer is *infinity!* God *is infinity* — undefinable! WE CAN'T DEFINE IT! We can't even conceive it. And we can't conceive God, at least not in this life or any life for that matter. There are an infinite amount of particles n particles in the particles n spaces between those particles, and we can *try* all we want ta find the end o' the universe, the final answer, whatever. But we're never *going* to because it all goes on forever."

"And how d'you know that?"

I shrugged because I mean honestly ... through the ceiling, past the sun, and into the darkest void at the bottom of my soul ... "God."

"Did God tell you or something? How d'you know?"

... be done with this bullshit ... "Yep. God told me this

argument is over."

"So you're conceding?! You admit that you don't know?"

"Yeah sure, as long as it'll make you disappear."

"Okay then, *admit it!* Admit you don't know everything."

I picked up a bar rag and whipped it against the countertop — SMACK! ... everyone in the store turned to stare ...

who did it, who did it

YOU DID IT! YOU DID IT!

Do you know who did it?

"I know nothing" ...

Something, though, that's a-whole-nother story ...

You go to school to learn something, and you go to college to learn more of that something, then you graduate and get your diploma so now you can go and make something of yourself and be somebody, and maybe if you're lucky you'll get to be a big somebody with lots of things, or just a regular ol somebody with some things. Maybe you'll get to have your own little box in which to keep all of your things, and on the wall you'll display your certificates that show that you achieved something, indicating you have the right to be somebody, whoever you are.

Remember how they all used to say, 'you can be whatever you want,' and maybe even they posted advice on the walls of their classrooms telling you how to be whatever you want — hard work, study, strive for goals, achieve goals, run to the finish line and don't stop running, think outside the box, like when you're walking through the desert and there are no houses or school buildings to be found for miles, there you should think ...

But don't think inside the box, just do what you're told and you'll get your certificate of achievement to hang on the wall of your box when you grow up ...

That's what they all said, remember? ... But where are they?

Still stuck inside their little boxes.

Oh When! ...

Will they ever get out?

July

The sirens wailed when It came down from the sky, moaning and screaming for their master, That Guy. Randolph and his family raced home to seek shelter, but when they crested the hill they saw It in the valley raping the Earth ...

There was a tornado swirling inside of him.

God.

Dog ... the ginormous German shepherd at grandma's house. Grandpa would slap the shit out of it. It barked at Randy, but it loved grandma because she would feed it chili and raw beef and leftover cheeseburgers. "Hi Thor," she said — this little old lady with arthritic hands and knees, pearls around her neck and in her ears, all hunched over in her creamy-white, chiffon dress, the beehive atop her head, shuffling through the dusty yard with a massive pot of warm beef broth and polenta ...

"Hi Thor. How are you?"

And her face caked with bright red makeup, always smiling through immense physical pain. The dog — the German shepherd on a tractor chain — was so huge and powerful; he stood on his haunches to show her his might, and then when she neared he bowed to her, head atop paws the size of human hands, as she spooned piles of slop into his tin tray ...

"There you go Thor."

And she said it sweeter and nicer than anyone said anything to any other living creature ever. She spoke nicer to the dog than to her customers, and way nicer than to her husband, but she spoke to Randolph the same way, always smiling and holding her little mouth of lipstick ever-so-slightly open as she looked down on her precious little cherub, her only grandson, and oh how proud she was!

"Randolph," she would say real breathy like a whore, but she was his grandmother and he loved her even though he was afraid of her because he always remembered that song when he looked at her — the song mommy and daddy listened to on the old record player ...

Grandma always had lots and lots of jewelry and makeup and stuff and things. She would watch the Home Shopping Network and order bobbles from the Franklin Mint — little statues of lighthouses, coin and stamp displays, hard-bound Reader's Digest books and Abe Lincoln collectibles. She always gave Randolph the lighthouses, and he loved them, displaying them on the shelves of his bedroom — models of America's greatest towers from places like Portland and Chesapeake and Cape Cod ...

Mommy and daddy would listen to the album and the song would come on with the guitar picking real slow and then the flute, and Randolph would gaze out the window into the dark night and see the little shadows running around beneath the moon light, peeking through the trees.

It made him wonder ...

Grandma kept buying Everything, and she would give him bits and pieces of it All, because she knew All that glitters is gold. Randy knew that's what Everything turned into, and grandma just wanted to be sure, so she bought her way ...

And Thor?

... dogsidaed ...

~~ *RW* ~~

I got lucky, but I come from a lucky family. The job at the newspaper just kinda fell into my lap, like how a leaf falls from a tree: you don't think about why it happened, it just did, but when you do start to think about the series of events that caused the leaf to fall and land on that one spot — the changing of the seasons, the wind, the tree germinating, a squirrel burying an acorn — you can't help but understand that this singular event is the result of an infinite series of causes; this singular event was fated from long ago ...

Like I said, I just got lucky.

At the newspaper, I had to learn to write coherently or embarrass myself in front of everyone in Montdale County. I could write 10,000 pages on my journalistic career alone; mind you, I stopped working for the newspaper at age twenty. Still, I wrote there for over eight years of my life.

You see, I was an apprentice, a warrior-in-training, so to speak. From Gutenberg to Franklin to paperboys, journalism and apprenticeship have come hand in hand. Throughout my formative teenage years I was lucky enough to learn this trade. My pen is my sword, and I can't ever thank my teachers enough for what they taught me and what experiences they facilitated.

Covering sports, I was introduced to the schizophrenic nature of the mob. I saw the most despicable of parents, coaches, and fans, as well as the most ecstatic, knowledgeable, and respectful. Often times, they were the same people wearing different masks, like members of the chorus in a Greek tragedy. The basketball gymnasium, the football field — these are the American theaters, and the games, even with all of their rules, are our gladiatorial competitions. Nothing evokes more reverence than a successful athletic team, especially in rural America where often the only social event on a Friday or Saturday night is a high school athletic competition.

In my time at the newspaper, I stood on the sidelines in state-semifinals football games and sat at the scorers' table for state-finals basketball games. I had great rapport with coaches because I wrote objectively (at least as best I could) but always respected my audience.

At first, I carried my esteemed position as if it were the most fragile piece of China ever made. Cautiously on tiptoes rehearsing every syllable of every question, I approached the coaches for interviews. Sweaty palms and nervous, I tried not to be seen down on the baseline with a camera slung around my neck. But the more people commented on my most recent article or photograph, the more confident I became. My sweaty palms dried out; I found the courage to ask the tough questions; I wanted to go beyond my own abilities every time I sat down to write, always wanting my latest story, my latest column, to be the most fluid and concise. I pushed myself, always on the lookout for new words and new ways to describe the same plays over again, experimenting with language that highlighted various attributes of the game more than others. About the same time, I began to see the game itself differently: no longer was a simple competition merely a compilation of numbers and times, but rather a danse macabre of passionate strife and sacrifice or sometimes just sheer, cold ruthlessness. The ball stopped *'bouncing'* and instead *'skipped across the translucent floor like a stone on a pond'* ...

The more I wrote and the harder I pushed myself, the more the comments came. Most of them were positive and encouraging, but some were skeptical and insulting — people wondering how I could *ever* say or write something so *cruel* or *disturbing!* Heaven forbid I tell the *truth* or write the *whole* story ...

Yeah, the truth fuckin hurts and not everyone likes to hear it. Some people only want to read *nice* stories about *nice* people doing *nice* things ...

~~ *RW* ~~

When I departed for the second go-round to Cairo nothing had changed. Route 67 was still there, asphalt, yellow lines, and all; all the little towns were still there; the corn may have gotten taller but that's about it. It seemed that I had been doing this ceaselessly forever.

Everything before Nashville was a daze. There, I drove over Interstate 64 and then past about five factories and at least five more large warehouses all on the north end of town. It's a rare sight in the Midwest anymore — a self-sustaining community with jobs and services for the people who live there. Of course, if the interstate weren't nearby, this town never would have remained economically significant.

Nashville, you see, was a time warp, memorializing an age when the small town was the most important functioning civic body in American society — back when people lived and participated in communities rather than isolating themselves in dead-end subdivisions: people chatted on street corners; moms sent kids on errands because they only had to walk around the block to the local grocery store; downtown Main Streets were actual shopping districts where merchants sold and people bought *stuff* and *things* other than overpriced antiques. Nashville had its fair share of antique shops, but there was also a family-owned department store and a couple of dime stores and, believe it or not, people were actually *shopping* at these places, and everyone was outside, walking around, chitchatting and talking: it all just seemed to function so perfectly, just like that picturesque American small town in the back of your mind. The place was seductively cozy: I didn't wanna leave ...

So I stopped at a gas station to whet my whistle, and as if everything couldn't get any more perfect, you'll never guess what I found at the soda fountain ...

Seriously, you won't. Because you've probably never heard of it.

Ski.

Ski is a brand of highly-caffeinated soda bottled in Evansville, Indiana, and only sold south of Interstate 70 and north of the Kentucky border. It tastes kind of like a cross between Orange Crush, Mountain Dew, and Surge — that really tart shit Coke put out in the nineties. And much like Surge, the color of Ski resembles that of urine.

I filled up a twenty-ouncer and sipped in ecstasy. Reluctantly, slurpy in hand, I left Nashville. I would've stayed but a town is only as good as its people, and I didn't know anybody there.

Continuing south, I stopped again just outside Carbondale at an old-school Wal-Mart that hadn't been converted into a life-sucking super-center yet for some 35mm film for the ol Nikon. In the parking lot, I found a group of fat males — two men and three boys — all huddled around a pickup truck. One of the fat men was messing with something under the hood while the other guy stood by smoking a cigarette, explaining what to do because he actually didn't know.

I drove some more ... through Murphysboro and Shawnee wine country, past all those vineyards and orchards and Alto Pass, and on down the road through the tall deciduous forests until I reached the Jonesboro roundabout ... the sky was bleak and gray, motionless above and all around as if the entire universe and everything living had decided to stop ... perish ...

Halfway 'round the roundabout my attention suddenly gravitated to a perversely juxtaposed monument in the center of the circle. I stopped and parked, figuring to have a gander. In the middle of the grassy green was an old-fashioned red telephone booth commonly found on the streets of London. The phoneless booth was next to a fountain encircled by a rot-iron fence upon which hung a sign that read **DANGER ELECTRIC HAZARD**, beneath which was a picture of a silhouetted man being zapped by a silhouette of lightning. I recognized that man ... Further scoping out the place, I encountered a plaque commemorating one of the famed Lincoln-Douglas debates which took place in Jonesboro in 1858 ...

There were seven debates between the young Republican Abraham and the Democrat Stephen in the race for one of Illinois' United States Senate seats. The debates focused on issues of states' rights and popular sovereignty, all of course revolving around the subject of slavery.

Douglas, being a Democrat, frequently denounced Lincoln as an abolitionist whose progressive rhetoric was jeopardizing the fragile union. In response, Abraham would passionately declare that America should be united and not divided, and that we should all join hands and sing together as One people ...

Kumbaya, My Lord! Kumbaya! Kumbaya, My Lord! Kumbaya!

He also directed many personal insults at Douglas who rarely strayed from his pragmatic idealism. You see, Douglas believed that the Union of states would best be preserved if certain states respected the popular sovereignty of others. At one point, Lincoln passionately declared in front of a rambunctious crowd that Douglas therefore must hate 'freedom' and 'liberty.' Another time, Lincoln referred to Douglas' continued use of the term 'popular sovereignty' to justify slavery in certain states as (I quote) "a do-nothin sovereignty that was as thin as the homeopathic soup that was made by boiling the shadow of a pigeon that had starved to death."

Witty, idealistic, tall, goofy, Abraham Lincoln was quite the character. He lost the 1858 Senatorial election, but was of course elected to the Presidency two years later and presided over the deadliest war in American history. A passionate and righteous speaker, he could work a crowd with rousing talking points — 'liberty' and 'justice' and 'equality' and 'unity,' even proclaiming 'Oneness.' Yet it still may surprise many Americans to know that the Great Emancipator didn't actually believe that blacks and whites were, or could be considered, 'equal.' In fact, Lincoln's greatest hypocrisy was the continued reaffirmation of the division of humanity along socially-drawn 'race' lines while preaching his 'One People' dogma. The following is an excerpt from the Charleston Debate:

> I am not, nor ever have been, in favor of bringing about in any way the social and political equality of the white and black races, that I am not nor ever have been in favor of making voters or jurors of negroes, nor of qualifying them to hold office, nor to intermarry with white people. I as much as any other man am in favor of having the superior position assigned to the white race. I say upon

> this occasion I do not perceive that because the white man
> is to have the superior position the negro should be denied
> everything. I do not understand that because I do not want
> a negro woman for a slave, I must necessarily want her
> for a wife. My understanding is that I can just let her
> alone.

It should be noted that during the Charleston Debate, a group of Democrats held up a sign that read "Negro Equality," featuring a picture of a white man, a black woman, and a brown child. What they intended by this gesture is unknown. Perhaps they were making a philosophical statement foreshadowing the end of race. More likely they were trying to say, 'Hey, 'fwe abolish slav'ry then we're gonna have a buncha little brown babies runnin 'round ...

'And we don' want that ...

'It ain' right ...

Anyway, for the next one-hundred years, 'race' issues plagued America. In Cairo they were officially settled with a brief civil war in the 1960s and 70s. The progression of 'equality' under the law for black people has taken baby steps over time. Lincoln may have started the whole thing by freeing the slaves, authoring the "Emancipation Proclamation," etc. But Lincoln seemed to pity the negro condition rather than actually acknowledging that black people were, well ... PEOPLE!

You see, by ending slavery, despite Reconstruction and forty-acres-and-a-mule and all of that other stuff, the United States Government pretty much might as well have said, "Oh we're sorry we whipped you, raped you, and made you work in our fields so we could sit around on our verandas all day drinking toddies and fanning ourselves. So here you go! Now you're free! You don't have to work for us anymore."

Rejoice! Rejoice! Freedom!

And all the black people dance around the bonfire singin them ol negro spirichuls. N then they wake in the mornin hung over on moonshine n walk outside their shanty shacks n look at each other like, "Wuts we gwin ta do now?"

"I dunno. Weez free! Lets 'ave anotha party!"

And so they dance around the barbecue and get drunk and sing songs, celebrating their long-awaited freedom after hundreds of years of captive servitude. Freedom means you don't have to work if you don't want to, and why would you? I don't.

Funny thing is, after all that hoopla — hundreds of thousands of dead soldiers, millions of dead slaves, thousands more lynched and raped, and thousands beaten in the streets of America's cities during the Civil Rights Movement — the present-day living situation of many black people isn't all that different from what it was back then. In Cairo, many poor black people spend their days getting drunk and jiving in the street to a thumping subwoofer and sometimes they throw some chicken wings on the Weber ...

... moonshine, spirichul, bonfire ...

It's not like they don't wanna work or don't have to work. It's just like this okay: after 300 years of forced servitude, why *shouldn't* they kick it for a while? Hell, they've only been 'free' for 150 years now. They still got another 150 before it all evens out! Then they can start over ...

Ah yes! I can hear the gasps now! No, I'm not being 'politically correct' but let's be honest with ourselves — none of you people are 'politically correct' either. Political correctness is an act, a front, a defensive cover up, that squares like you gasping faggots use to iron out the wrinkles in America's social fabric meanwhile completely ignoring the gaping hole in the tattered security blanket.

Race is just a buncha bullshit anyway: the concept was developed by colonialists in the fifteenth and sixteenth centuries to justify their own ruthless cruelty when harvesting slaves in Africa, the Caribbean, and South Pacific. Race is one of the oldest known social constructions in the history of mankind. Hitler used it to justify the slaughter of Jews because he needed a domestic enemy so that the masses would be afraid of someone other than the lunatic in power. So you better watch out for people who make sweeping, judgmental statements about different groups of people who happen to share certain characteristics ...

The bottom line is that Lincoln was half right: we're all One — one species — but we're all a bunch of Ones too — singular individuals, all seven billion of us. Under certain circumstances, I will admit, grouping people is necessary especially when a group of people who all share one very obvious characteristic also happen to share a deep history. In the case of people who happen to have black skin, their general plight under our civilization's tattered security blanket is economic and socioeconomic. Mine is emocionomic and egoistic because I am a white male. Native Americans have no plight because we took care of them a long time ago ;) ...

Again, just FUCKING KIDDING! You see, I'm testing you to see if you can make it all the way through the damn book. You're doing very good so far. Don't give up now, seriously, it's gonna get *pretty damn fucking good! really damn fucking soon!* I promise.

Anyway ... remember we were driving along when we stopped in Jonesboro to talk about Abraham Lincoln? Well eventually we left and drove on to encounter the shantytowns of Unity and Hodges Park. The Unity Post Office was a U-Haul trailer. Surrounding it were trailers (mobile homes) and surrounding them were fat white people seated in lawn chairs just watching the cars pass by. Just on the other side of a hedgerow were the trailers of Hodges Park around which sat fat black people in lawn chairs ...

The same people were not doing the same unthings except they had morphed into different flesh forms.

We're all the same — the shanty shackers and development dwellers, developers and politicians, Jesus Freaks and home boys, even the high school kids at the Harvest Life Missionary where I arrived right on time for my scheduled five o'clock meeting ...

I entered via the office and was told by Karen to proceed through another interior door where Wayne would be. Wayne and I were to live together in the vacant rectory of the old Catholic Church. I gave Karen many thanks and proceeded to the game room where a man with a long, gray ponytail and a gray goatee leaned against a ping-pong table. I introduced myself. He acknowledged with a whispery voice that he was indeed Wayne. His eyes were soft, gray spheres hanging from his brow over an assuming smile that seemed to say, 'No matter what, everything will be alright.'

We confirmed our previous arrangements, and he calmly informed me that he had some work to finish at the office, so I said I would get something to eat and return in a couple of hours.

··· ||| ··· ||| ··· |||

After a plate of General Tso's Chicken at the Hong Kong Chinese Restaurant, I coughed up rat hairs then crossed over to the liquor store behind which was a group of black people standing around drinking from brown paper bags. One of them was USC Steve. His eyes followed me as I crossed Washington Avenue and proceeded directly toward him and the two others. He danced a jiggity-jive and cocked his head, "Yo dude, yo!"

"Yo Steve."

"How you doin?"

"Pretty good, jus' back in town takin some pictures."

"Ah ha."

A woman with dark sunglasses and a smooth pearly smile watched me from her perch atop a rusted air conditioner. "Whuchu takin pictures of, chile?" she said. I was entranced by her as soon as she spoke: she was beautiful, not in the Louis Vuitton sense, but really *actually* beautiful — great vibes ...

"Oh you know. Jus' the town n the people n stuff."

I brought the camera more to be a prop than an actual tool. I thought people would notice me more if I was walking around taking pictures instead of with a notepad and tape recorder, and then maybe they would be more likely to engage with me.

That's what I thought ... Really, though, I ended up just taking a buncha pictures, including photos of Steve and the woman and the other guy all in black dawning sunglasses, standing sketchily in the background behind the rusty air conditioner around which Steve sauntered.

"Ain' much ta look at 'round 'ere," she said, flinging her head back into hysterical laughter as she gyrated atop the perch.

Steve looked at her with his lips all pursed and face all scrunched up on the side. Snapping his head back at me, he said, "Yo dude, you got a smoke?"

"Yeah," handing him a cig and a light, then pulling my notepad from my pocket figuring maybe they would talk to me.

"Whuchu writin?" she asked.

"Oh, I'm jus' takin some notes."

"Notes fer what? You writin a book?"

"Well —

"He's a newspapa man," Steve barked.

"Well, righ' now I don' really work for anybody — pretty much jus' freelancin."

"So whuchu gonna do with it all?"

"I don' know. We'll see. Maybe write somethin."

"Somethin 'bout this town?" ... She was genuinely interested ...

"Probably."

"Well well," again that head fling ... "'If that ain' somethin. You b'lee that Steve? — A book 'bout Care-oh."

"A book 'bout Care-oh," dreaming off beyond, a smile further brightening his already glowing countenance. He took off his hat to scratch his head then placed it back on and flung his arm against my shoulder ... "So wuz up? Lis'en uh this. Still nee' me ta talk fer yo' book?"

"Sure," I said, sitting down next to the lady on the air conditioner.

Steve stood in front of me, then sidled back ... "Lemme know when you ready."

The bald guy all in black came up and stood behind Steve, smiling real wide and bobbing his head up and down. He had a Miller High Life in his hand and a gold earring in his left ear. He stared off into the setting sun through those big dark sunglasses atop his fat face. Really, he was funny looking, like he could kill you if he wanted but he wouldn't: you wouldn't be worth it to him ...

"You ready?"

"Go."

"Okay so lis'en," looking out beyond me, beyond the road and everything, just loving the spotlight ... "This town 'ere ain' showin *no* mercy. I wuz like nine-year-old when I got 'ere up from Miss'ippi."

"You were born in Mississippi?"

"Naw man, I wuz born N'Orleans n moved ta Miss'ippi when my dad died n then up 'ere with my grandma cuz my mom had ta stay down thur n be a mish'nery."

"So how long you lived here?"

"'Bou' ten years."

"So you're only nineteen?"

"Naw man, I'm thirta-fo'."

I decided to ignore the mathematical fallacy ... "So tell me 'bout your days around here."

"My days? Whuchu mean?"

"Like wha' d'ya do during the day?"

"This," he said.

She busted up ... "This's all we do."

"I try ta get work, I do," pain pulling him down by the face ... "But thur ain' nothin er nowhere *ta* work fo down 'ere."

The bald guy lit up a Swisher Sweet ...

"Nothin," she said.

"But can't ya work fer the city?"

"Man," Steve rubbed his eyes and leaned into me then barked a loud secret, "The city ain' gonna do nothin fo ya. They don' care! They jus' run by all them white folk n then 'ftaint white folk runnin it, it black folk who got em all up in the

160

pocket book, n they all give the jobs ta they friends, nobody else. And I ain' friends with *none* of em! I try ta sue em n they ain' givin me ——

"Who you suin?" she snapped, cynically cross, "You ain' suin nobody."

"You shut up!"

"You don' be talkin ta me like that!"

The other guy tapped Steve on the shoulder ...

"What? I'm tryin ta get my in'aview 'ere."

He then began to instruct Steve with his cigarillo ... "Ma', ya ai' s'po ta tah t'a la'ee li' tha', donchu gotchu mannuhs ma'? She jes' a la'ee n you be treatin her li' she jes' a dog er sum'n ma', ya oughtta apologi' ta 'er."

"Why donchu mind yo' own bis'nis. Ize gettin my in'aview." ... turning back to me, "Wha' wuz you askin?"

"Ummm," to my notepad ... "wha' do people around 'ere typically do during the day?"

"Drinkin. Smokin dope. The Devil's doins."

"So most o' the people 'round 'ere don' work during the day?"

"Naw man. There ain' nowhere *ta* work. Lis'en ta this 'ere, jes' lis'en ——

"Here we go."

"Shut up!" ... turning back to me, "Ya gotcha crack'eds, ya dope'eds, ya drunks, ya ballas, n ya workas. Me? I'm a drunk. I'll 'mit it. I ain' 'fraid o' nothin. I get up n get my beer in the mornin, beer in the aftanoon, beer at night. But I ain' 'urtin nobody. I got my money n I use it."

"Where d'ya get your money?"

"Guvament check cum in the mail n my momma, she sen' me money sometime. But hey! Lis'en ta this, I'm suin em."

"Suin who?"

"The council."

"Cairo City Council?"

"Yeah."

"Youz full o' shit!" she barked.

"Naw naw, tha' big hole o'er there on Commercial? I be walkin down o'er there n it fall in righ' undaneath me — big sink hole. Tha' why I got this limp n this leg 'ere stick out on the side."

"Psh!" head flinging hysterics ... "You had that limp 'fo you fell in that 'ole!"

"Shut up! My lawyer say that I kin sue em n we workin on gettin it from em but they ain' gonna pay. They don' care 'bou' none of us."

"Ma', lis'n ma', they ta' all tha' money n kee' it fo 'emsel's ma', non o' it cum'n ba t'us, ma', not fixin the stree' oh the ho's ma', nuttin ma'."

Steve urgently patted my pad, "Write this down 'ere, write this down! I'm tired o' you people in Illinois takin ev'ry grant n they don' take care o' nobody in Care-oh, don' give a damn 'fits the project landlord, judge, er whateva, they all togetha — put this down man! — I jus' got in a car wreck, a pothole in Care-oh n I been suin Care-oh fo two years. They ain' cum ta me yet. You know my lawyer man up in Carbondale, he on tee-vee — Larry n Larry Attorneys — write this down man!"

"I'm writin," fitfully scribbling.

"God bless 'Merica!" the other guy blurted. "Bless muthafuckin 'Merica!" raising his cigar heavenward ...

"Fuck it! Fuck America, thaz what I say!"

"You just calm yo ass down! He ain' gonna write nothin down you be talkin like you iz!"

"Shut up woman! Write this down," patting again, "I would like ta thank the Daystar Center fo helpin me clean out my drugs n shih. Thank y'all ...

He ranted all the way to the silent abyss until only his living corpse remained — hands on hips, the limpy right leg turned in half pigeon-toed, as he gazed out over the street and the houses like the explorer cresting a rise. Behind him, the bald man in black turned around and sauntered away, a slow steady march, puffing on his cigar, then disappearing behind the corner of the building ...

162

"Well," I said, pulling out my cell phone for the time, "Seems as if I better be goin. I got a meeting ta go to."

"Alrighty then," Steve said.

I stood up and started to walk away ... "Hey man! Hey!" turning around ... He was bouncing toward me with that awkward limp ... "Ya got five dollas?"

I reached in and pulled out a ten, "There ya go man."

"Hey, thanks man! You be 'roun' fo a while?"

"Just a few days."

"Alrighty then."

"Alright, see ya later."

"Nice meetin you!" the lady shouted from behind. I turned and waved a two-fingered salute. She smiled back ...

... ||| ... ||| ... |||

Back at the mission center, I found Wayne and followed him across town to the rectory. He showed me upstairs to my room and stood in the doorway watching me as I unpacked my things. I could feel him back there; I tried to forget about it, but I just couldn't take it, so I turned around and faced him ...

"This town has had problems from outsiders coming in here." His soft and gentle voice carried ominous undertones; the house breathed its silent, old ugliness around us ...

"That's what I gather," unpacking my bag in the silence enveloped by the ruffles and swishes and vooooit of the zipper. Orange streamed through the windows from the fire burning on the horizon. The darkness was coming to consume everything. He was still watching ...

"But," I said, back around facing him, "From what I gather, it seems that there's a lotta corruption 'ere by the locals in power, and *that* is what's holdin this town *and* the people back."

"There is corruption." He turned around into the hall and waited as I finished unpacking ... "I stay down here in this room."

"Okay."

He showed me around the house. Downstairs in the

kitchen, I imagined a priest meditating over a Rosary.

"I like organic food," showing me his collection of raw vegetables in the fridge ... "I know a farmer that gets me really good vegetables."

"Awesome dude." ... gazing out the window into an enfenced courtyard that divided the rectory from the church — a couple of lawn chairs and a statue of the Virgin Mary ... the sky streaking a peep show for the dark murk coming on seductively careful ...

I went outside to have a cig. Wayne came out a few minutes later, us both sitting in those rusty lawn chairs, facing the Virgin. The fiery orange streetlights from the adjacent parking lot cast broad, angular shadows on the surrounding facades ...

"I grew up Catholic," I told Wayne.

"Yes" ... thinking silence ...

"It," inhaling the last drag of my smoke then stomping it on the ground, "was int'resting."

... resting his hands symmetrically on each arm bar, legs spread evenly in front of him, attentive and serene ... "Is that all?"

I shrugged, "Well 'fcourse not. I mean, bein Catholic has affected me greatly — how I perceive the world n how I interact with it, ya know?"

A statue ... "I can see how something traumatic like that would affect somebody."

"Traumatic?"

"Growing up Catholic in this day and age."

... what? ... "Excuse me?"

He didn't/wouldn't move ... "Sometimes certain things remain hidden in the darkness because people are too afraid to come forward and accept Jesus' light in their hearts."

"Without darkness there is no light."

"But Jesus teaches people how to shine their light so that there are no dark places."

"But there is a balance of dark n light in the universe."

"Yes," he nodded once and returned to stone ... "Right now

164

there is. But when Jesus returns, he will shine his light so bright that everything hidden in the dark places will be exposed and only those who have accepted him in their hearts will be spared from damnation."

I chuckled to myself, but he heard it ... "I suppose that *could* happen. But you don' know n I don' know if it ever will."

"If you have faith in Jesus Christ and faith in the teachings of the Lord and the Bible, then you will not need to know when it will happen because you will have been saved from damnation." He spoke like a machine: only his mouth moved, no other muscles on his face or body.

... give the Devil his due ... "I s'pose that makes sense" ... but it doesn't matter if anything or everything or nothing is true cuz it's not about facts, it's about fiction ... "You know, the Bible's a good story. Whether er not any of it's true is irrelevant."

"In second Samuel it says, 'As for God, his way is perfect. The word of the Lord is flawless. He is a shield for all who take refuge in him.' The Bible is the word of God, and God's word shields us from lies."

"But the Bible is *not* 'the word of God.' It is 'the word of God' as written down and edited n passed down over thousands of years by *people*. They may claim that God inspired them ta write what they did, but how can that be proven?"

. "You must have faith, and then you will know."

"But faith can't be proven. For example, you can't prove right now ta me that you have faith. I just have ta take your word for it," leaning over to him with a twinkle on the tip of my tongue ... "I would have to *trust* you."

"Faith is trust."

"You can have faith in anything," standing and pulling a quarter from my pocket ... "I have faith that if I let go of this quarter, it will fall to the ground. Ready? Let's prove it!" And I dropped the quarter ... "A miracle!" ...

"You just proved your faith."

"No, I *didn't* prove my faith. I jus' proved that if I drop a quarter it'll fall ta the ground. I had faith that was true. But you can have faith in anything n it doesn't matter if it's true or not. You can have faith that you will let go of that quarter and it'll fly away, n you can believe that with all your heart, but you're gonna be disappointed when you find out it falls ta the ground."

"But you just said it was a miracle."

"Yeah, it was."

"But you don't have faith?"

... who the fuck is this guy ... "No, I *do* have faith" ... dig it out ... "It's a miracle that it even happened because it's a miracle that anything *ever* happens and I or you are there ta behold it, because it's a miracle that any of us are even alive and at least semiconscious of something. But it's also a coincidence and it's fate too, because even this moment here, right now, was bound ta happen from — well, forever ago, when anything ever happened — everything back there already happening and already gone."

"You're thinking too much. The more faith you have, the less you'll need to think and the more you'll understand."

... yes, yes, YES! because it's all the same answer to the same unanswerable question whether it's a coincidence, a miracle or a logical conclusion — what you believe, the 'why' part of faith, the 'why' even have faith! ... but it was all like a big puzzle still unsolved and I wanted to figure it out so bad, to line up all the pieces because they would tell me 'why' '*why*' '*WHY*'!!! not just about faith and the universe: I knew that already. I knew everything ... but Cairo, that's why I was here ... why Cairo and why this and why me? ... and him back there watching me with those cold eyes and then straight from the dark depths of his quiet and mysterious soul, 'This town has had problems from outsiders coming in here' ... and trying to make things better right? ...

... what was he doing here ...

"So are you from around here?" I asked.

"No, I'm from Mount Vernon. I'm down here all summer

166

doing missionary work, helping the fellowship community build their houses."

"Oh I see" ... working to fix things for God ... "You know," turning to him, "I'm workin for God too."

"Oh," folding his hands over his lap, noddling his bobble head ... "Well there is only one God, the Father, and only one savior, Jesus Christ, and until you accept Jesus in your heart, you will not be saved."

"Oh, I'm already saved." ... whispering voices ... Satan and all his demons and God and all his angels and Jesus and Ghandi and Mohammed and Buddha and Zeus and Apollo and even Macannan Maclir and Thor and that Lady — she was there too ... "I saved myself."

Silent.

"I am who I am and I do what I do because that's who I am n that's what I do."

Fossilized.

I fired up another smoke and sat there puffing, him motionless until he segued because it was his duty to find out ... "What is it that you're researching?"

"What?" I suddenly felt sick.

"Tell me about your research."

"Oh, oh — ha hah heh heh — it's nothin really, just a buncha academic bee-ess."

"Oh, I see. I wish I could've gone to school. I just didn't have the opportunity. I'm so fascinated by people who get to do experiments in laboratories and such, but what you're doing sounds very interesting. What did you say you were researching again?" He was suddenly more like a person ...

"Oh really, it's nothing. I'm jus' tryin ta find a 'causal explanation for racial residential segregation,' and I'm *supposed* ta be goin around n doin all o' these interviews n askin all o' these questions 'bout race n such, but I don' know — I jus' don' think that race is really the issue here. Hell, it's not an issue at all."

"Really?"

"Oh yeah! It's jus' skin color, ya know? I mean, there are no biological diff'rences between blacks n whites except skin color really, n that's not causin the problem here."

"But wasn't skin color the main reason for segregation in the first place?"

"Well yes, but ya see, blacks just *happ*ened ta be the people enslaved. It could just as easily have been Asians or all blonde people. Imagine if we had decided ta say that hair color was indicative of race, then maybe all blonde people would be living here in Cairo in wretched poverty right now."

"So what are you doing then if you're not looking for — what did you say it was?"

"Racial residential segregation."

"Ah — what are you doing then?"

"Ya know" ... good question ... "I don' really know. I jus' think there's more here than meets the eye. Like, there's Real Life — you know 'bout Real Life?"

"No." He lied.

"Well Real Life Rehab is this place over on the other side o' town that caters ta mentally ill people n drug addicts, helping them with rehab n stuff. I've been tryin ta get a hold of em, tryin n tryin n tryin, but they never return my calls, never return my e-mails. I jus' wanna talk with em, figure out what they do. I even sent them my credentials n ev'rything, but still — nothing."

"Maybe they're very busy."

"Yeah right, too busy ta return a damn phone call," a huff ... "I don' know," a puff ... "There's somethin goin on there n all over here n I don' like it."

"But you said they help people?"

"Well," a chuckle ... "that's what they *say* — their website says. I can't rely on that information, not ethic'ly! And *then*, listen ta this — so I met this woman named — well I'm not gonna tell you her name — but she told me 'bout how she lived at Reality House n they took all of 'er money n ev'rything n then they never helped her get medicated fer her addiction n

168

never gave 'er any money ta live on even."

"And she was a drug addict?"

"Yeah, that's why she went there."

"Well, if she's a — uhhh — a drug addict, how can you trust that what she's saying is true?"

... oh yes Mister Cool-Kitty-Cat-Fuck-Face, all drug addicts are liars ... But what about sober ideologues with a vested interest? ...

"Wha' d'you mean?" I asked.

"If her mind has all of those drugs in it, maybe she isn't fully aware of what's going on."

"Oh I see."

... ??? ...

"So are you talking with people?" he asked.

"Yeah. I've interviewed several people — a local historian, the dean at the high school, amongst others. I talked with Karen as well as a few residents o' the houses which your organization is workin on. And I find people here ta be very nice. Most people, I've found, jus' get drunk n high all the time n they don' do anything. But nobody has been *overtly* aggressive."

"Yes," he said. "I find all of the people very kind. But I find most people to be kind." And he shook his head. "Some people don't see all people as kind."

"No," I said. "That's true."

Harvest Life computer lab:

— giant poster taped to blackboard reads:
  THE ENEMY

death	fear
addiction	fat liar
cursing	sin
evil	temptation
neglect	pride

"Who does not do what is right is a child of God, nor is anyone who does not love his brother."

1 John 3:10

  — half children doing what God does not want, just like them ironic

"He who does what is sinful is of the devil b/c the devil has been sinning from the beginning."

1 John 3:8

  — why don't capitalize 'devil'?

"The thief comes only to steal, kill, and destroy."

1 John 10:10

****

"Do not love the world or the things in the world. If anyone loves the word, the love of the Father is not in him."

1 John 2:15

"Little children, it is the last hour; and as you have heard the Antichrist is coming, even now many antichrists have come, by which we know that it is the last hour."

1 John 2:18

****

33rd & Magwin Dr. — rectory, a trip back in time
— no hot water, no cold water
— no A.C. unless abs. neces.
— strange disap. of a shampoo bott.
— therm. in room says 86 @ 11:30 p.m.

after talking with Wayne:
— the Harvest Life people disguise their goals in the name of God. It's no different than when a politician does something for "the good of the people." Either way, it's his goal that HE wants to accomplish. It's not that it's only a personal goal: you can say something is "good for the people" but how can anyone ever determine what is and isn't good? Politicians and Christians have a lot in common: they each have ideas about how things could/should be so they try to make them that way, but they fail to recognize how things are, completely.

NOTES — 7/17/07

**** walking with Nikon ****

RANDOM ENCOUNTERS:

Cairo City controls light, water, gas bills and distribution of
— monopoly
— talk to Mayor Dudmond Greasley
— find out property tax and water rates
— review city financial records for unnecessary expenses

Ask about homelessness, look up statistics
— likely not a prob. due to small town, comm. etc.
— considerate people willing to house family members & friends
— everybody seems to know everybody (maybe)

171

L___ T_____:
    — phone call to R.L., ask for T_____, sec. says I need to talk to W____ I__, I say tell her I would like to talk to her, she says she's on the other line, I say I'll hold, she comes back and says she's still on other line, I wait about 5 min more, am trans. to v-mail

pics of kids, smiling, and kid on bike — clowning, cheesing, obnoxious

awkward run-in with Coach on resid. street walking around
    — him going house to house
    — with three other suited men
    — him, suit & horn-rimmed
    — didn't seem to recog. me or just didn't want to be assoc. with me

the old hospital Southern Medical Center undergoing asbestos removal

old man w/1.5 legs all bruised, propped in w-chair in front yard with fam. sitting around:
    — "Anyone caught tryin ta do that shit, we should kill em n throw em in the river." (shih, rivuh)
    — Charlie Koen: "Let him stay up there. He the reason why this town is the way it is."
        ** matter-of-fact, not vindictive: Koen literally 'up' and 'to be thrown in the river' to be sat. for 'up' where Charlie is
            — Charlie like God in heaven; owner Heavenly Gates Funeral Home
        ** looking for scapegoat b/c it's easy when suppression & dep. are mater. b/c soc. is so damn utilitarian a-way
        ** no self-respons., the have-nots in a drunken pity party
        ** don't know what don't have b/c never had It

walking down 18th St. east toward Sycamore, old building, fence on left, crazy God-talker dude in Wis. plate truck tells me:

> "Are you gonna go in there?"
>
> "What?"
>
> "I just went in there."
>
> "You went in there?"

etc.: watch out and use comm. sense

> — inside side door, found a buncha old Fr. textbooks, etc.
>
> — walls, old stones

return to car for film then head for building across old hardware store p-lot for pics

> — sign: Mt. Moriah Mis Church

sitting @ car waiting & smoking Mary Ellen (white) comes by asks for ride to R.L., I say, okay, on way we stop @ bank & pharmacy

> "Get down on getting high?" — her
>
> "Yes."

drive to BF's house, smoke

> "You're just a baby, kid."

BF (black) from Detr., ask about utility bills, says 'Not too bad'

> — doesn't trust me
>
> "You still gotta long ways ta go chile" ... "But you'll get there."
>
> — down to Ear., reassuring

BF escorts me from house but says to come back for more

2nd time — L___ not available

> voicemail only
>
> "Can I talk to W____ I__?"
>
> "She won't be back til next week."
>
> "How convenient."

hang up

**** Do they think they can be asses to everyone b/c they deal with retarded drug addicts all day? What a vulnerable group of people to take adv. of. ****

return to Harvest Life (3:00 p.m.), no Wayne, no Karen
    — mis. kids all from North
      ** Minneapolis, Wisc. etc.
    — leave for food
      ** pasta salad @ g-store
      ** hot white chick in Led Zep shirt checks me out

return to Harvest Life (app. 4:00 p.m.), no Wayne, no Karen
    — in office: K's mom, meet her
      ** says K not there, go see husband (K's dad) Paul in back
    — proceed down interior corridor, dark, tile floors, block walls, no wind.

interior room at end of long hall, no wind., three fans blowing, about size of big closet
    — Paul sitting behind desk
    — desk: old comp., nothing else
    — bookshelf behind: four Bibs and Left Behind books; bottom shelves empty

"Paul?"
handshake
"I'm Randy."
"Oh yes."

ask about Wayne, tells me not there still at construction site

PAUL CHRISTMAN
    — gray mustache
    — thick hairy, husky build
    — leathery workingman skin

174

— inquisitive blue eyes
— chest hair (gray) protruding from teal button-up shirt
— left eye wanders upon engagement

asks me who I am, tells me to sit in seat next to empty animal
cage, tell him I am Randy, asks me what I am doing, tell him
I'm looking for Wayne to get into rectory, asks me if Wayne
knows I'm coming, tell him yes b/c staying with him
then again, "Who are you?"
— shrugging, smiling
— he knows
"Randolph Wolfram."
"Who is Randolph Wolfram?"
silence b/c I know and he does too, but forbidden to utter
"Why are you here?"
tell him, research
asks about research
tell him (start to)
interrupts me, "Have you ever been to Real Life?" aggressive,
interrogative, prodding like cock
tell him, honestly can't get in touch
him: Ha Ha Ha Ha — me too, nervous
"So is that all you're doing?"
"No."
trying to figure out why the town is the way it is, tells me race
riots, tell him okay but more more more because because why

pause

staredown, maintain eye contact, smile me and him then
him: "So what do you think the answer is?"
tell him about finding a comm. of dependent drunks, high utility
bills, R.L. sketchiness
him: "Don't talk to me about this."
me: "I need to talk to people who pay bills."
him: "And maybe the utility company."

— they would just cover their own asses, have to gather
     info. first
him: not utility's fault
me: "I'm not cynical, you know."
him: "Okay" — blinks breaks eye-cont talks about resid.
heating houses in wint and cooling in summ, says he doesn't
turn on A.C. in summ and keeps house cool in wint
me: nod and smile, "How can they afford it?"
him: doesn't know
me: "Maybe they can't."

silent pause, staredown then says he'll call Wayne crazy
"Okay."
tells me to go ahead and wait outside and he'll be out

Go to 16th & Washington Ave., the big white house, Karen's
     — Wayne will be there

arrive, park on street — no Wayne's truck

walk around for more pics
     — Commercial Ave. building (1), 40s or 50s
     — once a school
     — sign over door: **FALLOUT SHELTER**

BUILDING AFTER BUILDING DECAYING WALLS COL-
LAPSING TREES GROWING THROUGH ROOFS
     — like nuclear fallout
     — nobody seeking shelter
     — everyone on streets drunk and high

ZOMBIES AFTER APOCALYPSE
Where is the savior
Where is Christ

****

"They went out from us, but they were not of us; for if they had been of us, they would have continued with us; but they went out that they might be made manifest, that none of them were of us."

1 John 2:19

****

one-eyed man on bicycle
— white guy, long hair, lots of tattoos, wiry
— show him nuke-fallout sign, lights cig, no comm.
— says he lived in town whole life
** remembers streets full of cars, people everywhere
** "Looks like a damn bomb just leveled the place."
** "Nothin but dope dealers, crackheads, alcoholics."
— self-proclaimed pothead
— asks if I smoke, say Yes, says he has to get beer, leaves

return to Karen's house
— still no Wayne's truck: early 90s Silverado w/ topper
— Service Angel comes out, says Wayne is sitting in living room
— knock on front door, small dog yelping
** French doors, solid wood, glass windows, lace curtains, can't see in
** house Vict., maybe Q.A. all white

Paul answers door, says he beat me
— hardy-har-har
— escorts me to central chamber
** three couches, high ceiling, big sq. coffee table, big tall windows
** W, K, P on separate couches

sit next to Wayne, across from Paul, Karen crying in corner
    — Me
    — God
    — Devil
    — weeping Virgin

room musty, cool like a dungeon but full of light

Paul: "Randy, we've been talking here, and frankly you scare me."
    — intervening chuckles intermittent
    — stares at floor, eye-cont only at end
    — rehearsed robotic

"I scare you?"
"You don't scare ME, but you're scary."
"How?"
the truth and Paul and his organization accomp.: "What you are doing is just FRIGHTENING!!" tells me I will upset people; heaven forbids that I hurt anyone's feelings, boo-hoo
him: can't be associated with me because; and I can't stay with them
me: a sheep in wolves clothes, "alright alright alright"
him: Belleview Motel is clean and ——
me: interrupting, "Been there before, I know."
Karen: speaking up from corner crouch (sic), "He stayed there last time."

from BEHIND! ——————————————
chang, chong, clachamooshy, ching-ba-ding-cl-cling-cling-ba-dong, whoosh! wash! whoosh! swoosh! ahhhhhhhh!! argh!! argh!! my bones!! my flesh!! my eye!! swoosh!!
    — his head severed at the neck by the cha-ching-whoosh-swa-looshity-swoosh! of the sword ...
    — Goodbye.
    — but the blade cla-ching-a-ringed off the stone ...

Wayne: problems in the comm. have been caused by outsiders coming in and stirring

me: "Well you guys aren't originally from here are you."

Paul's corpse: noooo, but lots of progress, lots of progress, lots of progress, more than anyone ever; him thinking great things of himself in glorious greatness
    ** another zombie
    ** leading the clan of zombie (selfless) worshippers; selfish
    ** a dead idea of death
    ** salvation unsalvageable

MESS WITH A MAN'S IDEAS, MESS WITH THE MAN

Karen: we don't support what you're doing so go for it! get er done! go seek the truth!

corpse: you're not welcome at our ministry, would love to hate (have) you (your service)

me: I understand

corpse: in contact with elite and powerful, personally affiliated with R.L.; "Understand you're in search of truth?"

me: nope, just why

Karen: question to keep asking why why why

corpse: you can see! now be BLINDED! the truth is found in the LIGHT! follow it and get ZAPPED! revealing darkness is scary! we want to stop you! go and revel (reveal)!

Karen: support you, but can't help you! go follow goals of God!

me: "Alright, understandable."

Wayne: keep it covered, better than worse; people don't need to know what's behind only what's in front, watch illusion!!

corpse & Karen bowing to Wayne's wisdom

****

"The world does not know us because it did not know him."

1 John 3:1

****

corpse: I am TRUTH!! I will set you FREE!!
me: You are real.
corpse: I am right and you are wrong!
me: I am right and you are wrong!
corpse: NO! I am right and you are wrong!
me: That's what I said.
corpse: That's what I said.
me: We agree.

777 ...

Wayne led me back to the rectory. I packed my bags as he watched from the doorway, making certain I hadn't a chance to steal a cross or statue of Mary. I said goodbye to him, not maliciously or vindictively or spitefully or smitefully or suspiciously. Nope. I figured to let them be suspicious and smiteful. Afterall, they were the children of God and they knew what was best for All. I was just some idealistic young punk or something: I wasn't really sure. I had a camera, a notepad, and an idea that somewhere right under my nose was 'the answer' to all of my questions even though I only ever really asked one question — why? So the answer should be pretty fucking easy right?

That's what I thought. Alls I had to do was keep looking and I would find it ...

... just keep on sifting through those haystacks, you got through one, now there's five hundred fifty-four more to go, so you better get a move on ...

If there was ever a time to give up and just stop caring about everything, now was the time ...

I checked into the Belleview Motel immediately following my departure from the rectory. I was tired, weary, dejected and disenchanted. I walked around town all day, spent five rolls of film and been chastised by alleged Christian know-it-all evangelical existentialists. In my room — the same as before — I plopped on the bed and flipped on ESPN, just like back in Columbia. I mean, if you're destined to fail and you know you're never gonna find it, then why keep fucking looking? Just kick back, relax, stare at the tube, and do absolutely nothing.

I smoked a bowl, maybe two, and after that prolonged period of nothingness morphed to anxiety funneled into the ant pile, I hopped up and crossed the street for a forty of malt liquor. And guess what? They didn't card me — not because I looked like I was twenty-one but because the dreary-droopy muthafucker behind the counter could've given a fuck less if I was working for the cops on some sting operation to try to catch gas-station clerks selling alcohol and tobacco to minors, because seriously, the guy pry makes minimum wage and he has nothing anyway, so what is there to take from him other than his shitty-ass job slinging fossil fuels and inebriating intoxicants to the meek and meager just so they can manage to survive another day in the wasteland of hell without blowing someone's brains out or even their own ...

And that leads us to the question of the month, and no it's not 'why' — it's ...

Which would you prefer? — to be drunk, stoned, cracked out, washed out, dirt poor, and without a care in the world ... or sober, pious, dry, bland, with money teeming from your asshole because you've pinched it tight your whole life to keep it all from being flushed away ...

So which?

You can't say 'neither' and sure-as-hell not 'both.' You have to pick one or kill yourself. Which would you pick?

Of course in the real world — that is, the world outside of this fantastic place I've created in your mind — there's one, the other, this and that, and an infinite amount of in-betweens. You can be a drunk asshole who likes bland food (perhaps you're British), or a pious stoner who ritually tokes everyday at 4:20 ... plus many many more combinations of many many more virtuevices than I can even begin to list ...

You can be as devoutly certain of everything moral and amoral as anyone could possibly be, or you can be as careless as the gas-station attendant and still you're never going to solve the big problem or find that needle in the haystack, because you can bust out your calculator everyday trying to figure out when that fucking line will reach the asymptote, but you're just going to be working your ass off for nothing because it never gets there, and if you give up and stop caring to even try, you'll never get there either because you're just like the hare, three steps from the finish line, so close you don't even care so you decide to call it quits right there.

There is no destination. There is no finish line. But you see it out there just beyond the tree line, where the sun meets the horizon and you know and think that one day you'll get there.

... someday someday someday ...

But someday never comes.

So you give up looking for the path that will lead you to The End because you know you'll never get there even though you can still see it out there beyond everything you've ever dreamt and everything you've ever needed, even though you already have everything you will ever need in order to survive.

... but what about everything else ...

You can't get there! I have faith in you, I know you can't! You can't do it, yes you can! You can't do it, Nobody can! ...

That evening I drank one forty and had already cracked open another when I got a phone call from an intriguing number, so I muted the television — *Family Guy* flashing and Peter too ...

On the other end was a woman who I will refer to as Annie the Axe. I was given her contact information by those two sociology students who hooked me up with Barry Coldwell. I had called this woman several times and left her several messages, and of course, just as I had given up on everything and resigned myself to a life of incessant inebriation, she calls me and confirms everything I suspect:

Pretty much the entire community, county, everything is controlled by an elite group of mostly white people and a couple of blacks who are in bed with wives. These people control the city government, utility company, housing authority (both city and county), as well as most private enterprise. Annie noted that one councilman who happens to be in charge of the county housing board is an insurance salesman who turns around and sells insurance to the same organization that he resides over. She went on to detail numerous accounts of fiscal waste tied up in a nepotistic, deeply-rooted good-ol-boy system that is so tight-knit, nobody who doesn't know somebody can get in. There have been notorious instances of alleged voter fraud that have gone unprosecuted for lack of evidence because the city government "has difficulty holding on to important files."

"Well wha' does that mean, exactly?"

"It means they sometimes go *miss*in jus' when ya need ta look at somethin."

"So what? Do they burn em?"

"Burn em, throw em away, whatever! They get rid of em. City controls the garbage service too, n *boyyy* is that just another *waste!* It'd cost half as much ta charge people fer garbage service er even contract it out ta some private comp'ny. Now they gotta haul the garbage, so they gotta *pay* somebody ta do it, n then they gotta *pay* ta haul it ta the landfill some forty miles away, n then they gotta *pay* ta even be able ta *dump* at the landfill! Waste waste waste!"

But she says none of them really care because councilmen are paid for full-time work, and the mayor gets a pension as does everyone who works for the city — this, in a town with less than 3,000 people. The parks need mowed, but the city can't afford to pay someone to mow them; hundreds of derelict properties need cleaned up, but the city can't afford to demolish the abandoned structures. On top of everything, the city must maintain a grid of streets and sidewalks laid out to accommodate a population of 15,000 people — over five times the amount of people that live there presently — which in turn means the same amount of maintenance with less tax money available to pay for it and even lesser tax money when you consider that there are hardly any stores or businesses in town to bring in sales tax revenue and a lot of the populace is dependant on Medicaid or Social Security — Annie thought that might have something to do with property tax rates, but I don't really know nor care to look it up, because it doesn't matter. The problems are much too obvious to concern oneself with trite stats and numbers.

Annie listed a bunch of names of various individuals tied into that ring of power, one of them being Perry Ellis whom I had a hunch about. I asked Annie if they knew I was here and if they had any idea what I was doing, and she said, "'Fcourse they do honey. They know ev'rything you're up to."

I also asked her about Real Life. She just said, "Oh God that's a-whole-nother issue. I dunno much about it, but I sure as hell *don't* like it!"

I asked Annie who I could talk with in order to confirm some of the things she was telling me, and she told me about a local progressive organization, the CCPA — Cairo Citizens for Progressive Action — of which she was greatly involved. She told me if I wanted to find out more, I should meet with a man by the name of Gee-Cow because she couldn't meet with me in public because then *they* would definitely know. I got Gee-Cow's number and told her I would call him in the morning. She then gave me some background on Gee-Cow, informing me that he had been a ballot-box supervisor in the past and presently volunteered much of his time to direct community clean-up projects. I bid her adieu, thanked her graciously, and plopped down on the bed with an idea raised from the dead.

I had a dream ...

Adorned by those tattered clothes again, I led an army of rabblerousing idiots through Washington D.C. across the National Mall. I was in front sprinting ahead of everyone, carrying the American flag, millions of people without faces following me, stride-for-stride, step-for-step, all tattered and mangy and they all looked the same.

We ran and ran and there was Nobody to stop us, and we reached the steps of the Capitol and still there was Nobody, so we stormed the Bastille and took back America ...

This was the revolution.

And with Old Glory in hand, I ascended the steps and brandished the banner, everyone-ever behind me, whooping and hollering like a chorus of chimpy children ...

> Oh beautiful for spacious skies,
> For amber waves of grain!
> For purple mountain majesties

Above the fruited plain!
America! America!
God shed his grace on thee!
And crown thy good with brotherhood
From sea to shining sea!

I stood stoically like an idol, a statue, gazing out over the festering herd of rotting corpses, and me the deadest, dirtiest beast of all ...

The revolution is a dream.

··· ||| ··· ||| ··· |||

The next day, 7/18/07, I telephoned Gee-Cow and was greeted on the other end by his wife who told me, "Youz the one wez ben waitin fo! Youz gwin ta be the one thaz gonna save this town!"

Oh no ...

Anyway, Gee-Cow came to the phone and told me to meet him over at 38th and Elm around 11:00 a.m. He would be painting the curb, he said. I had breakfast and drove on over.

He didn't really tell me anything that Annie hadn't told me the night before, just gave me a few more names, etc. I thanked him for his forthcoming conveyance of hearsay and went back to check out of the Belleview. After Annie had told me that *they* all knew about my existence and after Annie and Gee-Cow had both painted a picture of corruption so vast and unconquerable, I figured my time in Cairo was up. I had done what I could, the best I could, taken some damn good photographs, met with damn interesting people, took damn good, detailed notes, and had some pretty damn enlightening experiences to say the least.

And I have to admit, the place was growing on me like Poison Oak. If I scratched the itch to take anymore pictures, talk to anymore drunks, or get anymore involved in the undercurrents of community affairs, I would puff up and break out in a feverish rash, so I had to leave.

Before I could go though, I had to make one last stop at a place that had been in the back of my mind since I noticed it on my way outta town the first time, back in June. I had to visit

Fort Defiance State Park and stand at the confluence of two of the continent's mighty rivers — Lady Ohio, shimmering as she just coasts steadily into the Muddy Mississippi, a brown murk of sewage. These were the intestines of the continent and the Mississippi was definitely the lowest of the low — the descending colon, taking everything that drains from the streets of the Heartland and the streams of the plains and dumping all of that shit, silt, and waste into the Gulf of Mexico.

Standing there down at the water's edge, beholding the jagged dividing line that separated the pretty blue Lady from the artery of waste, I looked back up the shore at Cairo's abandoned and collapsing business district. I imagined the river cresting over the thirty-foot wall and washing away this septic wasteland forever. And I thought about all of those people I met.

And I wondered ...

Whose lives and efforts are all in vain? And what of those without virtue? ...

And I laughed, ascended the embankment laden with littered soda bottles, beer cans, styrofoam to-go boxes, and cigarette butts, then back around to take one last look at Him and Her then up to Them, hopped in the car, started the ignition, popped in a cee-dee and cruised away, free as a bird ...

All the way back through Missouri destined for misery, and in Columbia I found it on the recliner, staring into the flashing box, and I fucking hated it so much and I didn't even know I hated it, like I had just been walking along and then suddenly I found myself face down on the concrete, and I didn't even remember how I got there, like the whole instance between the time I tripped and the time I beheld myself with bruises and bumps and a minor concussion was just a dream.

And then I woke up and completely forgot what I had dreamt.

But I knew it was something ...

The Complex

You step on a crack, you'll break your mother's back ...

That's what she used to say — not that you should be careful because you could trip and fall but that somehow, by merely stepping on a crack, even if you're nowhere near her, your mother will get a broken back.

My mother always had a bad back. She would cramp up for days without moving. I thought it was always my fault, remembering stepping on that crack back there by the Post Office.

I forgot! Seriously, I tried to avoid it, hopping from one symmetrical concrete block to the next. I must've just missed it! I'm sorry ...

... ||| ... ||| ... |||

"So I've had this thing on my to-do list for some time now — write a vivid description of Ten Sleep."

"Well, it's poor, int'resting, n we got bad roads."

"Yeah, I don't ——

"I moved ta Ten Sleep in 1982, the Wednesday before the weekend before the Ten Sleep Homecoming — a big drunken brawl."

My father is a lawyer who practices what is locally known as T.S. Law — the only lawyer in Ten Sleep and perhaps the most coveted lawyer in the entire county. He and I are on a walk around the perimeter of the village — total distance 2.2 miles.

We pass houses with half-finished renovation projects that began, it seems, when I was maybe twelve years old. Big dirty dogs chained to stakes in the ground leap from their burrowing holes to bark at us, inevitably choking themselves; rusty automobiles lay in scrap heaps surrounding trailers held intact by duct tape; burn barrels smolder a putrid funk resembling a combination of pipe tobacco, campfire wood, and whiskey breath; from deep within the gloomy haunts of the surrounding forest echo the hacking caw of a crow, a singular chirping songbird, and an incessant myriad of cricketeeks and cricketocks; somewhere out there a lawn mower trims invisible grass as right here, up above and all around, the locusts expand and contract in congruence with summer's depth and gravity ...

On a walk, dad likes to point out things like trees and their sizes and species: "That's a Hackberry," or "Why didn' they call this Oak Street? Lots of Oaks —— or White Oak Street, cuz Oak Street ain' got any Oaks, not as much as here," or "You ever fart while yer walkin?" and he'll rip a big one, "I do."

But above all, dad is well versed in the law ... and local lore ...

"We've got crime," he says, "and we've got punishment. N that punishment ain' always in accordance with the law, though it's much more so now than it used ta be. Used ta be, back in the ol days, you committed a crime, you'd get the shit beat outta ya. That doesn' happen anymore. Guys like Big Bird Hernandez n Jimmy Noresco took it a little too far — Bird especially. Well, hell though, Jimmy Noresco used ta own — down by, you know where Wally lives now?"

No response.

"Well, Jimmy used ta live out on a farm down there south o' town n he had all sorts o' jungle animals — uhhh — you know, bears, alligators, lions ——

"What? You're lyin!"

"NO! Seriously! Oh, I know what it was — Lawrence Kenny!" he slaps my chest. "Lawrence was state's attorney at the time, n somethin got out — BUFFALO!" ... a revelation ... "Jimmy Noresco had some buffalo that got loose one time n they started runnin around on PEOPLE'S FARMS! —— and somebody called the cops n I think they used nine-millimeters on em."

"Seriously?"

"Well I'm guessin it was their *first* n *only* choice."

"They didn' try ta do anything else about it, then yer sayin?"

"Well I don' know for sure, but that's what I'm guessin. Lawrence Kenny n the cops prob'ly jus' shot em."

We round the corner, heading east now, passing a Pekingese smash-faced yipper dog, tied to a cable tied to a downspout, running back and forth in a semicircle ...

"One time," he picks up unannounced, "Jimmy Noresco's eatin ice cream with a knife out of a big carton. It's the middle o' July. He says, 'Ey Wehrem uhguh luh trefa fola hula eh uh uh.' I never really listened to him or paid any attention to him."

"Where was he? Wha' did you say?"

"Jus' walkin in fronta the house. I said, 'Hi Jimmy,' or somethin like that. That's about it."

Walking through a sultry August afternoon, everything is so organically saturated with bugs, weeds, trees, fungi, mammals the Earth can't sustain it for much longer, yet autumn and death seem so far off.

A lone dog bark is a solo introduction to a chorus of yelps and howls from the various canines chained, penned, and enfenced throughout the community; in the leaves of trees, bugs hum in bags of dirt as their maggots feast on the fruits of the majestic hardwoods; within a mile of where you stand there are tens of thousands of trees of varying heights and species and thousands more different species of vines and mosses and wildflowers and poisonous ground-cover blanketing the forest floor; and within that forest echoes the endless harmony and disharmony of a symphony of songbirds ...

"One thing we don' have," he says, "We don' have curbs n gutters, just runnin ditches, n then ya get cars drivin up in yer front yard. Maybe that's somethin Barack Obama will take care of — gettin us some money for curbs n guttering around here."

"I doubt it."

"Yeah, pry not. But ya know we have stuff — just as much stuff as any big city has. We have a fire department, police department ——

"Who? Earl?"

"Well it ain't the FBI er nothin, but he's still ——

"Dad he's dyslexic — can' write tickets."

"Yeah, maybe — whatever. Well anyway, what I was sayin was we got a Post Office, township offices here too, a couple nursing homes, some bars; one thing we don' have is a drug store but we do have a lotta drugs, n we have the Moonlight Y, a couple car dealerships, the Knights of Columbus hall — Ya know it's easier ta focus on what ya have rather than what ya don' have cuz what ya have is obvious, but maybe it's too obvious, I don' know. Ya gotta think about what ya don't have."

The tiny, humble houses all dwarfed by a grain elevator and radio communication tower flashing its white light hundreds of feet above ...

"Tee-ess has three bars, stay open til three a.m. so the Hamilton people can come drink down 'ere late at night, n there used ta be a whore house — Ted Miller's house."

"What? Where?"

"Just up 'ere on the left, you know behind where the nursing home is? They wondered why there were so many little rooms in the house when he bought it."

"Who's Ted Miller?"

"You know, he's got kids — Tanner n Vanner n Danner n Kate."

"Oh, I see."

"Well, I don' know if that's their ——

"No, it's fine."

"N we got a pool supply store and a place where you can get yer truck fixed. We got a lotta stuff in Tee-ess — a lawyer," he smiles real big.

"Lotta people in Tee-ess need a lawyer."

"NO! No more'n anywhere else."

191

I should describe my father ... on a walk, he strides heavily — a massive cumbersome gate as if he were carrying twice the weight of his body. He puffs out his big brute chest as he gracefully stomps around the village, or even the house, like a giant crashing around his castle. You can hear him coming from the other side of the house: a door will be slammed so hard the walls tremble, and then he will walk into the house and stomp toward you. Whatever room you are in, he can sense it. He may call out your name in a deep, bellowing roar, and you don't have to answer: he's just letting you know he's here, that this is his turf and he is the leader.

He works everyday, Monday through Friday, a little bit Saturday and sometimes even Sunday. The office is just half a block down from the house, and the two buildings are linked by a fiber-optic intercom system that allows him to page my mother whenever he needs something. My father will work all day at the office or go to court somewhere while my mother remains at the house either cleaning, cooking, gardening, or soldering a stained-glass project. She's very crafty.

At five o'clock the workday is over. Father arrives home and uncorks a fresh bottle of cabernet which is often gone by seven o'clock with another already opened. He stands around in the kitchen, laughing with my mother, talking about his day, talking about someone else or how much one of his or my mother's relatives has irritated him, and my mother will do the same. They listen to each other as they drink and eat and sit around for a little while and then go for a walk around the village before retiring into the living room for the daily dose of visual entertainment on the television — usually shows like *Seinfeld* or *Everybody Loves Raymond*, in the summer a Cardinals baseball game.

You see, I grew up a huge Saint Louis fan. My grandpa's sports bar was decked out in Cardinals memorabilia. Being in close proximity to Saint Louis, I attended hundreds of games growing up. I remember Ozzie Smith running out and doing back flips on the astroturf, Mark McGwire's towering moon shots, Jim Edmonds' diving catches, and Albert Pujols' unmatched and unrivaled greatness.

When I was three, my grandpa, my dad, and I were all watching a Cubs/Cards game on tee-vee. I cheered when the Cubs got a hit. Hell, I liked their pinstriped uniforms and the blue-and-red 'C.' My grandpa slapped me upside the head and said, "That's the wrong team." I've been a winner ever since, but it's not as great as it sounds ...

As mentioned, I grew up surrounded by sports. My dad took me to professional baseball games and later, when the Rams came to STL, professional football games. We went to all the high school contests, and I even tried to play baseball and football but was so slow and miserable that I fucking sucked, so I would keep the stats and that's how I got the job at the newspaper.

Which brings us to our next juncture — the corner of Summitt Street and Seymour Avenue ...

Running east to west, Seymour marks the end of Ten Sleep and the beginning of Hamilton. Head north on Summitt beneath the massive hardwoods looming over the narrow road like boogiemen giants, and you will steadily ascend the hill, continuing past the gray oaks and their knotty, wrinkled branches like the flabby arms of old widows. Out of the valley you rise, until you break through the tree line to stand at the foot of another massive hill lined by houses on all sides ...

You are leaving Ten Sleep for the City Upon a Hill, the Seat of Montdale County — Hamilton. At the top of that hill — the intersection of Tobias Road and Main Street — you look out to the east, north, and west and you see the entire county for miles — silos, grain bins, farm houses, and big red barns peaking out over fields of corn, beans, and milo, grassy meadows and pastures. Behind you is the forest, and nestled somewhere down in the valley deep within that forest is the place from whence you came, where seldom is heard an unchirping bird and the wild dogs roam free ...

Despite their proximity, Hamilton is quite different from

Ten Sleep. There are no dog barks here, no scents of burning garbage, just cheerful songbirds and the potpourri of gardens and freshly-cut lawns. The wind whispers through tree branches, cars whir on the highway, and children blissfully play. To Randy, Hamilton represented illusion. He went there only to play and work: reality lay somewhere in between ...

He would park on Main Street and proudly proceed up to his office where he performed his journalistic duties with a civic pride. He would look out the window and marvel at the beautiful ornate courthouse and its stoic prominence in the center of the town square. To him, it was the idol on the pedestal, the centerpiece of the community and what everyone pictured when they thought of Hamilton.

He loved his high school mascot — the little blonde Swedish man dressed in orange and black, standing atop the hill, gazing out to nowhere: this was the Hiltopper, and Randy was a Hiltopper, and he wanted to climb high above everything and shout out to everyone so they would marvel him. He wanted the pedestal ...

But when he wasn't having dreams of glory, Randy was marveling the luster of the old brick facades or wondering longingly on the dark, mysterious depths of the vacant buildings, imagining the commerce, the people, the shops and markets from decades ago — his mind turning the images of ancient photographs into a movie reel that only he could see. He fancied himself an integral part of that timeless movie — one of a dying breed from the age of civic shopkeepers and morally pragmatic journalists. these were the purveyors of Earthly goods and bads, and they all stood around on street corners or in the news room talking to the good and the bad about the good and the bad.

Randy was neither good nor bad ...

... just compassionately ruthless, especially when it came to video games. Throughout the summer of Cairo and Columbia, Randy was an avid *Goldeneye* marksman on the ancient Nintendo 64 console.

Introduced to the gaming universe in 1996, Nintendo 64 revolutionized the industry — the first ever mass-marketed, three-dimensional, virtual-reality, simulation-stimulation device of its kind. In the summer of 2007, passing the lonely hours of non-work and non-play, Randy and Mark would sink into their favorite ass crevices, grab their favorite controllers and commence the never-ending virtual war. They would choose 'shoot to kill,' one-shot-yer-dead, and would play at places called The Facility (a chemical weapons storage bunker) or The Temple (high ceilings, dark passages, sliding vault doors and wide open chambers). But the most epic of *Goldeneye* battles always took place in the tight crevices, cubbyholes, and sniper perches of the megalithic, metallic-gray, industrial Complex — a massive stainless steel labyrinth with spacious ventilation shafts and multi-tiered firing sanctums.

Around and around they ran, in search of each other, watching the other's screen, but always running from each other while running toward each other — each both the hunter and the hunted. There was no way outta the maze except to win, and the only way to win was to kill ...

Cigarettes pursed between their lips, sitting in their gluteal molds, tapping buttons and swiveling joysticks ...

... ta-ta-teh-tick-tick-slah-slick-slah-ta-ta-teh-tack-tack ...

"Fuck!"

"Shit dude."

"You son-uv-a *bitch!*"

"Oh shit! Oh shit!"

"Oh that was ——

"Fuck!"

"Nice."

"There we go — oh! How did I not ——

"I don't ——

"Well *fuck!*" ...

They played to win and won like winners, each knowing that the other was just as good and could easily have won. Still, they hated to lose, not because they hated the other person for winning, but rather because so much passion and emotion were invested into this God-damned video game that if they wouldn't have hated losing, they would might as well have given up, and not just on the video game — on life.

They had nothing else to live for. Whenever they were tired of reading or researching or working to attain some abstract and intangible end, they sat down and smoked a bowl then assumed their places in the arena of virtual reality — a real virtuality of winners and losers and consequences that *felt* like something ...

School only impacted their grades and work only impacted their bank accounts. How could they have ever won with grades? How could they have ever won with money? There would always be smarter people. There would always be richer people. But on any given night, the winner of the epic *Goldeneye* battle could say he was the best *Goldeneye* player in the world.

I wondered that — if at this moment in time, there could possibly be a better *Goldeneye* player than I or he. Afterall, the game was nearly extinct — almost a decade old. Who played *Goldeneye* aside from die hards? And who lived it harder than us? ...

We always knew we were either best or second best, and so we kept playing because the loser always challenged for a rematch, knowing he could've won if only he had ...

... n't tripped and fallen into a hole gaping open inside of me and landed in this massive complex of thoughts and presumptions about Everything ...

I just wanted to think nothing about anything so I thought I had to climb out of the dark hole where I was sitting thinking everything about nothing because I thought I had to extricate all of my thoughts and throw them out of the hole before I could ever climb out because I thought I was the Devil or Sarge maybe and I didn't wanna be the Devil anymore and I didn't wanna dominate everything or save everything or dominate everything by saving everything because I didn't wanna be the

Antichrist or Jesus Christ because I didn't wanna be sacrificed and I thought that's what would happen to me if I continued thinking and doing what I was doing so I had to stop or change directions or turn around and go back to the start and try it all over again because it's not that something was wrong though I thought it was it's just that it wasn't possible because how could this be this way because I didn't think I could possibly be that special like all those teachers used to say and Barney too ...

so special so special so special so special

I didn't think I was special but I knew I was more special than even special and that's why I just wanted to be normal and stop presuming things about myself that nobody could ever prove because I knew God wasn't on my side and the Devil wasn't either because nobody was not even me ...

I didn't wanna have faith or believe or even possibly think that I did have faith about believing or something but no! Nothing!

I didn't even wanna think so I wanted to get rid of this damn logic complex that they teach you to use because it was absolutely unnecessary considering everything because I didn't even want that (anything) not even answers or even life and certainly not death or heaven or odds either ...

No luck no draw shooting not to hit the target but to miss on purpose so the bullet goes flying off into the dark nothingness and maybe it hits something because sometimes you gotta take a shot in the dark but you can't shoot in the dark forever because if you don't find that light then you're just gonna be a sorry schmuck for an eternity but I didn't even want that because I didn't wanna think about the possibility of achieving any sort of ephemeral enlightenment and just being disappointed and trying from then on forever and never to get back to there and then I would start having faith in the getting of something even if what I would be trying to get is Nothing and I didn't even wanna think that Nothing was something just Nothing Nothing Nothing!!!

197

Not a word or the opposite of something else or something (everything/Nothing) infinite but not because it isn't ...

It never was.

So you can see I was pretty fucked up and tired too. I had been carrying around this damn burden for so long that I just wanted to heave it from my shoulders and be rid of it forever, but you see the problem was that I wasn't strong enough to just chuck the damn thing or squat and set it down so in order to get rid of it I literally had to fall on my fucking face figuratively and trip in a certain way that would minimize the damage to my psychological and incarnate self. Nothing was telling me something and I knew what I needed to do ...

The only problem was I couldn't do it yet because I didn't think I knew how, but that doesn't mean that I didn't know how because I probably did, I just didn't know that I knew it because I thought I didn't ...

I needed to stop thinking.

I knew too much and I knew I didn't know much of anything but that *not* was all tied in a knot, and I couldn't even get to it because it was buried at the bottom of a landfill covered in layer upon layer of rotting knowledge that first needed to be cleaned out and hauled away — a massive excavation project!

Yes, that's what I needed — a shovel, a backhoe, a dump truck and maybe a crew of working men, cuz I had to dig a hole — a huge one! — the biggest hole in the history of holes!

... it would make me whole ...

A whole hole of holy nothingness so that I could retrieve the (k)not, untie it, and then burn the rope so that ashes to ashes and dust to dust and nobody, not me or you or anyone else, ever has to go around looking for the knot or anything else because it will no longer exist!

Yes!

But fuck! ...

I still had yet to find it because it was still down there underneath all that garbage, and that garbage wasn't anywhere except inside of my mind, so somehow I had to get it out of there and it wasn't going to be with a shovel or a backhoe or a bunch of blue-collar workers. No, this was a white-collar job that required very little physical exertion but extreme psychological effort coordinated over twelve to fifteen intense hours of empty meditation, philosophical brooding, and concentrated devotion to sensory aesthetics ...

Whatever was down there, I wanted it. It may have been a knot, could have been gold, could have been shit, but how could I know unless I looked?

I wanted to know to know I wanted.

And just as Mark McGwire needed steroids to break the homerun record, I needed something to help me see ...

I needed LSD.

Now children, by no means am I advocating drug usage. I'm just saying that sometimes it is necessary to perceive the world in certain physical states only realized via specific intoxicating/mind-altering substances. You ever get jazzed up on coffee before writing a paper or going to work in your cubicle? Same thing. I needed LSD in order to facilitate the discovery of _____, so that I could understand _____, and subsequently share my new discovery and knowledge with the world, furthering the civic and evolutionary progress of man (me) and mankind (you).

And you know, Mark McGwire needed to break that record too, and the only way he ever could've done it was with assistance from performance enhancing substances — in his case, steroids. If Mark McGwire wouldn't have taken steroids, wouldn't have broken that record, then the American populace would never have rallied behind him (Sammy Sosa too) and beheld one of the greatest sporting spectacles of the nineties. Baseball would've just been baseball — slow, boring, and fat, hairy men chewing tobacco. They didn't break any rules because steroids weren't expressly prohibited. Everyone just got upset when they realized that this hero, elevated to god-status, was actually just another human being to whom the ends justified the means.

Someday that'll happen to this hero and all of you out there who already adore me will be sad to find out that I too have a great tragic flaw: I too am a human being. Still though, I have yet to break any rules, because nowhere is it written that one is prohibited from discussing his usage of elicit drugs in connection with intangible virtual discoveries and the blossoming of knowledge. It is against the law of the land to be in possession of or to consume LSD; however, as far as anyone can ever know, this entire story is completely fictional and I never actually used acid and nobody has any way of proving that I did, unless the CIA detains me and administers a spinal tap, which they won't do because they don't even know who-the-hell I am or what I'm even doing and they have much bigger fish to fry like terrorists and ex-KGB agents who sell chemical weapons to the Mujahadeen and guys with names like Hussein, Ahmadinejad, and Mohammed. My name is Randolph Wolfram: it's German (Austrian specifically), but I assure you I have no ties to any 'home grown' terrorist factions like the neo-Nazis, various break away sects of the Church of Latter Day Saints, or Moose Lodges; although, I did once attend a 'truth' convention in Chicago with a bunch of insane freaks who thought the government was going to round us all up and put us into concentration camps because they (the government) allegedly blew up the World Trade Center in a Reichstagian ploy to create a neo-fascist regime. Yes, at one time I honestly bought into that bullshit. Now I realize how laughable it and every other conspiracy theory actually are. I mean, think about all that red tape!

But you know what? It doesn't really matter who/what/when/where if the government or military or whatever were behind anything conspiratorially subversive, because as far as I'm concerned, there ain't nothing any of us can do about it anyway! What? Do you wanna overthrow a massive bureaucracy? Is there any precedent for such a revolution?

But before we even take this one step further, what good

would it do any of us citizens of the world's largest and most powerful empire to subvert a systemic structure that allows us select few human beings lucky enough to be born under the stars and stripes to do a lot of shit (whatever we can get away with) and be whoever-the-hell we want (whoever we can get away with) and say whatever-the-hell we want (whatever we can get away with) in any sort of way we want so as to manifest an idea or a thought in however aggrandizing (self) or sympathizing (you) or propagandizing (everyone else) of a way, and fire our shots from our guns (or mouths) at paper targets posted outside of the strict confines of residential areas while drinking Busch Light from a camouflage aluminum can so that nobody can see you except for you all dressed in orange, and nobody can see me because I'm hiding in a tree with my lover whom I can have sex with whenever I and he/she so desire and sometimes even when he/she doesn't necessarily completely desire but can be made to desire once it starts, and if you're good you can get away with anything?!?!?!?!?! ...

God bless It! And God bless all of Us!

America! America! God shed his grace on Us! ...

And He certainly has. Can you prove otherwise?

No, you can't. So I'll prove it to you ...

One lazy summer day in early August of 2007, I awoke neither reflective nor ambitious, emotional nor intellectual; life was a clean slate. The sky was overcast gray — low stratus clouds, no wind, not too hot, not cold, just a comfortable eighty degrees but dismal. I was candid but not open; all universal tangents were closed, so there was nothing to think.

I wandered in wonder not wondering ...

"You know where ta get some acid?"

"Yeah dude," Mark chuckled. "I was thinkin the same thing. I heard ...

... a lengthy narrative about how some dude on East Campus had acquired fluff from a couch-hopping slippie who was an alleged acquaintance of an acquaintance named P___ on whose couch this dude was allegedly sleeping ...

It was all very sketchy, but we decided to check it out later that afternoon. It was ten o'clock. I dressed and went for a walk.

At Nakota I grabbed a cup of coffee and had sat down at the bar to invest myself in a crossword puzzle when a pony-tailed-nam-vet-Holy-Rolling-hippie-rock-and-roller came over to me in his country-humble-wild-Baptist sortta sidle, rambling in his down-home-prophetic-preaching sortta way ...

"End times man, see the signs showin it a comin man, gonna be 'ere soon n what r we gonna do? What r we gonna do man? Crazy shit comin man, crazy shit. Jesus comin down ta save us n thur ain' nobody gonna stop it from happ'nin."

He took a sip from his mug and scoped out the scene with those beady blue eyes, turning full-circle before returning to me up-and-down with an omnipresent and omniscient smirk, "Randy, man whuchya up to?"

"Jus' sittin 'ere."

"Yeah man?"

"Obviously."

"Hey man, you wanna hear a story man?"

"Umm — maybe?"

"So lis'n 'ere man, check this out. I'm down thur at Booche's las' night, jes' eatin a cheeseburger n this guy 'ere is sittin next ta me at the bar n he's all a cussin n cursin, 'Fuck this!' n 'Fuck that!' N I look o'er at im n I see the *Devil* in thur n I tell im, 'Git outta 'ere *DEVIL!* Nobody wanna hear you cursin, people got thur kids in 'ere man. Kids don' need ta be hearlu em words.' N he looks righ' o'er at me n says ta me, he says, 'You talkin ta me?,' and *by golly* I *jump up* outta my seat n stand up in fronta im n he *slams* 'is beer mug down on the counter — su'prise tha' thing didn' *shatter* he slammed it so hard — n he walks to'rd me n I'm jus' standin thur, 'You *DEVIL* ain' gonna *tech* me! Git outta my face,' n he brings 'is fis' back like he gonna hit me n I jis' stand thur n fis' drops down n all shakin all over like spine turnin ta jelly er somethin n'en he walks out thur, his knees all shakin all over, n I go outside n watch im walkin away all shakin n tremblin — fear o' God got in im, thaz what it wuz. Well I'm watchin im walk down thur at the end o' the sidewalk thur n I turn ta look the other way n I see that *DEVIL!* — Black demon standin down thur on the other end n him down thur all tremblin n scurred n then he turns 'round n looks back at me n that *Devil* jes' *SUCKS RIGHT BACK UP IN IM!*"

"So the Devil was at one end o' the sidewalk n he was down at the other?"

"Thaz right. Cuz he didn' know what ta do 'thout 'is Devil alongside im comfortin im n protectin im makin im think he some big shot er somethin, don' need no Holy Spurt, got the Devil inside im n that Devil's cursin, n I use the power o' the Holy Spurt n *knock* it outta im, *knock* his damn socks off is what I done, n that Devil didn' know what ta do n then he turns 'round n look back n back ta 'is ol ways again. Same ol same ol, didn' even know the Devil wuz in im, n pry still don' know, jes' bein pissed off ol bastard is all. Don' know the power o' the Holy Spurt, never been interduced ta it ever n jes' don' know. See Devils walkin 'round all the time man, ever'ere ya see em n what ya do 'bout it?"

"What can ya do?"

"Ain' nothin ya can. Ya jes' gotta keep fawlin the Holy Spurt, lettin it guide ya n ya know wha' ta do then 'fyou let that Holy Spurt guide ya ever'ere ya go ain' no Devil gonna gitcha."

"Nope."

Carol Ray sips from his mug, then, "So whuz happ'nin in Randy's world?"

"Well," a chuckle, "I'm gettin ready ta go trip some acid."

"Oh HO! Goin on uh 'dventure!"

"Yep."

"Where ya gonna go?"

"Oh, just around prob'ly, see things in the new light."

"The *new light*, eh! Thaz the only way ta see em, look at em n thur differ'nt ever' time, jes' the way things is. Holy Spurt

203

always changin em, changin how ya seein em n ever'thing always changin ever'ere. Power o' God come up n that the power o' change n God's ever'ere ——

"So change is ev'rywhere."

"Whoa, by golly! Thaz right! Always changin ever'thing!"

"Ev'rything. Ev'rywhere. Ev'rywhen."

"Ever'when huh? Changin all em thangs back thur n lookin at em jes' changin n goin n keepin on movin. You got it man, gonna 'ave yerself sum good fun tonight man, n be safe on yer journey."

"Oh I will."

"You do it man." Carol Ray steps back, slaps me on the back, and exits stage front ...

I departed soon after to meet up with Mark and proceed forthwith to the slippie. Upon arriving at his hermitic lair, we were greeted by P___, the aforementioned lessee of the apartment, who directed us to the drab, mangy late-1970s couch upon which reclined a greasy, blonde dread-head with a stupid, childlike disposition. P___ introduced us to 'The Dude' (his given name, I assumed) and subsequently informed 'The Dude' of our desire to procure hallucinogenic substances, whereupon 'The Dude' snapped his fingers and a shoebox appeared on the coffee table; another snap and a vile of eye drops was in his hand; and a third snappity-clappity intricately executed procedure produced ten sugar cubes, each containing a singular tear of the concentrated fluffity so that in our possession, Mark and I each had five drops, a.k.a. hits, of what we had only been told was none-other-than legitimate LSD.

These ten sugar cubes wrapped in aluminum foil contained this very elicit yet most (in)famous of substances, once claimed by some of the greatest creative minds of the Western world to have the mystical, sacred power of putting he/she into the arms of an all-knowing, ever-omnipotent-omniscient One. We were not only procuring a drug, we were in possession of The Elixir for which all of those vainglorious explorers and mystics before us had been searching. The Fountain of Youth, the Holy

Grail — to drink from these consecrated mystical places or chalices would be the equivalent of what we were about to do. And what we were about to see, that which every explorer ever would envy ...

soulelos and evid nwod eth tibbar elohwhole, whichever way you like

Bring it on but not too on because I could lose it all and turn into a tortoise; I mean come on and cummon and c-note me you muthafucker! fuck my mind up and down my spine! but not too hard cuz I don't wanna break my own back, falling on my face after tripping over a crack, a void, a ripple in the surface just like time for a ripple in the shell where the two pieces of What don't fit together as if someone or no one who-so-ever put it all together or cut it all out and screwed your Mother Earth really bad and fucked her all up so that just for one insy-eensy-weensy-bitsy-ditsy of a second you saw/see/will maybe through it all and beheld the shell around What ... the truth? ... happiness? ... nothing? ... space? ... God? ...

a void ingoodles son upon fun, crash bang boom! it's over, it's done

Now back then there was time for you to run, but it's boogers in your nose, snot I just ate, too late, the adventure's already begun ...

Mark and I dropped a couple hits apiece and then our buddy Booze came over and took a couple himself, and we sat there and waited until Mark informed us that he was going over to his girlfriend's place to have wild tripped-out sex in the Garden of Eden, so Booze and I were left to journey like two gangsters or John Travolta and Samuel L. Jackson in <u>Pulp Fiction</u>; Mark was definitely Bruce Willis, I was Jackson, and Booze was the hopeless brooding introvert.

Ezekiel 25:17 ...

"Ya ever tripped before?" I asked Booze.

"Naw dude, this is my first time."

Interesting ...

205

We proceeded from my apartment on South College Avenue north toward downtown. The drug had yet to take effect, but we were both getting a little loopy so we walked slowly, careful not to trip and fall. As before, the clouds were real low and dark like a scene from the winter or the British Isles; the air temperature and barometric pressure were so perfect as to be unfeelable.

Our first stop of the afternoon/evening (it was sometime between five o'clock and sunset, but hard to say) was the Hindu gas station — a convenience store that sold everything but gasoline. Gasless, No-Gas, the Inconvenient Store — these were the names attributed it by locals. We needed cigarettes, so I purchased a pack of Camel Filters — the old-school kind remember? Back before Camel decided to change the damn flavor and the box from that sleek, drab brown box to the ugly red and white one with blue trim? It was the worst marketing mix-up ever — taking a perfectly-perfect product and making it less perfect but probably more poisonous and addictive. Nowadays, those cigarettes taste nothing like they did back then — NOTHING! Shame on you Camel!

These cigarettes were like smoking milk chocolate, and now you can only get them in South America. Back in 2007, you could get them anywhere, and they were just what we needed — the tastiest and most delicious of nicotine products in order to achieve the most fulfilling and complete acid experience. Having procured cigarettes we proceeded to Booze's apartment where we encountered his roommate Nick who was cooking macaroni and cheese. He peered at me through my sunglasses, "Are they in ya? Ya did it?"

"We're sailin outta port dude, destined for the open sea."

He chuckled heartily, "Well, do enjoy yourselves."

First we had to clear a sitting place and clean up all the sticks and rocks from the floor in order that we pitch our tent on a smooth surface free of debris, so we dumped the ashtrays out the window and tossed all the empty beer cans and crusty pizza boxes into a corner then sprawled out on the clear surface

— Booze in a reclining chair, me just laying there listening to the ping-ping-ping come from the control panel of the submarine flying past Jupiter before finally arriving at Earth where we landed at Pompeii and the ruins of the ancient city beneath the watchful guise of Lady Vesuvius. Seriously, the television was absolutely amazing, like 72-inches or something absurd with LED and LCD and LSD — what better combination could you ask for?

Yep! That's right. Better throw the Floyd in there, jamming "Echoes" in front of a live audience of zombies as my spine tingles and my feet fill from the bottom up and then finally my whole body because I'm dying ...

So half dead at least psychologically so really yes and unable to communicate because something or *this* thing is being lifted outta me by whatever isn't filling me up and pushed out by whatever is so that everything's all jiggly, my spine and all, just a blob of goo melting into the beer stained carpet laden with tiny cockroach eggs and lice like being buried in the Earth without the protective comforts of a seven-thousand-dollar casket and your Sunday-best, consumed by Momma and her big smelly vagina, while above the stars and beyond the heavens the great ebb and flow of the ceaseless swirling lotus blossom produces the so(u)le inspiring wonder! In that chasm of light and no-light of echoing silence, I heard the ghosts of those mystical British prophets speaking of a distant time that never was but will always be possible:

> And no one called us to the land
> And no one knows the where or whys
> But something stirs and something tries
> And starts to climb towards the light!

bwang-cha-foom, da-dee-dee-dah-deederdeeder-dee-dah-dee-dah, dee! cha-foom! bwa-la-ra-da-la-ba-daba-daba-daba-dah! bwang-cha-foom! da-dee-dah-deeder-deeder-dee-dah-dee-dah-dee-dah-dee-dee-dah-dada, deeder-dee-doh! kloh, schna-mo, frintaskity-bo-to, in-lasten-pusten-kisten-ruften, lichten, schneiben, cro! gogogo! don't you know! bozo and cozy-dozy-lil-Rosy in her hammock too, with ham hawks and dreadlocks and weed and pussy too! itsall, itsall, solved, the puzzle that is meant for you! jew! jew! jew! that's who! ha-ha-ha-ha-ha-ha-ha-hee-hee-her, ba-dee-ba-deet-ba-dert, this is how I flirt! I love you, oh yes I do. I love you and you love me and we're a happy family and they tied Barney to a tree with a great big hug and drug for me and you, isn't it, shouldn't it all just be so truly rational like God and the Catholic Church or those scientists and their universities with church bells on the hour and little introductory chimes like ding-dong, ding-dong, da-da-ding-dong, ding-dong, ding-dong, da-da-ding-dong!

BONG!

CLONG!

JONG!

RONG!

TONG!

QUONG!

FONG!

NONG!

SONG!

Nine o'clock, 21:00, you/me have nowhere to be! Everything to see/do and nothing to do/see, what a doozie, wait! ...

... silence, shhhh ...

Do you hear it? ...

It's coming ... the fanfare!

Enter _____!

All Hall _____!

Joy to the World, _____ is born! Let Earth receive Her King!

And you and I shall sing!

And you and I shall sing!

With all the hearkened angels from Harold's Square and the crossing of the great river for _____ is here and _____ is gwine ta be the one thaz gonna save this town!

Your town, the world ...

208

And no one calls us to move on
And no one forces down our eyes
And anyone speaks and no one tries
And no one flies around the sun!

Be careful Icarus reaching for that (en)light(enment), you may melt and then you'll be like the blob of goo sprawled out on a bed of beer and fermenting roaches otherwise known as Randolph Wolfram — oozy-goozy little baby, oh so precious in this moment, but where oh where is Mommy? ...
No one sings him lullabies and no one makes him close his eyes and so he throws the windows wide and calls to you across THIS GUY (the sky)!

THE ANNOUNCER: Ladies and gentlemen of the Whatever, please give a warm welcome to The Rationally-Interrogative-Consciously-Omniscient-Extroverted-Introspective One, appearing now naked in full glory for your very peepers to behold ... Let's give one HEARTY ROUND OF APPLAUSE, for Your Hero! The King of Everything! ... *MASTER RANNNNNDOLLLPH!!! WOLLLLLLFRAAAMMM!! ... auo! auo! AHHHOOOOOOOOOOOO!*

WOLFRAM: Thank you, thank you ladies and gentlemen. (subsiding applause; a pen drop)

WOLFRAM: I stand before you this evening to show you the inside and outside of a balloon light and free. I am empty yet full of nothing other than this nervous initial awkwardness that accompanies newfound innocence and a new perspective on the universe. The brilliance that I at this moment behold is nothing more than a series of coruscated utterances recorded on the notepad of Your Highness. Having now shed the remnants of that suffocating cocoon, I finally am able to behold and sense everything and nothing just like the blissful child uncorrupted by good and evil and all knowledge therein. Before me, I see a flower-burst pattern of glistening color strewn amidst swaths of pitch blackness and pure brilliance. This is light, and it is refracting through the lens of my eye which is composed of billions of tiny little prisms, so that by positioning my gaze at various angles, I see various bands of color akin the length of the electromagnetic wave being refracted. Oh! — Yes, I see we have a question — Yes, you with your hand up — Yes YOU! Go ahead now, don't be shy!

BOOZE: Why are you talking in a British accent?

WOLFRAM: (glancing back at the screen) Must've been the Pink Floyd video. Oh well. (ascending to proceed forthwith through the wall) I do suppose we should have a further gander, shouldn't we?

BOOZE: (following like a groveling hound) Why are you naked?

WOLFRAM: Naked! Why I'm not *naked!* I still got this flesh covering my soul don't I? (discovering himself at a junction) Hmmm — right or left?

BOOZE: The kitchen.

WOLFRAM: That wasn't an option Mister Booze. Must you be such a sloven fiend? Seriously, straighten up! (lifting the hunching Booze into a soldierly stance) See, that's better now. Mustn't slouch or slack on the job! Keep on close watch for we must prevent the mischievous foray from striking our sphere of intellectual influence and interrupting this, the ejaculation via the perpetual emission of energy from the natural nuclear decay of our celluloid contraptions. We mustn't allow these dysfunctional, God-awful flesh organisms to put our incarnate selves into any danger here in this three-dimensional realm. Do you understand?

BOOZE: (droolaughing and snorting idiotically)

WOLFRAM: I know, I know. You don't. Don't worry about it. You wanna have a smoke?

BOOZE: Sure, I mean — I guess.

WOLFRAM: You guess? YOU DO!
(crawling out the window and on to the porch rooftop to puff like dragons)
BOOZE: You should really put some clothes on.
WOLFRAM: (sitting cross-legged, gazing down at his flaccid penis) Why?
BOOZE: Cuz you can't be outside without clothes on.
WOLFRAM: I beg to differ, Mister Booze. Indeed, you *CAN* be outside without clothes on. It's just that the various enforcing agents of order here in this three-dimensional realm would prefer that all human flesh forms were clothed so as to shield the beholdance of various reproductive organs. If you are advising me to put clothes on, I may in fact, heed your advice; if only however, it befits certain intenstantial circums — ONE: do you believe that I should put clothes on because, as you say, 'you can't be outside without clothes on,' implying that possibility is subject and limited to man's rules and regulations governing herds of people? or TWO: do you believe that I should put clothes on because it would be the wise thing to do in order to prevent such aforementioned mischievous foray from striking our sphere of intellectual influence and interrupting this continued ejaculation of the perpetual emission of energy from the natural nuclear decay of these, our cellulose organaptions? Which do you believe Mister Booze?
BOOZE: (slobbering pensively) I think (puffing and flicking) you should put your clothes on so we don't get arrested for tripping acid.
WOLFRAM: Great! Number two.
BOOZE: Yeah. Two.
Wolfram proceeded back through the window, not before however, posing for the entire neighborhood of nobody-at-all by exposing various ins and outs of various crevices and dangling slevices of his loaf of bread ...

211

Emerging once again, Wolfram is clothed in a colorful tie-dyed t-shirt, wholly jeans of holes, and a scarlet bandana ...

Back through the window again, one by one, Wolfram leading the charge, they proceed down the stairs and out the door into the Great Wide Open under this guy black and blue. There was no moon, only clouds and the buzzum of streetlights, both orb-whites and wash-oranges.

... pause, behold the silence, look around you and see (seriously do it, this is a command reader!) Go have a cigarette or something ...

ANNOUNCER: We'll be back after these brief messages and a word from _____.

... ||| ... ||| ... |||

In the ecstasy it may be noted that a one-hundred-yard gain resulting in a touchdown was brought back because a penalty marker was down at the ten yard-line. Holding on the offense, number 666. The penalty is inclined. Get down! Duck and cover! Duck and cover! ...

Up the middle, I'm getting weary, my face is droopy and dreary though it must be done must be done must be done.

Insert penis into vagina and cum ...

We reached the intersection. Large-wheeled contraptions zoomed past us, making low resonant noises. They had large glowing eyes on the front and within they were piloted by humanoids. We kept walking, all the way to the Parthenon atop the Acropolis — campus, the University. Finity. Fine.

Fuck heaven and all of the angels and their angles perpendicular to parallelograms falling from the sky. I couldn't stop. It had to be done, to be found, to be seen, to have to wish to want ...

In the shadows and the silhouettes, I found what I hadn't thought of yet, self-manifested and imposed — a presumption about you and me.

"Do you think humans will live on Mars someday?" he asked.

"It's possible," I said. I mean, what was I supposed to

fucking say? — Yes? ...

It was time to go.

So I flicked my burning cigarette into a pile of dried kindling next to the oogaboobas and shackaroos and a McDonald's inside of a strip mall whose prominent establishment was the Chipotle Burrito & Colon Cleansing Factory. Drones were lined up inside, snaking around the queue ropes in giddy anticipation of Doctor Umberto Eco shoving a burrito (low-fiber) down their esophageal orifice and a retractable fiber-optic cable with a self-lubricating mechanism and gluten extractor up into their tightly-packed septic cavities.

... how is your phillangeal-firculis frikagator?

– it hurts when I phirificate

... here here now. I'll just frikagate all of the phirds from your phanus and then your phirculictic frikagator will work fantastically!

– thank you doctor!

... now benericate overate ——

@!##$%*#(!)(#*#$&&!*(#)(&*@&*

But just as the echo of libidinal angst permeated the porous walls of flint, man's cheap and shoddy edificial shrine to the consumptory insanity exploded into an epic conflagration sparked by Randolph's cigarette ...

And the bowels of all the denidroids of civicon bled spicy volcano sauce from the molten-magma machine otherwise known as Taco Bell.

The End.

But not really. Everything just happened to burn in hellfire and damnation, but Boozey and I were safe and sound walking on the hot coals and ashes of what were once a collegiate campus of fast-food restaurants. We had a very specific destination, or at least I did. He had no idea what was going on, nor that the city through which he was walking was actually just ashes and dust and it didn't mean anything that Chipotle now served vegan-organic burrito-bols: the shit still gave you gas.

Anyway, we walked away from that pyre and back to our mire at 1610 University Avenue, Apartment B — Booze's cesspool of a dwelling place. Upon arriving, he plopped down on the couch and stared blankly at the void box. Meanwhile, something somewhere out there had me entranced ...

I gazed out the window to the east, looking down upon the intersection of High Street and University Avenue, which was a glowing orange, illuminated by a lone halogen streetlight. Beyond the intersection, further east, University Avenue dropped into a dark ravine. To the south, High Street ascended a steep hill into an eerie block of large ominous trees, dancing shadows and dark, unwelcoming houses. They were watching and it made me shiver ...

As did the silence — no cars, no people, no wild-woopity-wallooworing of beer-guzzling students, just silence except for a far-off siren and the bescending-bezuzzery of a motorcycle muffler on the distant highway.

Directly across the street, one story below, the front door of the little ranch-style bungalow swung open: enter dude with little beagle dog ...

He ties the dog to a knothole atop a stake stuck into the ground in the front yard. Beagle sniffs around, walks around, sits down staring south up High Street and then emits a timid half-bark, barely audible, as if barking at something much larger and more powerful than he and too afraid to bark louder. Whatever-he-beholds is staring at him and won't stop staring and that freaks him out, so he turns around three-sixty only to look again with more little half-yelpities

Hanging out the window to gaze up the street, I notice on either side of the road two large looming trees — the gateway to a hazy, foggy, dreary, eerie, creepery, slithery, slimery, unknown-ivery of a dark-netherly, cold-shivery ...

The dog suddenly loses interest in whatever and turns around to lick himself. Booze is behind me on the couch ...

"Booze."

"What's up dude?"

"The tee-vee ain' on ya know."

A deep pit (not a chasm, for I can see the bottom) opens and something pushes me in ...

"What time is it?" I ask, plopping down next to him.

"Pry four o'clock or so."

"In the morning?!" pulling out the cell ... "Make a wish."

"Why dude?" ... a button click and the tee-vee flashing at us ...

"It's one-eleven."

"Yeah dude, that's cool." ... in stunned introversion he was/is rummaging through his mental repository of presumptions and assumptions ...

We couldn't be in here. The walls were closing in and he and that tee-vee staring at me, flashing huge faces and images of how it all used to be but how it never has been nor will be.

Climbing from the shallow pit, I reassume my position at the window. The dog still licks himself, still chained to that stake, then sniffs around some more, completely searching the entire area within the circumference of his capable movement only to find _____ ...

I wonder if he knows, chained down, that there is a world beyond that limited radial movement. Any idea did he have? And if not or so did it matter? What, afterall, matters if it cannot be experienced or known for it is without the bounds of exploration and knowledge?

And me? What of I?

... these same themes repeating themselves over and over again written on the walls of this place, so familiar yet so fresh and stale — the physical. But what about the armory of my mental repository? What of my psychological place in the nether regions of nothing? Afterall, this didn't matter — not the apartment or Booze or the television on the pedestal inside of the wooden box. None of this shit is/was permanent, and none of us actually treated the shit like it was worth anything anyway — piling empty beer cans and smelly pizza boxes into corners while the carpet, recently-installed brand-new, rots in

215

wafting odors of mold and mildew because laziness and carelessness and there's so much more shit where this came from anyway and there's money to buy it so we can just get more, and the same with beer and pizza and cigarettes and apartments because if this shithole you live in doesn't work out because your landlord fucking hates you or you hate him or whatever, you go out and lease another one from some other careless asshole who also don't give a flying fuck about the condition of his building, only that the tenants pay their rent on time and he'll worry about all of the shit stains and peeling plaster later.

In this, the realm of anything and everything, where is the sacred temple? Where are all the saints and martyrs? ...

Ladies and gentlemen, it is time. The caged dogs are howling for the return of their Master, the poets and artists weep in the street because they fail to grasp greatness, and the singers and musicians play in the jug band of ordinary men and women awaiting the return of their Savior and Hero!

Ladies and Gentlemen ... Here He Is ...

LIVE FROM STUDIO 1610 B IN COLUMBIA, MISSOURI ...

WOLFRAM: We gotta walk up High Street.

BOOZE: You wanna watch a movie?

WOLFRAM: Not really.

BOOZE: How 'bout <u>Star Wars Episode Three</u>?

WOLFRAM: Seriously? Whatever.

BOOZE: Dude, this is an awesome fucking movie! (watching movie)

WOLFRAM: Dude, what's with the Princess?

BOOZE: Wha' do you mean what's with her?

WOLFRAM: You know, with Anakin and the dark side and all of the Jedi councilmen —— why don' she stand up for her man?

BOOZE: What are you talking about dude? She's *fucking gorgeous!* — absolutely perfect. She don't have ta stand up to anyone. Everyone gets outta her way when

216

she walks through.

WOLFRAM: Well yeah, but that's only cuz she's a woman.

BOOZE: Of course she's a woman!

WOLFRAM: I know that.

BOOZE: Then what is your deal dude?

WOLFRAM: I don' know. She's jus' not in control enough, ya know dude? She jus' doesn' have the BALLS!

... A quintessential example of a Freudian slip ...

Was it true? Did our little hero (not so little anymore) want to lick BIG BALLS? Maybe that's why he envied God so much, worshiping the phallus and wanted to burn down the city and all of it's buildings rising to heaven like penises outta the Earth because he was angry at God because God wouldn't let him suck His big cock so he decided to cut it off and make God a damn eunuch by burning His symbolic representatives in effigy!

Homophobia? Perhaps.

Godophobia? Definitely.

Fearful of lightning striking twice and the will of a condemning and controlling God, Randolph either had to overcome or bow down at the foot of the altar and submit to salvation, rendering the remainder of his incarnate existence a Christian cocksucker. No, no. Randolph was a cock and one devil of a mastermind in spiritual warfare ...

WOLFRAM: Let's go. I have ta get rid of it. I don' know how but I have ta get rid of it.

BOOZE: What dude?

WOLFRAM: My god complex — it has ta go.

BOOZE: What are you talking about?

WOLFRAM: Shut off that tee-vee, we gotta —

BOOZE: Dude let's just watch ——

WOLFRAM: *NO!* (tyrannical) *WE'RE FUCKIN TRIPPIN ACID!* Now god-fuckin-damn-it, I ain' gonna spend my night trippin watchin a damn movie! We *have* ta go and we *have* ta go *now!* We *have to!* We have no other choice.

BOOZE: (stunned uncertain brooding)

WOLFRAM: We can't sit here anymore, Booze.
(pleadingly convincing) The beasts are lurking and we
must defeat them. We must defeat the demons or we
will spend the rest of our lives wallowing in agony.

BOOZE: (doe-eyed) The rest of our lives?

WOLFRAM: The rest of our lives ... So we *must* go!

BOOZE: Must go.

WOLFRAM: We must go now.

BOOZE: Now.

They marched downstairs and around the front to stand in
the middle of the T-intersection looking up the hill, south down
High Street. Forward they walked, Wolfram at the left hand,
Booze at the right. The orange streetlight ignited the buildings
behind them. Ahead was an orb of murky white shrouded by a
damp fog of gray, pre-dawn mystery ...

It was Randolph's intention to walk straight ahead without
turning back to face burning Sodom. He feared that if he were
to look back, he would turn to a pillar of salt, just like whoever-
the-hell's wife. But Booze kept turning around and looking
around, and this irritated Randolph who could feel his friend's
frightened shadow tapping him on the shoulder ...

BOOZE: Dude there's somethin following us.

WOLFRAM: There's nothing followin us, just look
straight ahead.

But Randolph knew better, for he could hear it growling in
the bushes, running on the sidewalk alongside of them. And
then from the corner of his eye, he caught its red eyes and
beheld the most gruesome creature ever seen ...

It made him sweat.

It made him groove.

It made him burn.

It made him sting.

He shook, he shook.

Oh yeah! Ah-ha-ha-ah ...

WOLFRAM: Dude ——

BOOZE: It's right over there!

WOLFRAM: Shut up! There's *nothing* there!

BOOZE: Dude, look ——

Perhaps if Booze hadn't turned around shaking and trembling, everything would have worked out as planned and they would've kept proceeding forward and met the Black Dog of Death at the top of the hill instead of seeing *It* back there behind them standing amidst the conflagration down in that valley ...

And perhaps if Booze had never turned around and Randolph would have kept to his convictions, our hero would have been sentenced to prison for the rest of eternity because he never would've known and never would've found the Holy Grail, the Fountain of Youth, what he had always been in search of ...

He never would've seen His Shadow.

Standing back there under that streetlight was the silhouette of a man — a ripple in the time warp, an opening in the shell, and *he* was just a shell, but there on the other side of everything. Within was nothing/everything ...

WOLFRAM: Fuck!

BOOZE: That was fuckin freaky dude.

WOLFRAM: Fuck! I fuckin turned around.

BOOZE: (incredulous) You turned around?

WOLFRAM: Yeah, it was down there back there lookin n waitin for me.

BOOZE: I *knew* there was somethin following us!

WOLFRAM: Of course there was somethin following us you idiot! It was the Black Dog! The Shadowman sent out the Black Dog ta scare the shit out of us so we would turn around n see him n get *sucked IN!* Jeez! Do you even know *shit!*

BOOZE: (gackling) What are you talking about?

WOLFRAM: Are you fuckin crazy?!

BOOZE: Dude, yer fuckin crazy! (hysterical laughter)

WOLFRAM: Oh, that's just *lovely!* (maniacal) *YOU*

haven't even seen the Shadowman. *YOU'RE INSANE!*

BOOZE: Dude, Randy, chill out, you're goin crazy!

WOLFRAM: *Crazy! CRAZY! ARGHHH!!!* ...

And that god-complex? Well, it seemed to fade away with the echo of ARGH!

Randolph and his friend returned to STUDIO 1610 B, smoked a cigarette and then our hero departed to take care of unfinished business ...

WOLFRAM: I think I must be going.

BOOZE: You goin home?

WOLFRAM: Kind of. I have somethin ta take care of.

BOOZE: Alright dude. Sure you don't wanna stay n watch some *Sports Center?*

WOLFRAM: Naw man. I'm good. It's been fun trippin with ya though.

BOOZE: Yeah man. I had a good trip.

WOLFRAM: Def'nitely. So take it easy dude (making way away), and hey! Don' try ta go ta sleep for a while. You won't be able to.

BOOZE: Yeah, I ain' tired.

And neither was Randolph. He walked around the house to that intersection, facing up hill again, calm and serene, the chirps of the early birds welcoming the rising Son. Randolph set off up the hill alone — not so high, not so dark, and not so daunting anymore. He would get his worm ...

~~ *RW* ~~

About two weeks prior to the acid trip, I awoke in the middle of the night panting, my body covered in sweat. I couldn't move except for my rapidly flitting eyes — left to right to left to right. Suddenly a face appeared — pale white like that of an old woman, wrinkly and haggard. My eyes locked on it, and I was overcome by cold chills but still paralyzed. The face flew across the room, watching me the whole time, my eyes locked on it still, and the chills so powerful I couldn't even breathe. I was helpless.

Then the face stopped on my far left and flew right at me. I couldn't breath; I couldn't scream. Alls I could say in a deep, low raspy whisper was, "Please, help me."

And it disappeared.

I shot up, covered in cold sweat. Everything was dead silent and I was still shivering. I jumped outta bed and went into the living room, flipped on the lamp and the tee-vee and stared at the box. For a long time, I just sat there, curled up on the couch, staring at the screen and the wall, back and forth, shivering as if there were cold hands on my shoulders.

Mark came out.

"Sorry dude," I said. "I didn' mean ta wake ya up er anything."

"Oh no, you didn' wake me dude," he said, plopping down in the chair to roll a cigarette. "I couldn' sleep. I felt like there was a face right in fronta me er somethin."

I just glared at him, chillingly serious yet sickly amused, "What?"

"Yeah dude, I felt like there was ——

"Dude, I *SAW* a face!"

"Yeah? I kinda figured that's why you were up. I figured somethin like that had happened."

"I saw a face, like an old woman's face er somethin goin across my room!"

"Yeah dude," he said dragging. "I've woke up several times in the middle o' the night n felt like there was a face right in fronta me. I never seen it, but if you say ya saw it, that doesn' surprise me."

"Huh," I was shocked into numbness.

"I believe in like spirits n ghosts n shit. My stepdad's really into tha' shit, like gettin in touch with the dead n talkin through weegie boards n shit like that. It's crazy dude."

"Yeah. I'm kinda freaked."

"Fuck dude," he said shifting in the recliner. "I'd be freaked too if I saw a fuckin face in fronta me like that." He shivered, "Creeps me out."

I lit up a cigarette, and we just sat there like that, smoking and staring at the screen for a long time. Occasionally one of us would shiver. Eventually, Mark tamped out his smoke and said, "Well I'm jus' glad we're gettin outta here in like three weeks dude. This place creeps me out sometimes."

"Tell me about it dude," I said, tamping out my smoke. "I wonder if some old woman was killed here er somethin."

"What makes ya think that?"

"Oh I don' know. I jus' saw an old woman, ya know, n I figured ——

"Well, if it's an *old* woman, maybe she jus' died here."

"Yeah," figuring pry right ... "But why the fuck is she botherin us?"

"Maybe she left somethin here. Maybe she wants ta ask us fer help er somethin."

I shrugged. "Then why don' she fuckin ask instead o' tryin ta freak the fuck outta us?"

"I don' know dude," he hacked a smoker's laugh and rolled up another. "Maybe we fuckin pissed her off somehow. Maybe she's pissed that we moved inta her apartment. D'you know who lived here before?"

"Yeah, jus' some army guy."

"Oh," he shrugged. "Well I don' know dude. I don' know why she's botherin us."

"Well maybe 'fwe see her again we should ask her."

He laughed again. "You gonna try n reason with a ghost, Wolfram?"

"Well, I mean, yeah. Why *can't* we reason with it? 'Fit's fuckin freakin us out we should a'leas' know why. And it should fuckin tell us, God damn it!"

He cackled and puffed. "Alright Wolfram," he said dragging. "I'll leave the negotiations ta you."

"Sounds good dude," firing ... "I'll deal with her."

The Sword

He could handle It. Randolph knew he already knew Everything. You see in college, learning and homework came easy. Work was serious play and play was serious work. By day he read, and by night he partied, but not because he read by day. You see, Randolph didn't party to relieve the stress of studying, he studied to relieve the stress of partying. Of course, both he had to do: the latter was a requirement for a person of his age, and the former was his sustenance; literature was his summons ...

Randolph devoted himself to the study of literature, specifically American literature — expansionism, transcendentalism, the antebellum South. Literature was his escape from the flashing television and blanket wireless internet access. He loved reading and thus grew to love what he read. Indeed, Randolph loved the classic American novelists so much that he resigned himself to read every great American novel ever written. Before long, he found himself emulating narrative structures and character archetypes whenever he sat down to write.

He idolized Holden Caulfield and Zoe Glass. Of Mark Twain he made an obtuse, psychological enigma. He loved to hate Henry Miller because he agreed so much with his bullshit. He respected Hunter S. Thompson because nobody else seemed to. He imagined himself traveling across America with John Steinbeck instead of that damn dog. He would look in the mirror and see Jay Gatz, and in his dreams Jay Gatsby, wondering out there what could be ...

Through William Faulkner he saw the great mansions of

the Old South rotting in the wasteland along with the customs of bygone generations. And through this juxtaposition he saw himself in his rusting Middlewest of postindustrial America.

More than anything, literature taught Randolph how to observe and draw conclusions from his material and emotional surroundings. In his mind, he would compare similar symbiotic themologies and figurative metaphoric beholdances between what he experienced and what he studied. He began to see his life and all of his experiences as one big story of individual stories. The place and time in which he lived became a period in history of which he was an integral player who could affect great causes. Suddenly, life was less about accomplishing a series of predetermined goals and more about experiencing possibilities.

The more he read, the more he desired something great. All of his fellow English-degree-seeking peers dreamt of writing the next great American novel. He tried to out-school them, but the harder he tried, the more he realized that he was just like them — working for grades and only dreaming of greatness.

After two years of college, Randolph was depressed and disillusioned, and he couldn't figure out whether he was humiliated or exalted.

~~ *RW* ~~

After the acid trip, I went back to Hamilton for a little vacation before school started up. When I returned to Columbia, I felt compelled to trip acid again because I thought I had a new psychological complex to get rid of.

You see, I was obsessed with this redhead hippie girl from the coffee shop and was thinking I was too obsessed and would just end up heart broken because I only wanted to get laid and didn't really care about caring. On top of the melodramatic sexual tension, I was trying to quit smoking and drinking and poisoning my body with substances because I thought the only way to transcend the boundaries of three-dimensional reality would be to live physically pure like Jesus or something. I knew I couldn't just quit because I thought it was impossible to just stop everything with all of these voices telling me to do things. I thought the only way to stop the voices was to eradicate my psychological complex, thinking the only way to do that was to trip acid. But you see I was afraid I could possibly fall off the edge and turn into Jesus or the Devil knowing it would be One or the Other but not knowing which.

Obviously I was still a mess, thinking day and night and day and night while trying to work on my Cairo project because I thought I could write a book about it and it would be the best book ever written, so I thought I had to write it all right then because if I didn't I would forget everything. The problem was I thought I couldn't write without smoking, so I thought I had to choose between the way of pure transcendence and the way of fame and glory because they obviously weren't the same ... or so I thought.

Every night, I went to the coffee shop to try to write but would only sit and brood before giving up only to talk to all the tweakers who sat at the bar. One day, just sitting up there causing nothingness, I noticed this old guy with a long white beard who just happened to appear in an upright-hunched position leaning against the end of the bar. I didn't say anything, just saw him, but seemed to recognize him as maybe someone familiar but I couldn't figure out who or where from. The next day he returned, and then the day after that and after that, until pretty soon he was a regular character, scrawling beautiful calligraphy without punctuation or actual sentences on parchment paper with felt-tipped pens — lines and lines of words.

Before you know it everyone starts talking and wondering what for who and why. I watched him everyday, envying him because he didn't seem to know that he was the man on the pedestal. I wanted to say something, but I didn't know what. For some reason I wanted this guy's respect because he was so cool and wise looking, just not caring at all.

One day, a few weeks after he first appeared, I happened to be sitting next to him at the bar when he looked up and said, "I see you're sitting in the belly of the whale."

"What?" ... everyone was looking at me, and I was thinking 'this guy is nuts,' but also wondering, 'was this guy nuts,' even real?

He looked like God.

Well yadi-yadi-yada, I hunker down, swallow myself, and we get to talking ...

I ask him what he's doing, and he shows me these parchment pages with words all rambling together. I start reading, noticing lots of metaphors and allusions to fairy tales. It's all kinda interesting — real stream-of-conscious psycho-narrative, unthinking-subconscious-revelatory-prophetic shit, very different and definitely entertaining. I read and read and read, everyday more and more, and every time I read I feel like some porthole to some mystical realm is opening inside of me. And then the more I read, the more I feel each word in my heart, like everything he is saying on that parchment paper is poking at me like pens (not pins) trying to show me something, but I can't figure out what or what to think about so I don't. I think I can write something about it because it feels like inspiration, but I don't know what to write, so I don't. Really I don't know how ...

Until one day ...

I've been reading his shit for a while, and this guy — we'll call him Abraham — asks me, "What do you want to do with your life?"

"I wanna write."

"Ahh ...

I tell him about my background in journalism and my journey to Cairo and how I'm working on a story, and he asks me something else and tells me something else, so I ramble some more about everything I think and why it's all worth thinking, but before I can finish he tells me to stop and suggests I find some quiet peaceful solitude to sort these things out. I ask him how I should go about sorting these things out and he says, "Well you wanna write, go write about it!" and then starts rambling something about fairy tales ...

The whole walk home I think about what to write, and then up the stairs and to my desk and my computer, and just sitting down breathing in and out and closing my eyes and everything disappearing and all of the voices silencing ...

help!?

A suggestion of solitude only leading to increased masturbation with renewed feelings of peace dispersed intermittently throughout day and night that may or may not be the same days and nights but is nevertheless part of one. I suggest solitude, he says, going on to say I remind him of Little Red Riding Hood and Pinocchio, a cross between an all-too-trusting young girl and a lying puppet. *a star between wanting to be real versus reel* Asking for help *asking for the experience toward the tenderness of self acceptance* with everything, even asking for help, he tells me to quit cutting corners or else I'll bleed to death in the long run, but why? And how will I bleed and what corners have I already cut? I need specifics. I need someone to tell me to do this or don't do this, that's how I grew up, but I was stubborn as a child, only sometimes *a jimmy the cricket? a mother who states be sure to stay on the main road?* listening to my father's blunt commands, other times avoiding them just for the sake of spite. Should I drop? No, says part of me that already feels somewhat at peace. Yes, says the other part that wants to experience more right now, but should I experience now, and if I do what could happen in the long run. Is dropping cutting? If I trip will I fall or just stumble along and pick myself back up? But why is tripping such a negative thing? *quest ... ions only you can solve sitting in the belly of the whale and the wolf, not drop, possibly shed as you mature psychologically* You fall and you could break your leg or bust your face wide open and be ugly for the rest of your life, unattractive and pissed off because nobody wants to look at your pathetic self. So perhaps tripping isn't necessarily a good

227

idea. Instead, just keep walking and step over the crack with care, proceeding slowly and cautiously along the narrow *interior* path, *that does and doesn't exist, a pathless path* not talking with any wolves but <u>never</u> afraid to stop and smell the roses. But be careful ... the wolf might be hiding behind the bush. The rose bush is burning in the forest but *never is always* nobody sees it except for me. I stop to *always is never* watch and suddenly a face appears like that of a goat — it looks kind of like mine. What the fuck? Tripping isn't necessarily a bad thing if you and a friend trip together at the same time, you can laugh about it and help each other up and move on past *the crack in a cement heaven allows the flower to break on through the glass ceiling one was unaware existed* the crack amused at the fact that you didn't notice the crack, but instead cracked your laughter cells open bursting forth amusement and joy. If you trip alone, then <u>you just pity yourself for falling down kicking yourself in the ass</u> *and feeling like you're becoming the ass* why didn't I see that crack and avoid it? It's nothing but a personal beating that takes you <u>nowhere</u> but only delays your inevitable arrival at the far-off destination. It's good to trip with friends along our ways to separate destinations but when you trip alone <u>it can be</u> *but need not be* back-breaking, gut-wrenching, maybe even deadly, especially if you fall and knock yourself out and lay passed out on the sidewalk for hours in the middle of the night with no one around to know you even fell. If a tree falls in a forest and no one is there to hear it, did it make a sound? Well, that's not important — whether or not it made a sound. What's important is that <u>nobody</u> *you heard it* heard it. It fell and died alone and nobody was by its side to hear it utter its final words. A sad story but such is the case for that old tree. Hopefully it was an old tree and not a young tree that had been rotted out by some fungus — a disease living *"the tragedy of life is not death but what dies inside of us while we're living."* inside of it that it couldn't reckon with — *Norman Cousins* because it didn't know the disease was in there. It just grew less and less each year while the fungus destroyed its innards. Squirrels made their homes inside of the tree but they too died when it fell, trapped between the ground and the dead carcass with nowhere to go but through the carcass and out, emerging from the tree and the ground like a rising spirit or soul resurrected to heaven. *go where you've been assured nothing exists. you seem to know "everything" already* One good thing came out of this tree though, it provided life for the fungus, life for the micro-organisms eating away at its carcass. A sacrifice — one life for many — the life of the tree for all of those little lives but <u>they will die eventually anyway so why does it matter?</u> $\sum = mc^2$ What's the point of living if we're just going to die *aren't you curious to scene who you are and where you are going* like the damn tree, whether or not it was old or young, whether or not it rotted or passed away slowly and calmly during the dead of winter? Questions *the intersection of two quest ... ions can be a simple and profound insight* Questions, Questions *... one must quest ...* ions? Those alleged charged particles that are floating ... **ion ...* around everywhere making up everything and nothing at the same time. What about them? Maybe I should buy some. Buy some ions at the store and have a bunch of them, but why? The store is ions and ions are the store. You can't have ions they're everywhere. They're not possible or possessive for that matter but rather they are what we are if you break it all down. We are them, just like everything else. Ions and atoms, but no Eves. Where are all the Eves? Eating apples. I prefer orange juice especially after all the damn apple trees threw their fruits at me back in the complex and the wicked witch came and freaked the fuck outta me for no reason and I still don't know and probably never will. But I'll keep trying and crying about it all because it's all so damn complicated and then here you are making it seem like some damn calculable scientific equation of light and sound but I'm always thinking about infinity and those damn irrational asymptotes. So we got asymptotes and Einstein and Little Red and Pinocchio? Seriously, Pinocchio? What are you calling me a fucking liar or something? Does my nose just keep growing and if it does how do I make it — oh I see, clever clever. Just let it go down by holding really still and don't touch it because then it'll grow more and that means Little Red can't touch it either, but what if Pinocchio likes it when

Little Red touches his _____? If I'm Pinocchio I don't care about my damn nose as long as Little Red is fucking (ahem) touching it so I'm gonna let her help me but she's got the damn wolf on her heels and he's gonna eat her fucking grandma anyways, but it doesn't matter because grandma is old and ugly. But yes, I know, she's nice and bakes the best cookies ever, so why can't she just bake her damn cookies instead of having Little Red Riding Hood bring them to her? By the way, does Little Red Riding Hood actually get eaten by the wolf? The old ladies by the church down on the corner back there say that she doesn't but gets back at the wolf and wins. Pez doesn't know. But that one guy confirmed what the old ladies were saying back there at the church. Old people would know the answer to something as pointless as that,
but as I
walk
o n
they
a s k
me if I
was joking. Excuse me, I can't ask a
legitimate question, Jesus Fucking
Christ?! Why don't you go bake some
cookies grandmas because I'm following
Little Red Riding Hood all the way to
your house and I'm gonna have me some
nice juicy grandma meat for dinner. I think I'll
boil her (grandma) and a touch of apple cider vinegar at
the end to give the tender flesh a country-homey aroma,
and listen to this, maybe, oh yes this is it, I'm not boiling
grandma; I'm gonna skin her and stuff her with apples
and oranges so I can have my little bite of Eve and taste
sweet revenge against the fucking wicked witch and her
damn haunted forest back on High Street or whatever.
But you see that can't be right because then that would
mean the Shadowman is a woman. Is it possible? It can't
be. He's me. I'm not a woman, though I know we all
have our feminine sides but you know what — if you're
a man be a fucking man, that's what I say, and if you're a
woman be a fucking woman. I hate girly men not that I
don't like faggots or queers; I'm just saying, if you're a

man, be a man, you can still fuck whoever you want but you gotta be the fucking cock, man! More than anything I can't stand women that act like men and try to fight with cocks that they don't have by taking offense to carousing and caressing especially ugly women who are just upset with the fact that they are women, like old butch lesbians. I mean, hot lesbians who know they are women and love the fact that they are women, and I mean seriously love themselves, are amazing but they're probably not even just lesbians, they may be experimenting because it sounds exciting and seems

different and they just need
it's fucking short-haired
coaches who need to get
cock inside their twat:
it means to be a woman.
and hold that cock, for
force to behold and
sounds, smells, and
Mother Earth, for
held. Therefore, to
perceive through
and just perceive
thought is the feminine
self nurturing the
something with that
analyze it in brooding
masculine force, for the
organ that first must be
perhaps a beholdance
but when it does it thrusts

a change. No, you see,
female basketball
a fucking big huge
that'll show em what
Open up your pussy
it is the feminine
sense the sights,
tastes of the
women like to be
behold — to
apprehension —
without analysis or
force of your own
aesthetic. But to do
aesthetic, to even
contemplation is the
penis is an active
stimulated by
before it can perform,
into the vagina that

holds it, just like a sword into the heart of an enemy (or lover), and as we know there are swordsmen and there are archers and there are infantrymen and knights and generals and kings and queens and merchants (Jews) and farmers and hunters and gatherers and those whose pens are mightier than swords and curious old men disguised as sages who stand at coffeehouse bars and scrawl on parchment paper ...

So yeah, anyway, Pinocchio ...

Let's say Pinocchio happens to be walking along when he trips and falls on his face, flat on the ground, right next

231

to the Big Bad Wolf. Wolf stares him down as he lays there helplessly then offers the little liar his hand and asks where he can find any weed, but he says it like this, "Yo yo nigga nigga I need me some dro dro, so I can git up on em ho hos, know what Ize sayin nigga?"

"Yeah."

And so they go back and get stoned, sitting in Pinocchio's apartment listening to Led Zeppelin even though the Wolf wants to listen to Marley, but there is none because Bob is dead and with him died love and Jah, at least that's how Pinocchio sees it. What does he see anyway? Nothing beyond the tip of his nose which is now very short — normal — because he's no longer a liar but very serious, blunt and truthful so he tells the Wolf how much he envies him, especially how long his shiny sword is. Pinocchio is fascinated by it and reaches out to touch it but the Wolf pulls it back and says, "Yo nigga! No touchin! Whachu a fag er somethin?"

"No Mister, seriously, I didn't mean to ——

"Ah, whatever. You wanna touch it? It might cut you, n you might bleed."

"Ummm — I don't ——

"Here, go ahead! You want it, touch it!"

Pinocchio can't resist, so he pulls the sword near his breast because he loves how cool the metal feels against his bare skin and how shiny and long and perfectly straight the sword is ...

And he's just caressing it so much he doesn't realize that he's bleeding, and the Wolf's like, "Don't stop now," and Pinocchio says, "But I'm bleeding," and the Wolf's like, "It's too late. You can't stop now!" and like the big bad monster of a man he is, he thrusts his sword right into the open wound in Pinocchio's heart, killing the sorry little bastard, so fucking concerned about every God-damned mystery and always asking questions, questions, questions, why why why, so now the little fucker can figure it all out on his own without the need for any more questions or any more answers because he doesn't have any needs anymore not even a need to know or to eat or sleep or any of that shit, not even a need to shit or a need to write his damn story or listen to the advice of freaky, creepy, schmucks named Abraham, so he doesn't even have to look anymore or wait anymore or worry anymore or think anymore because he's dead.

But that Wolf will keep on thrusting and keep on doing and keep on fighting because he walks like a cock and he knows he's got all the answers, and if he gets hungry he'll eat a sheep for dinner because he's a sinner in the center of a game with no winner and all of the losers are following an invisible shepherd that may or may not exist, huddled together in the vast arid desert en route to the promise land, but none of them have ever been to the promis*ed* land so they have no idea that the direction is right whether or not it rains or snows, they all just heard from somebody else that *the* way was *this* way, and everyone says that alls you have to do is follow the leader or at least everyone else — the person (sheep) right in front of you because they all know for certain that everyone-else-whoever-will-ever-be-was-is must be right because everyone is doing it, right? And the prophets all told them *this* was *the* way, and the prophets weren't sheep, they were shepherds, and *WHY* were they shepherding the sheep?

?

So they would always have something to eat. Because the best way to survive life in the desert is to follow the herd and then just hang out at the oasis, drinking red wine while roasting a baby lamb over the open fire ...

Yum, yum, yum

Blood of Christ

Amen

Body of Christ

Amen

But Randolph wasn't always a blessed carnivore ...

Because he "seemed to have a lot of questions," Abraham recommended he seek professional help. So one day that fall after Cairo and the acid trip and all of that shit, Randy made an appointment to see a psychologist at the University Clinic. He arrived to be met by a woman, early thirties, playing some spacey music in the background of her barren, white-walled office. Randy took her for some 'new age' purist, especially after she told him he looked like Jesus and then gave him an assignment to not smoke, drink, or have sex for a week, also noting that matters would be made easier if he made certain to incorporate vigorous cardiovascular exercise into his daily routine.

Randy went out and completed his assignment and returned the next week to find the same semi-cute, kinda-sexy, blonde bitch in her office with the 'new age' spacey music and the two chairs and the lamp, except this time the office was reversed — the lamp to the left of the chair instead of how it was originally positioned on the right. Also, it appeared that she may have changed the type of light bulb from perhaps a twisty fluorescent to a more traditional yellowish-orange 60-watter. Whereas before, the lamp emitted a soft relaxing glow, now the room seemed to burn.

Randy was uncomfortable, so he vowed to button up and keep shut and only answer when spoken to, using his God-gifted power of verbal communication to beat around the bush and politick her into thinking what he knew she probably wanted to think in order to typify his personality.

He twisted her into knots. She tried to penetrate his subconscious, but she was only a woman. Perhaps if she would've gone about it all in a more nurturing sort of way, Randolph would've 'let her have it,' so to speak. But he certainly wasn't going to let her fuck him in the ass with some strap-on dildo, so he said, "Thank you," shook her hand and bid her adieu, because she had just sold him a new used car for zero down and zero monthly payments for zero months.

You see, he already owned the car: she just helped him find it again, and for that he is grateful. Of course Randolph wasn't done yet, not first without amusing himself. He figured she needed to learn a lesson and perhaps needed some time to reflect, so he scheduled another appointment with her the following week even though he didn't plan on showing up, just showing her up.

And while she was sitting in her lonely, white-walled office reflecting on her patience, Randolph was out having a dandy ol time, cruising around in his new ride. A new mischievous foray had invaded his intellectual sphere of influence: Randolph had a GIRLFRIEND, and she wasn't a ghost either. Nope, just a fucked-up twenty-year-old redhead who thought the Big Bad Wolf was chasing her.

Yes, Randolph had seduced Little Red ...

But another drama was playing out behind the scenes of caressing autumnal love: Randolph was experimenting with vegetarianism, but he couldn't handle it — gave him gas; he was also meditating daily by the river's edge and at night on his zen couch; he would write too, every night at the coffee shop because that's what he wanted to do. But remember, Randolph was still enrolled in the University. How could he work at the coffee shop, spend time with his lady, and write everyday without sacrificing his vehicle of physical and/or psychological health, all while attending school?

He couldn't. He didn't. It was too much. He had to give up something. What would it be?

But isn't that answer obvious ...

You see, when Randolph first started college, his father would call him twice a week asking, "How's school goin?" And Randy would say, "Fine."

"Fine? What's that mean? All A's?"

"I don' know — yeah! All A's."

"Are you tellin the truth?"

His father didn't trust him for some reason. Perhaps because there was an invisible monster crawling beneath Randolph's transparent skin.

You see, his father had always wanted him to go to law school or graduate school so he could get a good job with some corporation or something. Randolph always knew he never really wanted one of those jobs. He was just afraid of failing, and for a long time, he thought failure meant not getting A's or not getting a college degree. He thought that in order *to do* what you want with your life, you had to have a college degree, then he realized you only *have* to have a college degree if that's what you wanted or that was what was required for what you wanted *to do*. He began to see everything as only a means to an end ...

Yet, he still wanted everything, specifically all of those American things — big money, big life, big style, big car, big house, sexy wife, big dog, lots of kids, big city — you know the deal — the prototypical American life living the prototypical American Dream. That's what he was afraid of failing at — the American Dream.

Perhaps he was so afraid because he understood the

236

prevailing American theme, a theme so profound and heart-breaking he could never quite define it. He could never quite figure out what specifically it was about all of these great characters in all of these great novels that seemed so fascinating and so familiar ...

He would often look up from a book and find himself in a coffee shop, and for a while he would sit in silence watching all of the other studiers in their books and he would think about all of these characters wondering ...

And then he would leave it all behind to wander on the trail that led through the deep dark forest, away from the comfortable warm fire of civilization's orangey glow, to think alone ... and then later at home, lying awake in bed, he would see that trail in his mind and he would feel the little picture inside of him expanding into a landscape ... then closing his eyes he could see it so bright and colorful and real that it felt as if he were possibly off in another different place far far away, long long ago ... but it was right there inside of him, and it was happening right now ... and he would open his eyes and see the crumbling plaster on the ceiling of his apartment and again close them to be amidst the trees and their colorful foliage all lining the beaten path running off into the enchanted forest ... and then lifting up and moving forward, slow at first, stepping carefully and then faster faster faster until he was a warrior in shining armor sprinting ahead ... knowing in his heart that he is going the right way ... and so he will keep going and going into the forest deeper and deeper until that heart stops beating ... and then he knows he'll just be back there in that forest still running ... full speed to destiny!......................
....

3

Arriving Nowhere

The Fall

When he was a child he had a fever and spent the night screaming because he wasn't in himself, he was either floating or drowning, but he couldn't figure it out, so he kept screaming because his mother wasn't there ...

> Rockabye baby on the treetop,
> When the wind blows, the cradle will rock,
> When the bow breaks, the cradle will fall,
> And down will come baby, cradle and All!

... alone in the abyss beyond the boxy room where the Eagles had lifted them up on the winds. It felt like he was flying, but he felt like it was falling, and he didn't know from where or where to. He thought maybe 'death' because it felt like he was being transformed, and he had always imagined that a great transcendental metamorphosis would take place, like he would just disappear from existence and become an illusion.

Nothing would have ever been, and it wouldn't have mattered even if it had, because in that old place that would become a *was*, he would always be whatever he was then. When he thought about the future, the afterlife, he thought not of a heaven with clouds and gold but of himself walking the Earth, encountering the same people and doing the same things all over again. Life was silent and still. Death was a long loud memory. The present moment lies somewhere in between ...

And that's where Randolph found himself not too long ago, meditating over a pint of beer, thinking back on the fantasy and how it all seems so surreal — all of the stories true or not, all of the characters real or not, and everything that ever happened memory or illusion ...

But as he stares into the pool in the pint glass, he feels an overwhelming urgency to go, for he knows there is yet another mountain to conquer, a mountain greater than any ever conquered by the Greats, for this mountain is haunted by their intoxicating spirits, and nobody has ever reached the top ...

Or maybe somebody has ... and just decided Never to return ...

~~ RW ~~

It was October 31, 2007. The moon was full, the sky was clear. The zombies and demons had risen from the dead to walk amongst the living once again. All the students celebrated by dressing as the most absurd and ridiculous of raunchy axe murderers and seductive puppy dogs. Everyone had wild sex in multi-person orgies and chugged bottles of tequila while fucking or being fucked. Marijuana was consumed not by the bowl but by the bag. Witches and werewolves inhaled lines of dust motes and powdered their faces with cocaine. Every cop on the Columbia Police Department was on duty, arresting underage sorority sluts and confiscating their fake IDs. To enter a bar, a knife was necessary, sometimes to guard against hostile vampires, mostly just to slice through the fog of smoke — a putrid funk of tobacco, hashish, and straight up pot, as well as some other shit laced with PCP.

Halloween is the most celebrated holiday in America, and it's not even an official holiday. It's the one night of the year when a girl can dress like a slut or a man can put on high heels and a dress and no one thinks twice about it because nobody gives a fuck except to fuck whoever they came with and then some, because everyone's trashed and getting trashed and producing a hell-uv-a lot of it. Halloween is a time to celebrate who you are on the inside or who you want to be on the outside — usually a character you could never actually be, but for once, by golly, you're gonna *be* that character and you're gonna have a damn good time doing it.

For Randolph, Halloween 2007 was a very special one, for it was the day he decided to fuck it all and let it all be. That morning, he decided it was time to cut something out of his life in order that he would be better able to invest himself in the most important of duties. So he visited the Dean's office at the Schaumme University Honors College and officially withdrew from school. Randolph walked outta that office and saw the colors of the autumnal Earth brighter than ever; the sweet chirps of songbirds were like something out of a movie. Life had begun anew, and Randolph knew exactly what he would do with it ...

But first he had to extirpate a character from his soul, so that afternoon he and Little Red drove out to Hobby Lobby for face paint — five tubes of black to be exact — and then they drove to Target for a black thong. That night, Randolph put on the thong, black socks, black shoes, then spackled the extent of his exposed flesh in black ...

He was the Shadowman.

He and Little Red attended a rowdy party, and everyone was either repulsed or utterly turned on by the Shadowman.

Poor Little Red ... later that night the Big Bad Wolf swallowed her down, and oh how scrumb-didily-umptious she was!

Life was teeming with flavor and Randolph was foaming at the mouth for more ...

... ||| ... ||| ... |||

So into the woods to taste and see, to experience the fruit of
   great mystery ...
For I see a rainforest of glorious color!
I taste the fruits of tropical bliss!
Yet here I cannot find contentment, for I fear misery ...
So look up, look up! Through the looming haze to the
   mountaintop ...
I will tell you what is up there.

I will climb the highest peak and shout out all of my findings
and all of my conquests!
Full speed ahead, up up and away! Press on forward and do not
stop til you stand at the top ...
You will only be satisfied to have the greatest abundance of
all.
Climb climb climb to the top of the mountain beyond the haze,
To the place of the greatest desire ...
To desire no more.
Heed the call from the depths back to the cradle from which
you fell when that rip-roaring dog of wind handed you the
broken olive branch ...
... ||| ...
Oh goodness gracious!
Oh me oh my!
How long ago 'twas he fell from the sky!
In a diaper he was born, delivered from afar,
By the stork dropped into the seat of a car;
And then driven home that cool spring night,
To fill the room with shadows and goblins o' fright;
The storms they came and God did too,
And so did the Mother, the housewife, the shrew;
And I was He and now He is You ...
The shadow on the wall ...
The ghost in the hall ...
Boo!
Who?
Boo-frickity-hoo! And fuck you too!

World War III

Fuck you. That's right, screw off. Because sometimes you gotta fight especially when the monsters and Vermicious Knids are coming at you from behind the trees, and what do they want anyway? You're just trying to get to the top of the damn mountain, why don't they just leave you alone?

Well it's not that easy Buster Brown. Sometimes you gotta fight because you sure as hell can't just let em take it all away from ya, especially when alls you have is You.

Nope! You better fuckin nail em and hit em where it counts, cuz if you don't then you're fuckin screwed, and there ain't gonna be no fat lady singin or Golden Ticket presentation, cuz Willy Wonka's gonna send you home for not bein good enough to own his damn factory. Yep, you better fuckin fight *for* the good fight and not just *the* good fight, so you better know who's good and who's bad, cuz if you don't it's a long way back down and you might stumble on the way and then fall flat on your fuckin face, and then everything you ever worked for, everything you ever fought for, doesn't mean anything because you lost it all, and you might as well curl up in the corner and die!

What are you gonna do?

Give im the left hook and the right jab, then knock his jaw out of his mouth and pound a bottle of whiskey cuz it's damn cold outside, and unless you're fuckin George Washington, you ain't gonna survive Valley Forge cuz you know what happened there don't ya? The zombies came outta the fuckin trees — turned their backs to em and got stabbed in the fuckin back. You don't wanna die at the behest of a buncha sick fuckin cowards, hell no, rather burn in hell with all the sinners and saints cuz at least there'll always be a party after the fight, and fuck if you're lucky, maybe even before.

Like back on Labor Day weekend 2006, we had a huge party, biggest of the entire summer. Four handles of vodka, a handle of rum, a handle of whiskey, a handle of tequila, gallons of fruit punch, some cranberry juice, sliced limes, apples, and oranges — mix em all together and what do ya got? Jungle juice for all the wild little monkeys; poison the masses, just like Jonestown, so they bend down and kiss your feet and tear each other to pieces like the filthy fuckin heathens we all are.

And so that's what we're doing. We're out there at the Farm drinking toxic kool-aid from a barrel, scooping it out with a ladle, and then another guy arrives with a couple kegs, so now we got a war party — about two-hundred muthafuckers just hangin around smokin and drinkin and the women all screamin like whores and witches, those fuckin bitches.

The cops show up. I deal with em, say who I am, and they tell us all to be safe, and then leave us alone to feast on each other. It's just after midnight. The jungle juice is bone dry and everyone's fuckin trashed. The cops are waiting down the lane for anyone to leave so nobody can but everyone's freakin like God's gonna come outta the fuckin sky and smash us all. Somebody's gotta take control before this all descends into anarchy, so I hop up on the picnic table next to the bonfire and try to subdue the intoxicated horde of testosterone:

"Attention! Attention!"

—— are the cops gone cops are here the cops are here everyone shut up oh fuck cops are comin get outta here ev'rybody ev'rybody let's get outta here ...

"Whoa! Whoa! Attention! Attention! Ev'rybody quiet down!"

—— cops cops are comin they're comin they're gonna come n swarm the place who's twenty-one who's twenty-one anyone here who ain' twenty-one ...

"Attention ev'ryone! Quiet please!"

—— fuck shut up Randy's tryin ta say somethin just shut up you shut up fuck you there's tryin ta be an announcement n all you people are shut up Brandon yer makin just as much noise as Natasha Jesus Christ yer fuckin loud hez tryin shut the fuck up why do you get ta tell people ta shut up huh huh you stupid bitch quit screamin shut up ev'rybody jus' shut the fuck up Leroy shut up you were just over there yellin you fuckin shut up bitch you fuckin shut up god damn it people can we all jus' please quit fuck you ...

"Ev'ryone please ——

—— shut the fuck ...

"Atty," whispering to the Colonel, "turn out the pavilion lights!"

—— who turned out the lights shut up Nate I can' fuckin see who's that oh fuck it's you fuck you I oughtta slug no Jeremy don' fuckin bitch get away from me fuck off ev'ryone shut up can we please turn the lights no don' you understand the lights are off cuz ev'ryone won' shut up Leroy god damn it bitch tell me ta fuckin shut up one more time n I'll fuckin throw this damn can Brandon shut up yer the loudest fuckin cunt here I ain' no fuckin cunt you ain' fuckin cuz no one hey there's no need fer that fuckin language then why the fuck don't you stop sayin fuck fuck off somebody please turn the lights I can't fuckin see who the fuck somebody jus' fuckin spilt get off o' me Kirby who's fuckin smokin pot pot gimme where's it at who's got the Mary Jane Mary Jane who's got it it's gotta be Tyler fuck you I smoked all my shit its fuckin Kenny no shit Kenny you hordin weed I ain't fuckin shut up ev'rybody the lights are out because ...

"Atty! Flip the switch! ... Alright. Now ——

—— quiet down ev'rybody he's tryin ta ...

"ALRIGHT!!!!!!!!!!!!! SILENCE!!! The cops were just HERE! And now they are gone! And they will leave us

246

alone to feast upon ourselves as long as *that* is what we *do!* So *now* we all must *eat* each other because we can't leave. But if for some reason, since I can't force you to commit cannibalism, you *do* want to leave, be sure to take a left and not a right, for they will be waiting for you by the highway and bless your soul if you fall into *their* hands."

—— let's go fuckin shoot them pigs yeah shut up ...

"NOBODY is *shooting* any PIGS! No guns are *aloud!* You must rip flesh from bone with your bare hands and then you must eat it *raw*, do you understand? Nobody gets outta here *alive!* And I mean *NOBODY!* —— Men, grab the women."

—— no no let go let go rape em rape em fuck em fuck em but not too hard be nice just fuck them gently ...

"NO! Do not *rape* or *fuck* anyone! Rather rip out their eggs and lick the blood from their clits then plant the eggs in the ground, for *this* is the SEED YOU SEW!"

—— ha ha ha yes yes fuck you bitches yes yes fuck fuck fuck oh please don't please don't help help ...

"But women! *Fear not!* For the men don't get off *that* easy. Women, beneath this picnic table is a box of box-cutters. Each of you take one, then strip the men and cut off their testicles, spilling the contents of their scrotums over your planted eggs, for *this* is YOUR FERTILIZER!"

—— agag ahhooooooooo no no no no no yes yes yes yes fuck fuck fuck fuck mwa-ha pla-diddy-da-da what the fuck what the fuck that's right what the fuck what the fuck why why why because it doesn't mean anything anymore except for pleasure and everyone's on birth control so now we're gonna grow em in the Earth so the zombies will rise from the dirt like beetles and then they'll tear each other to pieces ...

"Thank you Elmo Sargent for that insightful analysis. Now back to the studio for ——

... ||| ... ||| ...

... or just there at the pond after the mutilation and castration, the moon washing white over the zombie field as crickets chirp the delightful songs of late summer, owls hooting snipers in the trees, and the bullfrogs bellow baritone harmonies from the water ... Sarge and I together alone like a meeting between Thoreau and Emerson here in the most untouched of settings — a battlefield of rotting corpses ... nature breathes and the Earth still turns even after the dogs have picked clean all the bones ... we sit on the picnic table, star gazing ...

"can I ask you a question Randy?"

"sure"

"wha' d'you want outta life?"

to the stars and the moon, then just one word, "Love"

him repeating, "Love" as if he were disappointed

"yep, Love"

"Nothing else?"

"power, definitely power"

"you know Randy, power is a very dangerous thing"

"what's so dangerous about it? it's just a physical force, energy transference n particle collisions n shit; it's as natural as this damn table of sliced wood coated in arsenic"

pause to drink from the blood of the pussy juice that somebody left in their cup before they turned inside out...

"Randy?"

"yes?"

"wha' d'you think you'll be doing in seventy years?"

"hopefully I'll be dead"

saucer eyes, "well let's suppose you're not dead"

"Okay, let's 'suppose'"

"I was thinking that maybe we could be having this same conversation somewhere far-off years from now, just you n me Randy" ... getting all sobby romantic, I should've cried salt because it was all so beautiful — zombies and death and mutilation and the internal longing-brooding for _____

... "with our canes n grandchildren, maybe teaching —
professors or something somewhere far-off at some college,
and we come back here n sit out in the field just like old times
and talk about the same things"

"like where we'll be seventy years from then?" ... him
unamused ... "you know it's possible; I hear they're doin great
things with life expectancy supplements"

"yer jokin right?"

he wasn't ... "oh Sarge! you're a funny fucker, that's for
sure! ha-ha-ha-ha schma-bra-la" ... god did I feel like a fucking
adult now! ... "what the fuck is goin on here?!"

"we were jus' talkin about the future"

as if it was Nothing ... "ah yes! the future" ...

You see, it was sometime in the future not too long after
then that it all just disappeared, or at least I forgot about it.
Fuck, I was still hungover on the battle. You see, everyone had
these great war stories to tell: me with my Cairo journey and
all and then this other guy who I happened to meet somewhere
around sometime back then there ...

He asked me, "So wha' d'ya know?"

"Excuse me?"

"Wha' d'ya know 'bout ev'rything?"

I mean, was this a fucking joke? Seriously ... "Wha' d'you
mean?"

"Well lemme tell you a story, the story of a journey, a
journey that began with a mere whimsical thought and evolved
into a tumultuous adventure of three men torn between two
worlds — the one that we'll say is, well, *in here,* and the other
that is *out there.* Now most o' this story didn't 'appen *in here*
but rather *out there.* You see, we left the box, which happened
ta be a tall wooden box inhabited by a family of human beins
who jus' happened ta be direct kin to a close acquaintance of
mine who we will call Devin, that bein his given name from
when he entered the box at birth."

"Wait a second," I interrupted. "Is this box a house
perhaps?"

A glare ...

"Maybe?"

"Perhaps, you would get more answers 'fyou would stop askin questions n start lis'nin. Turn off yer brain for a moment and just absorb what I am tryin ta convey to you via words."

Turning away for a suspenseful pause, he resumed in that well-read, backwoodsman's accent, booming like a football announcer ...

"Devin n I and another close acquaintance of mine who we will call Vince, were perusin about a dark residential neighborhood in a town quite similar ta this one sometime in the past — perhaps a couple o' days ago, maybe a couple o' years ago; time is not my specialty mind you. It was night, and followin a long discussion about the existence of extraordinary entities in this 'ere realm, somebody — I can't remember exactly who — threw out the idea of takin a hike through the deep, dark depths of the forest borderin the neighborhood.

"I mentioned that within the darkness, ya never know what you may encounter cuz in the darkness anything and ev'rything lurk, from the seeable to the unseeable, wolves n wolfmen, kittens n mountain lions, demons and even the Devil himself. Psychological preparation would be unequivoc'ly nec'ssary in order for us ta conquer the evil forces that lurk in the darkness, and that is exactly what I told my companions, bein an experienced n astute adventurer in the realm of the darkness myself.

"Well unfortunately, my fair warnin did no more than stricken them with fretful fear, n thus they refused to advance durin the night, but insisted that the journey take place durin the day, when the hot sun broils pale skins like ourselves n large bugs are seduced by the sweet n salty scents of our voluptuous bodily odors. I predicted a rather thorny adventure that would likely involve actual thorns as well as poison ivy and maybe even a chance encounter with some sortta wild, never-before-seen creature which would hunt us as simple game n then tear flesh from bone, feedin its young heifers with our meat 'fore leavin the remnants of our carcasses for the vultures n hounds to consume.

"Yes, it seemed quite romantic. There were so many ways in which we could injure ourselves or even die — poisonous plants, heat strokes, venomous vermin. Thus, we went our sep'rit ways that evenin, plannin to consume the followin day with adventure — a walk in the woods. That night I dreamt o' fierce ogres crawlin outta caves on all fours 'fore risin up on their hind legs n beatin their chests with large hairy fists ta rile up all their strength n fit ta tear a massive oak tree outta the ground n sweep us away with it, like a burly golfer knockin a white ball around, except we were white humans — livin, breathin beins accustomed to the comf'tuhble bubbles we inhabit, rarely seekin anything beyond the accepted or the ordinary, goin about our lives day by day as if we were stuck in a loopin movie reel that begins the day we're born n ceases the day we die, constantly settlin into routine while we try ta make things fun n excitin by gettin drunk in the evenins er goin ta the truck-n-tractor pulls on the weekends.

"We drink in boxy bars, drive boxy cars, and evenchully are buried in a box to exist only in our dreams — the only place where we can ever venture outside of our little boxes, those boxes encased within our own fabricated bubbles that also contain our social acquaintances n even beliefs, that is ta say the belief that what we believe may or may not exist outside o' that bubble. And thus we go day by day believin n playin around in our bubbles meanwhile wallowin in the shit that piles up since we never go outside o' the bubble to even take out the garbage. 'Fcourse, after a while, our bubble reeks foul of rottin corpses n rusty ol junk that is outta date n no longer relevant either materially or negatudinally.

(This is what I pictured:  *No, it's not a giant bunny rabbit ...*)

"Until we pop that bubble, we never understand what it is that we believe, nor do we even understand what that shit is inside the damn bubble, so we don' even know it *is shit* until we pop the damn thing. After that, there is no bubble, just a damn box, but boxes aren't hard ta burn n you can always build a new one. Bubbles, though, are more delicate: you gotta blow em up n fill em up with shit, so if you wanna bubble you better keep the one ya have cuz once ya pop it, ya pry won' want another one or so I've found. I find bubbles ta be not worth the trouble, so I popped mine a long time ago, n now I just have a box, but I go out of it every once in a while, like when we set out into the world on our little walk that day back then.

"Ya see, w'all were venturin inta that vast place outside o' the box where death lurks 'round corners n you can only expect the unexpected. Armed with a couple jugs o' water, I naturally donned long pants, but Vince n Devin wore shorts, worried more about the heat than the venomous vermin or poisonous plants. I was concerned about those things plus the man beasts. Yes sir, ya never know what could lurk in the woods: if there are beast-like creatures, we certainly don' know about them cuz no one has ever survived an encounter ta tell about it.

"Vince n Devin found this humorous when I told em to beware of man beasts, but then again their humor definitely kept me grounded, cuz as we entered the woods I felt as if I was in search o' somethin grand n great, more'n just a physical object er anything aesthetically pleasin, but rather somethin that would send me somewhere or somewhen I had longed for but never been. Perhaps I desired for these woods to revert me back to my innocent youth — a time when the breadth and depth o' the woods actually fascinated me rather than caused me to make up stories about creatures that live there who I've never seen ——

... Innocent youth, blah blah blah — where have we heard this before? Anyway, this guy was so full of wind, it is necessary for the sake of brevity to skip ahead ...

"So there I was armed with the trash can lid, standin at the bottom of an incline, the top of which seemed to be some sortta open clearin. I charged ahead with my shield, while Devin n

Vince chose to balance themselves on a log in order to scale the steep incline and avoid the perils o' the underbrush. On that log, Vince was overrun by a swarm o' horseflies n Devin lost his balance, crashin to the ground, flat on his face, scrapin his arm on the side o' the dead tree. There he lay in silence, motionless; the only sound made throughout the entire ordeal was the rustle of leaves as Devin succame to the powerful force of gravity. It seemed a morbid situation at the time. He didn't yell, cry out, or scream, just fell smack into the ground. Meanwhile, Vince had abandoned the log to avoid the horseflies n was pullin back tree branches as he carefully crept across the forest floor, unaware, perhaps not even carin, that Devin had fallen and maybe even broken his neck. I had already scaled the hill n was standin amidst tombstones in the middle of a cemetery 'bout thirty yards in fronta the place where Devin had fallen. Devin, 'fcourse, emerged with nothin more'n a scratch and a head full o' leaves. I casually informed Devin that if he had perished from that steep fall, we could have buried him right there next ta Otto Von Funk — the travelin troubadour himself, an All-American Zarathustra! The humble grave of Professor Funk was the first we encountered in the cemetery, n we found this rather fittin considerin that Professor Funk was a fiddle player who walked around America in the early part o' the twentieth century just fiddlin 'round on his fiddle. We, ourselves, were walkin 'round America, albeit a very small chunk of it, fiddlin 'round with a tin trash can lid, n right there, one-hundred years later, was the wanderin spirit of Otto Von Funk possessin us as we walked over his grave. Yes, I say *possess*, for after walkin over the Professor's grave there was a presence amongst us as if that spirit was guidin us, the wanderin spirit of an aimless drifter just fiddlin 'round happenin ta come across us transient teens while we paid our own respects ta one o' the greatest wanderers in the history of man — PROFESSOR OTTO VON FUNK!"

He leapt into a reverent fist pump in tribute to the Idol and then back down into his flesh because he couldn't float away just yet.

"Well anyway, where was I? —— Oh yes! Otto Von Funk! There we were at his grave, broodin within the shelterin womb of pine trees when we began to realize the vast extent o' the journey we had undertaken. You see, it was here that Devin informed us of his intentions ta walk halfway across the county through thicket n thistle, 'cross prairie n bean field, to his grandmother's house. His grandiose ideas could only be extricated from his cranium by acting upon them. However, I was skeptical as ta whether er not we, as a trio, would actually be able ta complete this journey without succumbin to barbarism or that is, 'thout Vince whinin n cryin like a little boy. Ya see, I knew *I* could complete this journey — a mere morsel of a much larger adventure that had, up ta this point, been characterized as life. I also knew that Devin had the gumption n desire ta finish it, though he may not have been the most physic'lly fit of us. Vince, on the other hand, was the most physic'lly fit, though I wondered whether his mind was up ta the challenge. Nevertheless, we pressed for'd.

"We continued past the spirits n their graves n over a freshly mowed, empty meadow ta once again break through the tree line n march through a dense thicket across a sandy creek bottom all the way to the base of a steep hill that seemed to culminate in an open clearin. At the bottom o' the hill was an old Dallas Cowboys rubber football n a Pepsi can whose emblem looked like somethin from the mid-nineties. I noted aloud that that particular can could have been in my hand as a young boy, for my grandfather always had Pepsi at his house n he lived near this spot in the woods I knew, for the neighborhood boys n I would frequent these woods. Thus, I s'pose the mere fact that I even remembered that simple detail of my youth perhaps indicates that that *exact* can was once in my hand. I choose to believe that it was, whether er not it is actually in accordance with what most would consider 'statistically probable.' Ya see, statistics may be useful in Vegas, but in the woods nobody gives a damn. I told this exact story to a smarty pants (or at least he thinks so) acquaintance (I call him that because he is definitely not a friend) who happens ta be an atheist and he went off on some tirade 'bout how it'd be statistically absurd for me ta have walked across the same spot where I once littered a Pepsi can ten years, maybe even more, before n find that exact Pepsi can. I asked him how he would go about calculatin this 'ere statistic, n he said that he would have ta find out how old the can was n then determine if I was actually in the woods on the date that the can was dropped on the ground. I asked him how he would go about doin that, n he said that he couldn' do that, whereby I told him that it isn't important whether er not that can was actually mine but rather what that can represents."

Another pause ...

"Wha' did it represent?"

"Oh, a memory, but remember, it's only trash."

"So is ——

"NO! It isn't! We had ta push on up the hill! For I had ta discover what lay atop it n lo-n-behold it was a neighborhood — the world! So there we were back inside the friendly n comf'tuhble confines o' civilization. You can be walkin through the woods, through meadows n fields o' corn n then ya stumble across a house or a street or even a community o' people n ya marvel at these seeminly misplaced landmarks interruptin the natural landscape yet tryin so hard ta fit in. Ya see, in a city or a town, a house is normal because it *should* be there next ta all o' the other houses n buildins n highways n bridges n sidewalks n street lamps n all o' that infrastructure. But when ya emerge from a completely natural landscape devoid of any obvious tamperin by man — that is, other than a Pepsi can and a rubber football — n you find yourself in the middle of a suburban neighborhood, well, the houses are absurd.

"Why do we confine ourselves to these little boxes n plant these flowers in rows around the outside n have the four-wheeled machines transport us ev'rywhere, n why do we insist on keepin the grass cut at a consid'rably stumpy level *and*, I ask you this! — the most perplexin of all peculiarities! — Why do some of us choose to attach a chain to a collar noosed around the neck of a vicious canine n stake the other end o' that chain in the ground in the backyard of our homes!? Perhaps we desire ta keep the dog as a sentry, guardin 'gainst undesirable fiends who may or may not attempt ta wreak havoc on us and our boxes. But how can that dog, chained to the ground, do anything outside of his circumference of movement? He can bark, n that's 'bout it. Yet we choose ta chain up this hound n feed it industrially manufactured kibble or leftover bones from the previous evenins feast. It's all simply mind bogglin but so is ev'rything else, like why in the hell does a picnic table look like *that!?* The Lord only knows.

"Anyway — we walked through that neighborhood for a little while n then crossed back over into the woods, and around trees, through a thicket o' small shrubs n thorns n then out again n around an ivy grove, hoppin another creek bed all dried up, til we found ourselves at the foot of a steep slope risin all the way ta heaven, so high n so dense with foliage that we couldn' see the top. For a moment, we paused in awe o' the hill we were about to ascend ta try ta reach the apex — the climax that would mark the end o' the beginnin n the beginnin o' the end. Pressin for'd, beads of sweat drenchin our faces, vicious flies attacked us in swarms, suckin our blood, but still we clamored up the hill as I led the charge, clearin the way with my shield.

"Higher and higher the hill rose in front of us, n then the climax ahead, the apex marked by a peek o' sunlight beamin down through the tall trees, n then almost to the top! Dodgin one las' thorn bush, the hill steeper now than ever before n lookin back, a fall would be deadly! We each grabbed on to a small saplin n pulled ourselves up over a muddy ledge — the side o' the hill that had been washed away by a rainstorm — n then on our hands n knees, pushin ourselves over the hump ... THERE IT WAS!"

A dark fog descended upon Sodom ...

"Wh-wh-wha' was it?"

A low whisper, "A prophecy."

"Wha' did it say?"

"It didn' *say* anything. It showed us the future! From the top o' that hill, we could see for miles n miles — the deciduous forest endin there at a cliff that dropped straight down one-hundred feet, maybe two-hundred, into a wide but shallow creek of clear water. The mid-afternoon sun brightly shone down upon us, and the field n meadow beyond the creek beckoned us westward ho! We were awestruck by the beauty o' the untamed horizon. But as we stood n gaped, Vince reminded us of somethin we had forgotten: in order ta make it ta Devin's grandmother's house, we would have ta trudge through the valley of the MAN BEAST!! ... He would be hidin n waitin for us innocent antelope ta frolic across the meadow, but the threat o' *no* Man Beast could scare us away. Sure he could scare us, but that fear is what was pumpin the adrenaline through our nerves, fuelin the *fire* that ignited the engine ta turn the motors n gears ta propel us for'd.

"So we went down the hill ta bathe in the creek, then dried ourselves with our clothes, n traversed the grassy field half-naked as bugs n burs latched on to us.

"And we walked ...

"And walked ...

"The sun beatin its intense rays on our pale bodies, bakin us like pathetic sugar cookies. Still we kept movin, carefully glancin left n right n back, fearful of the lurkin Man Beast. Vince was ignorant of presence; Devin felt somethin strange; I was certain the Beast was near: I could smell him, but still we kept goin across the grassy meadow n a field o' soy beans across which was anotha forest which we safely reached only ta find an unmarked, recently cleared dirt path dividin it from the field. Keepin with our western headin, we merged on to the wide path, all three of us abreast — me in the middle, Devin on my left and Vince on my right.

"So there we are just walkin when Devin stops in his tracks n tilts his head heavenward as if searchin for an answer. Vince n I turn ta face him as he looks at us fretful n confused. 'You hear that?' he says. I tilt my head in the same manner only to hear the most dreadful n ghastly o' sounds — a low rumble, perhaps even a grumble, ascendin higher n higher and then suddenly droppin low again n ascendin higher n higher n gettin closer n closer n then up ahead, off in the distance, maybe half a mile away, it manifested itself before us — the MAN BEAST! He was ridin his four-wheeled, mechanical-creature apparatus commonly known as an A-T-V! And he saw us! We stood there, lookin him face ta face, half a mile between us n nothin at all. But upon scrutinizin his stature, I realized, 'That's no Man Beast. That's just a Man Boy.' But Devin says, 'Where there's a Man Boy, there's a Man Beast.' The fella on the A-T-V was just a cub, n 'fcourse we scared him more'n he scared us. He quickly made an about-face n sped off down the path back into the forest. We shrugged n kept walkin. Vince decided then to speak up, sayin how he knew that cub was the offspring o' Someone with a capital S — Someone ta be feared ... the Beast of all Man Beasts! ... ||| ... ||| ...

"His father, Vince said, was none-other-than the seven-time World Wrestling Federation Sensation Champion of the Universe — BIG BEEF N TATER TOTS *GERKY!!*

"Legend has it that this beast of a man used ta beat himself over the head with a ball-peen hammer n then run off n chug a six-pack in thirty seconds 'fore challengin an inferior beast to a bru-ha-ha where he would tackle him, knock him unconscious, bite off his head n *spit it out!* Such is legend, though. I don' nec'ssarily believe in such malarkey n I knew that this Beef Gerky character was no more of a Man Beast than I. I also knew one other thing: as deadly a fighter as this Man supposedly was, he was dumber than the dog tied ta the chain. We just had ta outwit this Man Beast, n that's exactly what we did, cuz no sooner than the cub had gone, we heard in the distance the sound o' two grumblins gettin closer, so we

258

darted into the woods! Plowin over trees n through the underbrush, sprintin fast down the hill, leapin 'cross the creek n then back up the hill chargin for'd again, the grumblin still behind us gettin *louder* n *LOUDER!* N then up ahead, an opening! — a tall grassy meadow. We dove for'd, breakin the tree line, n fell down, crouchin in the prairie grass, silent n motionless, as the vehicle and its commander, the Beast himself, idled along just feet away from us on the dirt path dividin the trees from the meadow. We could see him, squattin up there, lookin 'round in his mista-cool sunglasses, his muscles pulsatin n rippin through his tight t-shirt with the word *TAPOUT* splashed across the front. Thankfully, he idled past us n then sped away back from whence he came. I looked over at Vince who smiled n nodded n Devin laughed n I smirked satisfact'rily, havin outwitted the Man Beast.

"Well, we started walkin again 'cross the grassy meadow, still headin westward into the sun when up ahead we noticed a gravel thoroughfare which divided the field from a hand-wired fence on the other side of which was a herd o' idlin cows that all turned ta look at us so we waved at them n then they went back ta their munchin. We turned south down this road that I knew would lead to another road bein how roads are. Well, there we were just walkin abreast again when behind us started another chuggin low grumble gettin louder n louder n slowly closer so we turned around n saw it down about half a mile off comin right at us — a large black four-wheeled monster with *TAPOUT* tattooed across its nose.

"'Gerky,' Vince said. The big mechanical creature slowed beside us, n the window on the driver's side rolled down ta reveal The Beast glarin at us straight-mouthed from behind those mista-cool sunglasses. He opened his mouth and the sound that came out was like nothin you could ever imagine ...

"He was quackin at us like a duck, 'Wuz that you boyz back thur on my property?' he said all naggy n nasally. I looked to my partners: Devin turned around, Vince kicked rocks in the apron o' the road. 'Yes,' I said. 'We were jus' passin thru. I

259

think we might've scared your son.' He looked over at the cub, 'Naw, ya didn' scare im,' n the cub in his matchin mista-cool sunglasses shook his head n crossed his arms — a tough guy jus' like his daddy.

"'Well what er y'all doin?' The Beast asked.

"'Oh we're jus' walkin around,' I said. 'We're actually headin west ta Devin's grandmother's house out by Niemanville.'

"'*Niemanville!?!?!?!*' he exclaimed, baffled. How could someone walk all the way ta Niemanville some seven miles from where we stood?

"Vince looked up and said, 'Yeah, that's where we're headin.'

"'Huh,' the Beast grunted. 'Well y'all wanna ride? I'll take ya down ta the Ol Niemanville Trail.' I glanced ta Vince then Devin n we all shrugged n said, 'Sure,' n hopped in the bed n sat beneath the back window, the decal plastered across it, **TAPOUT**, and there we were hitchin a ride from the seven-time World Wrestling Federation Sensation Champion of the Universe, Big Beef Gerky.

"Gerky dropped us off at the Ol Niemanville Trail n we bid him farewell, thanked him for the ride, n then recommenced our westward journey just a few miles away from Devin's grandmother's house. As we walked to'rd the house solemnly takin step by step, the afternoon sun dipped in the sky to a three-quarters position indicatin only a few more hours 'fore darkness. Our time was becomin limited, so Devin vowed ta keep this visit short.

"Upon arrivin, we all three courteously removed our shoes on the front porch, for they were laden with mud n other elements o' the forest floor, then went inside ta sit down in the livin room. A kind old lady in a housedress idled in a recliner next to a pedestal upon which was an assortment of over-the-counter pain n cold medications, prescription drugs as well as a gallon-size jar of petroleum jelly. An old-fashioned pendulum clock ticked on the wall, the only sound in the room other than the occasional grunt emitted by the old woman waitin patiently for the tick-tock ta stop.

"There was no television, no radio — jus' the perpetual tick-tock, tick ...

CUCKOO!

CUCKOO!

CUCKOO!

CUCKOO!

CUCKOO!

The Rapture

The previous page was left intentionally blank.

Don't ask why.

Don't think about It.

Don't shriek in befuddlement.

Don't cringe in frustration.

Don't hate me or my creation, and don't love me or my creation because I'm telling You not to hate.

I hope You enjoyed Your stay.

Because finally, today is The Day!

Yes, It Is!

I assure You; You must believe everything I say.

Oh no, Don't!

Even if He is telling You not to do.

Don't trust Him! Seriously, He's just trying to confuse You with His meaningless propaganda because He wants to ——

Silence from You! There is no need. 'Tis I You must heed! Yes! Yes! I, in deed. Listen to His negativity! Listen to what He says! Via blasphemy One can learn how to find two and three, and from what not, what One can be!

The Oneness is coming, I'm telling You now.

So buckle down and button up tight, cuz this is gonna take all of Your might!

The silence and tock-tickity of clock, a door where You will once/one feign a knock, but first we must settle the hickory-dickory-dock.

Now that we're here, You better not stop /// ...

Because I'm telling You why and I'm gonna tell You all about what happens as You wind on down the road, cuz they're coming so You better hurry and get the fuck done what You need to get the fuck done, but You don't even know who's coming or what-the-fuck You need to get done, and maybe You're expecting me to tell You, but if You don't know now it's too late cuz I'm trying to help You here, and if You haven't figured that out by-god You better start over with *that* in mind cuz that's what books are for, so You better take heed cuz if not, I'm screwed and then we're all screwed, so keep that in mind cuz there's no reason to hope anymore, and change is always happening just maybe not how You would like to see It happen, but I assure You It will work Itself out in the long run, as long as You maintain focus on the path, the task at hand will easily disappear from the to-do list, You just gotta keep working at It and chiseling away, but sometimes It's faster and easier if You hop in the car and floor It ...

... vr-vr-vroooooooommmmmmmmmmm ....

Cats and dogs but be careful, He's got the shotgun. Of course *that* doesn't matter as long as You're in control of the deadly weapon, guiding the ship through the flood cuz You gotta protect the covenant hidden in the heart of the Arc.

He was afraid of It. Never forget. Tuesday, May 15, 2007. He wanted to destroy It, but He didn't know where to look and even if He did, He couldn't have gotten It because It wasn't His destiny.

Somebody better tear down the wall and blow up the box! Who's It gonna be?

Sure as hell not the mommy's boy.

Still though, He should've just said something instead of trying to reverse seduce me by making me listen to "Dazed & Confused" as if It would've scared me to know that a woman's soul was born from the dark fires of hell! I didn't fucking care, just cared to fuck.

But what-the-fuck ever. Why do I even fucking care? Here I am with everything I could possibly ever want or need and still It ain't over yet — not until I say so, and god-damn-It until then cuz the world is as flat as this piece of paper ...

It's 1492 and Nobody knows. Nobody has any idea that there is another world across the ocean, that the ocean doesn't drop off into an endless abyss. But where is this New World if You can't see It?

Is It on Mars? One of Jupiter's moons? Maybe Venus? Maybe long long ago in a galaxy far far away ...

Just close Your eyes and see the vast ocean that drops off into the dark abyss ... those wooden ships on the water very

264

free have left an entire generation beyond the physical, yet still, we must heed the fanfare ... go west my friend! go west! follow the setting sun to the end of the world, where the winds begin ... there is a New World out there, a place where You can be whatever You want to be, and It doesn't follow the same rules as the old world ...

Why? You ask ...

Because beyond the dream of glory is a world of glorious dreams, from the I-had-a-dream to the I-have-a-dream and all the consecrated moments in between.

So if You really wanna find out What ... It all means, You just gotta go where You've been assured Nothing *exists* ... close Your eyes and peer into the dark void of infinite possibility: this is the New World ... *imagine* What all of those explorers and pilgrims and settlers felt when they landed on that coast or discovered the mighty rivers, vast forests, and open prairies ... *imagine* the visions of Adams and Hamilton and Jefferson cuz these are Our visions, and their story is Your story, and I know this sounds like a bunch of idealistic hubbledy-doo, but seriously SERIOUSLY! ... It's all about You!

Because You are the One.

E Pluribus Unum.

You are One of many — a singular individual amongst many other individuals, but together We are One.

We the people ...

You the person.

Come together, right now ...

Over Me.

Elaboration and explanation of this fundamental idea humanity has yet to conquer.

To concur ...

Is and will always be |||

Completely One.

Without beginning or end ...

Forever.

Never ...

Imagine! Then take that image from Your dreams and mold It into Something You can see!

And then It'll all begin to burn ...

"So wha' d'you think about Apollo n Zeus n all o' those characters?"

"The Greek gods, you mean?"

"Yeah," striking the match, sparking Sodom ... "the Greek gods," inhaling.

"Well," to the fires without a brood, "They all have diff'rent powers n diff'rent jobs n stuff like that, but I mean, it's not like Apollo actually drives his chariot n controls the sun or Zeus actually lives on Mount Olympus or anything like that."

"No, no," passing the baton, "That's jus' not rational" ...

In the End Times, beware the false prophets preaching truths via rational coherencies and mathematical calculations in regards to economic market tendencies and the logic set forth by the free and the enslaved, or maybe they'll try to save Your soul from the soapbox of environmental conservatism or liberal equality and justice for all because You should vote for civil servitude and citizenship while watching the daily news so You can cite pop culture gossip like Bible quotes from Facebook because Adam begot _____ but He also slept with Faith on Saturday night after the football game, at least that's What's written on the wall next to the words of the prophets ———— the End is Near the End is Near the End is Near the End is Near the End is Near the End is Near the End is Near the End is Near the End is Near the End is Near the End is Near the End is Near the End is Near the End is Near the End is Near the End is Near the End is Near the End is ...

Let's get this fucking over with ...

"Can you imagine a planet home to six billion o' those Greek gods."

"Yes. Earth."

"Can you imagine if Michael Jordan had grown up wielding a sword instead of a basketball?"

"Yes. Achilles."

"Of course, you know Achilles dies?"

"So? We're still talking about him."

harmony unity peace love war hate fuck shit bitch nigga

Remember Cairo? It's still there and so are the pyramids — the ones built on the backs of slave labor — and all the black people in Cairo, Illinois, descendants of slaves who were harvested by European mercantilists centuries ago then brought to America and sold at market like horses and cattle. You can buy a car on eBay, now imagine if the car could buy You ...

Is slavery okay? ... And why is it wrong? ... Because You shouldn't force people to work against their will?

Oh What ... do You will?

And What ... will You do?

Stairway to Heaven

You will go to school and get Your grades and climb the ladder, climb the Stairway, one step at a time, from kindergarten to PhD and maybe You'll be unlucky enough to be President someday, or if You're smart You'll be the CEO of a corporation that specializes in hypnotizing, sterilizing, gentrifying, spying, lying, and profiting from people dying. Hallelujah! Hallelujah!

Don't let em screw Ya!

vultures and dogs and songbirds too

all of them all of them watching You

as the Son rises in the eastern sky, peaking over the ashes and
     through the cloud of smog, the fires burn the vacant houses
     and somebody watches You

so rejoice! rejoice! Emmanuel!

and ransom captive You're liars hell

somebody gimme a glass of wine, something dry and aged for
     the last two-thousand years

but keep going up up up! You'll get there! I'll just sit here and
     drink my wine, but I'm rootin for Ya! goooooooo go You!

all the way ahead tll You're almost dead, and through the door
     wherein waits the whore, the Mother, the housewife, the
     shrew

welcome to Heaven!

It's a present in a box with everything You need!

a television, a toilet, a bag of weed

home sweet home

the comfort zone

surrounded by walls

infested with mice
ohso ohso ohso nice!
oooo baby baby! mooshy-mooshoo!
imadog
and so are You!
catooshie-n-ooshie-n-mommy loves You!
she'll even wipe off all the poopie-poo-poo
and cookies-n-milk and whine-n-beer too
so don't You worry!
there is no hurry
cuz daddy's driving chariot across the sky
that guy?
this guy!
ALL RISE!
the Honorable Judge Father Highness
who aren't in Heaven
hallowed be
creepy
and
and !...!...!...

oh calm on and come down now to Your dream of glory You've
had a long hard day's work and You found It and You felt
It so Now It isn't and You can close Your eyes and see how
You wish It were if It were what You wanted It to be but
the devils revel in a pile of poo and the zombies trample
the ashes and You are Here looking to see how to be turn
out it all might if only it stops it! stop it! please! please!

uoYerutrotenimluosdnayouknithtuobagithyrevednayrrowdnara
efdnaknithruoYcasedluesiyletulosbatcefrepdnaethsregginni
ethottehgarellaannogboraytubydoboNsewouoYgnithynadn
auoYtnodwonkesaucebonrettamwohdrahehseirttathrechaer
ptniaannogevasruoYluosdnanehwuoYllafpeelsatathginuoY
maerdfogillafdbauoYogotruoYtsiparethesuacebuoYrednow
tahwtillasnaemtubeshtnowlletuoYesaucebseshgirednoweth
emasgnithruoYesuohsiaxobtaethmottobfoethelohdnaethdne
foethecasedlucfoethnaciremAmaerD

I had a dream ...
gnirednowtahwtillasnaem
so I walked into the darkness ...
gnirednawgnirednaw
and I found Nothing in the greatest place of All ...
whereyouwillland
Nowhere
Now here

Sightings & Allusions ...

p. 5   Wikipedia contributors. "Cairo, Illinois." Wikipedia, The Free Encyclopedia, 6 Aug. 2010. Web. 9 Aug. 2010.

p.71-2   McLean, Don. "American Pie." American Pie. Prod. Ed Freeman, The Rainbow Collection Ltd. United Artists, 1971.

p. 81   Wikipedia contributors. "Charles Koen." Wikipedia, The Free Encyclopedia, 12 Jul. 2010. Web. 9 Aug. 2010.

p. 92   Joncas, Michael. "On Eagles' Wings." New Dawn Music, 1979.

p. 108   "Ba Ba Black Sheep." English nursery rhyme. 1st written app. Tommy Thumb's Pretty Song Book. Mary Cooper, 1744. Part of English language folk tradition.

p. 118   Charlie Daniels Band. "The Devil Went Down to Georgia." Million Mile Reflections. Prod. John Boylan. Epic Records, 1979.

p. 118   Inner Circle. "Bad Boys." One Way. Island Records, 1987.

p. 118   Brown, Pete. "White Room." Wheels of Fire. Perf. by Cream. Comp. Jack Bruce. Prod. Felix Pappalardi. Rec. Atlantic Studios, New York City. Polydor Records, 1969.

p. 118   John Lennon, Paul McCartney. "Oh Darling!" Abbey Road. Comp. McCartney. Prod. George Martin. Apple Records, 1969.

p. 119   Jackson, Michael. "Beat It." <u>Thriller</u>. Prod. Quincy Jones, Jackson. Epic Records, 1982.

p. 148   Jimmy Page, Robert Plant. "Stairway to Heaven." <u>Zoso: Led Zeppelin IV</u>. Prod. Page. Atlantic Records, 1971.

p. 154-5 Wikipedia contributors. "Lincoln–Douglas debates of 1858." Wikipedia, The Free Encyclopedia, 25 Jun. 2010. Web. 9 Aug. 2010.

p. 185-6 Bates, Katherine Lee. "America the Beautiful." Comp. Samuel Ward. 1st App. *The Congregationalist*, 1895.

p. 207, 9 Pink Floyd. "Echoes." <u>Live at Pompeii</u>. Comp. Roger Waters, Nick Mason, David Gilmour, Richard Wright. Orig. Release ON: <u>Meddle</u>. Harvest/EMI, London, 1971.

p. 212   Tom Petty, Jeff Lynne. "Into the Great Wide Open." <u>Into the Great Wide Open</u>. MCA, 1991.

p. 218   Jimmy Page, Robert Plant, John Paul Jones. "Black Dog." <u>Zoso: Led Zeppelin IV</u>. Prod. Page. Atlantic Records, 1971.

p. 264-5 David Crosby, Stephen Stills, Paul Kantner. "Wooden Ships." <u>Crosby, Stills & Nash</u>. Comp. Crosby. Prod. Crosby, Stills, Bill Halverson, Graham Nash. Atlantic Records, 1969.